Books of Merit

Icarus

ICARUS

A Novel

LOUISE YOUNG

Thomas Allen Publishers
Toronto

Dedicated to Albert Emerson
for unfailing love and faith

National Library of Canada Cataloguing in Publication Data

Young, Louise, 1947–
Icarus : a novel

ISBN 0-919028-49-7

I. Title.

PS8597.O63413 2002   C813'.6   C2001-904263-9
PR9199.4.Y6813 2002

Text Design: Gordon Robertson
Editor: Patrick Crean
Cover image: Julia Hember/Photonica
Author photograph: Albert Hurd

Published by Thomas Allen Publishers,
a division of Thomas Allen & Son Limited,
145 Front Street East, Suite 209,
Toronto, Ontario M5A 1E3 Canada

Printed and bound in Canada

Acknowledgements

I would like to thank Patrick Crean, my editor, for publishing *Icarus*, and magically improving it. Thanks also to Katja Pantzar, Denise Anderson and Gordon Robertson for their diligence and expertise, and to Doris Cowan for her meticulous final edit.

It's impossible to put into words the help my husband has been, the innumerable times he salvaged a draft, inspiring, nurturing, and resuscitating me. While many others have sustained and fostered me, I am especially indebted to Caroline Adderson for bringing *Icarus* to Patrick's attention; without her help I would be languishing in a slush pile. And Judith Stamps was invaluable for her insight and acumen and for rescuing me more than once. Other friends I would like to thank are Rachna Gilmore, Mary Tilberg, Steven Heighton, Lucy Bashford, Jay Ruzesky, Anne Green, and finally, Debra Ward, my soul's sister, for her drunk ascending a staircase.

Let me also acknowledge the following mentors: Rachel Wyatt, Leon Rooke, Adele Wiseman, Don Harvey, Guy Vanderhaeghe, Bill Valgardson, Derk Wynand, Lawrence Russell, and Rachel Wyatt, to whom I am deeply grateful.

My family has steadfastly nurtured me. I want to thank Richard and Kay for love, loyalty and shelter from the storm; Lesley for her encouragement; Scott for his aeronautical expertise; my father for being a masterful storyteller; and my mother for her unconditional love and the gift of clairvoyance.

Lastly I would like thank Catherine Yolles for finding me in the *Malahat* all those years ago and telling me I was a novelist. Thank you.

Part One

ICARUS

Icarus settles at the bottom of the crumbling steps alongside the usual lick of cigarette packages weathered soft as cloth. Gathering his strength he lifts one foot then the other to begin again, but quickly gives it up. Hard to tell, swollen as the ankle is, if the circulation's stopped.

1

A quiet chill drifts in. Darkness breaking along the horizon cracks the blackened shell and light bleeds through. From a shadowed heap of bush a fox creeps out and disappears. In the distance headlights appear, small annoying eyes weaving along the road, and soon the growling whine eats its way to him.

The road dips between two hills and the lights expose the lay of land. The range is virgin yet, left to scrub cattle and mustangs from carelessness as much as preservation. When he died, the old man willed the place to Gibson and Ana, and Icarus rarely returns—he and Laird, the eldest of the three brothers, live in town in a bottom-rung hotel, home to junkies and certifiables. Icarus ended up there after the old man died and Laird followed him. Laird worries more about what he imagines the old man slipped Icarus when he wasn't looking than what he handed Gibson when he was.

Gibson climbs out, leaves the motor running, mumbling something about Christ. Ana leans across to switch off the old man's Hudson. Its familiar throat-clearing kvetch burbles as the engine dies. Outside, the air is still—any second now the yard will come apart with birds.

"It's not goddamn locked! Since when don't you walk in and make yourself at home drinkin my scotch?" Gibson wheels drunkenly to study Ana, slinting his eyes back in the direction of Icarus, then yanks himself toward the porch while Icarus waits, squashed against the bottom step, for someone to open the door and care enough to help him up the stairs.

"Goddamn cats in goddamn heat, makes me goddamn sick!" Gibson doesn't say but believes the only reason she hooked up with him was because of Icarus. Women like the careless way he slouches through a room, never saying much worth remembering, thumbing through a person's story line as carelessly as he would pages of an out-of-date magazine. Indifference lends him a coolness the other brothers don't own. Gibson calls him Elvis to piss him off. Or Rake or Stick. He's raw-boned and six two. Icarus of course insists he'd never screw around with his brother's ol lady.

Ana stops beside him. "You're bleeding," reaching to touch his face, her voice gentle waves shushing the piling of his chest. "He's hurt," she calls to Gibson, opening the torn jacket for a closer look. "What happened to you, anyway?"

Icarus waves her away. "Nothin new, that's for sure."

Gibson pauses at the railing. "You look worse'n dog meat."

Icarus shakes his head, regrets it, and wipes his leathers ineffectually. The jacket and pants are shredded, encrusted with gravel and blood. "The bike's probably fucked!"

"You need to go to the hospital." Ana raises her voice softly to Gibson. "Tell him he needs to see somebody, he might listen to you."

"No way some quack's workin me over with bleach'n a wire brush. Need to take her easy for a day or two is all." After he finishes spitting up some blood, he eyes Gibson. "Came by to see if you'd see to my bike. Some asshole's bound to rip her off if I leave her long."

"Where is it?"

"Back on the turn-off to Klippert's gravel pit. A little more than halfways down."

"Piece a shit anyways."

"Klippert's is a good ten miles!" Ana wails. "How'd you get here— did someone drop you off?"

Gibson leans against a weathered beam. With his cheek jammed against his collar, he resembles a ginger cat with an impacted molar.

"No one's gonna see it down some gully. Even if they did, nobody but you'd bother haulin it out."

"Punks," he swears, suddenly motivated to try and stand, and having to sit back down. Slower than he'd like. "Punks is who! They're always out there screwin around."

"I can't understand somebody just dropping you off—and leaving you!"

"She's a damn fine bike. Lots itchin to get their hands on a bike halfways as good as her. Needs a little work is all."

Somewhere near, a robin starts. The sun drags free of last night, while all around the clouds catch flame. Somewhere else the other robin takes up.

"Suppose I'll need the winch."

"Yeah," he says, "you'll need the winch."

Gibson shakes his head and swears under his breath.

Inside the house, the reek of burning fish and garlic scores the air, a lazy claw unwilling to let go. Sore in his chair, Icarus tests his wrist, turning it slowly one way and the other and around. At the time it had been the least of his worries, now it hurts as much as his ribs. Musta used that arm to haul himself out.

Gibson hunches over the stove, a broken metal flipper in his hand, upright and purposeful as a baton he hopes to pass. In the background Miles blows something Spanish, a melancholy horn elbowing through the greasy air.

"You need to clean that gravel outta there." Ana works on buttering a stack of blackened toast. "Before it gets any more infected."

"Quit worryin. I don't need another mother. Gib's enough."

Gibson dishes out the fish. On each pirated cafeteria plate, a carbon-brindled trout swims on a sulphurous effluent. Ana takes hers to lean against the sink, a bare foot resting on a knee. Halfway through, Icarus stops, grimaces and spits out a tooth. "Shit," he says.

Ana stacks the plates in the sink. The way she carries herself, she seems out of place. She belongs in a lecture hall, or possibly doing the weekend show-jumping circuit. It's the arc of her nose, the directness in her gaze. There but for bumping into Icarus and

Gibson at a Dylan concert. Ana grabs a moulting sheepskin jacket from the rack and a couple galvanized pails by the door. "Those chickens need seeing to." Stepping into a pair of mud-dipped rubber boots, she says, "We're going to lose a lot more if we don't keep on top of it."

"Yeah," Gibson tells her, "you go on ahead. I'll be right along."

Ana's commotion as she busies herself in the yard fuses with the hum of the furnace and refrigerator. The brothers settle into a familiar silence. Another pot of coffee. A few more cigarettes. Sprinkling of hashish. Take a ride down Cripple Creek, along John Wesley Harding, right on through a lot of Coltrane, *A Love Supreme*.

"I figured out where she is, the mine," Icarus says, and when that doesn't get a reaction, he adds, "the Lost Lemon Mine."

Gibson snorts. "Right! Where have I heard that before?" rubbing his hand over his sheared ginger head.

"No, you're not hearin me right. I know where she is," he repeats quietly, his eyes staring straight at Gibson. Gibson leans back in his chair, flinging his arm over the back. "Another one of your bright ideas?" he asks, rolling his eyes closed. Icarus is a creature of hunches and suspicions. If he gets wind of something, it pays to let him track like a gun dog with a good nose.

Icarus pulls a map out of his back pocket, shoddy and browned. "I been talkin to some old guys that used to prospect that tract and nearbys." He lays the map flat on the table. "I got it pretty much figured."

"Like the ol man always said, the definition of a gold mine is a liar on top of a mountain!" Gibson glances at the map, then looks again. His eyes narrow. "Where'd you say you got this map?"

"I made it," Icarus boasts. "From talkin to that pair of ol Stoney guides that hang out at Klippert's and those busted-up prospectors I run into down at the Cecil . . . and from doin research at the library."

Gibson lets the chair fall forward and leans over the map, his arms two tidy triangles beside the chart of mountain canyons and flats. "You been to the library, have you?"

"And the archives." Icarus rolls another cigarette. "I scoped everything they got. I mean to do her right this time."

"Right."

"It's pretty well documented . . . the general area."

"The entire area!" Gibson throws himself back, pushing his chair away from the table. "The whole entire vicinity's been overrun with oil men and guy wires and ranchers, not a stick of grass they ain't been over a thousand times. Anything worth findin they already found. Ain't nothin left but gopher turds and beer cans. I'da thought playin mule behind the ol man woulda taught you that much."

"According to those ol timers we were wastin our time all those years with the ol man. Turns out we took the completely wrong turn every time."

"Story of his life. Where'd you say you got this map?"

"I told you I made it."

Gibson grabs hold of the map. He's quiet looking at it and Icarus slouches over his arms watching him.

"You didn't make this."

"All right, someone gave it to me then."

Gibson whoops and slaps his hands down hard on the table—it rocks slightly back and forth. "Why'd they give it you?"

"What's it matter? It's right is all that matters."

"I didn't catch that. What exactly d'you say?"

"Like I said, I found it."

Gibson keeps looking at him.

"Where's the big deal? I found it."

Gibson keeps looking at him.

"In a second-hand store."

"Right!"

"Inside a book."

He nods his head for him to keep going.

"In a old Bible."

The two brothers stare at one another. The kitchen's quiet as a dropping stone. Finally Gibson shakes his head. "You're one crazy bastard!"

"What's it matter—it's right!"

Gibson stalks the kitchen, silently pacing to the fridge and back to the sink, stuffing his hands in his back pockets and then slapping them under his armpits and starting to roll himself a cigarette and putting the tobacco in his shirt pocket and stopping opposite Icarus.

"Let me see that map again."

"I did some research."

"Nowheres near enough."

"I mean to find her come spring."

"You don't know shit. Here, gimme the map, I'll show you what's wrong. The whole entire thing's screwy."

"I got a feelin here, Gib."

There are days Icarus feels like the top of his head is an enormous rotating dish programmed to follow stars or track orbital debris, a dish receiving a hundred different channels, other people's conversations, arguments, scrambling his own suspicions about places, things. The everyday drifts by smoothly, one accident-cum-conversation spilling over another, a predictable groove, familiar enough, where the other, the sensory uproar transmitted through the satellite dish, is devastating. During those episodes, he's seized by an epileptic paroxysm of the psyche, impossible to ignore. He oscillates between consciousness and blacking out. If, for instance, he's been reading and suddenly comes across a name or phrase and his vision blurs, slips in and out of focus, and his heart chokes and then takes off at an accelerated clip, instantly he knows this name, this phrase, will have a profound impact on his life. It's never wrong, never to be ignored. It is too painful. Typically it takes more than a couple of hours before the tremors completely stop. A moody residue lingers sometimes for days, even as long as weeks. Invariably the phenomenon signals a crossroads if you like, a turning point.

It happened when he first came across the map in the Bible. Ordinarily he wouldn't have paid any attention to it. Hell, ordinarily he wouldn't have detoured through that ritzy part of town!

Wouldn't have glanced through the window! But no sooner had he noticed the bookshop's expensive window display than he sauntered inside, heading straight to a section hidden behind racks of rare leather-bound books, as though he knew the shop, as if he'd been through it a hundred times, drawn to one large, ancient Bible as if by a magnet. As soon as he saw it, his vision fell in and out of focus and his heart shuddered, like an engine fighting to ignite then abruptly taking off. He couldn't move. Fierce trembling hampered his reaching for the book. When he finally touched it, and was able to lift it free of the shelf, he couldn't hear for a savage ringing in his head. He didn't see the cover. The book was unimportant. It wasn't the book, he knew that much. He was paralyzed. Holding the book, he floated in space, a passenger in a fragile balsa-wood plane which was breaking apart. Once he opened it, he knew.

As the pages turned, it was as if the plane had fallen into the sea. He felt violently sick. Then a page flipped open and there it was, a cheap sheet of paper, folded once, neither straight nor well, and recklessly shoved into the book (he knew that much). Before he lifted the map free (for he knew immediately it was a map!), he knew the man (for he also knew it had been a man, a man in his fifties who some hundred years earlier had folded the paper and shoved it in the book, and the man hadn't cared which book he'd chosen, the book was unimportant) had been in an unaccountable rush and before he unfolded it to look, he knew this patch of paper would change his life forever.

These indelible moments stake him, this side, that side, claim him entirely.

Silently Ana enters the front room to mirror Icarus and Gibson crouching, heads dipped, limbs splayed, like long-legged beasts siphoning a waterhole, probing maps yanked wide and laid one upon another. Storm-wrecked aerial maps are deposited like silt in a flood zone trailer park, coloured geological charts pool under ruptured pipes of detailed maps, unrolled and fixed with shoes, ashtrays, mugs and beer bottles. On the sun-grilled porch, more sheaves unspool in a tiresome breeze down the front steps and hard-packed grassless ground. Magpies strut across the satin paper, oblivious to winter and sun breaking all around them.

———————

"Who are you callin?"

"Like I said, I'm calling Hill."

Icarus brakes alongside Gibson. "Hill? Are you outta your mind? What are you thinkin, callin Hill?"

Gibson pins the phone between his ear and shoulder and looks Icarus square on. "Another thing, I might as well tell you . . . I called Laird."

"Laird? You talked to Laird?"

"No way around it, come hell or high water—he's our brother."

Ana appears in the doorway. "I tried to talk him out of it."

"I can't believe you'd . . ."

"Blood's blood . . . good, bad or notherwise, just the way she is . . . true as the ol man said."

Icarus walks out of the kitchen. His stride is off, like he's missing a boot heel. The smell of bacon and onions rides the air behind him. In the distance, a siren of hounds fades in and out, and his eyes follow the trail of howls. It'll be dark before long. The best part of the day broken and gone, nothing left but to sink into getting things sorted and settled.

"Quit hangin around out here sulkin."

Icarus keeps leaning against the porch rail, staring out at the hills.

"You know what your problem is—I'll tell you what your problem is."

"I need a fuckin job."

Gibson takes the answer like a punch. "Damn sure couldn't hurt. Like I said, you got nothin better to do but waste yourself day in day out."

Icarus takes up chewing the inside of his cheek. He keeps his eyes on the hills. Used to be he knew every curve, used to be he spent every day, all day, roaming around them.

"Your problem is you never got around to growin up."

"Spare me your fuckin outfall."

"You never got over him handin me this place. That's what! You thought it shoulda been split three ways fair and square, but the ol man had sense to see you'da wasted it. You'da never got it to work."

"Settin up a half-assed chicken ranch is gettin it to work!"

"Fact is, he'da left it any other way, Laird'a killed you to get your third. You know it, I know it."

It's true, Laird's a miserable felon whose violations verge on the mythical. On the opposing side, wearing the cool James Dean jacket, Icarus slouches, picking his teeth with a Swiss army knife. The two are at each other's throat like a Chinese yin and yang, forever rolling one way and another, leaving Gibson lost in the middle, a fine line separating the two.

Laird was named for his paternal grandfather and Gibson for the ol man, while Icarus was intended to be named Helmut for his maternal grandfather, but when he was born, he arrived with such ferocity that he slipped free and tumbled onto the floor. His mother screamed, You've kilt him, you've kilt him sure! until the babe started squalling and the ol man, relieved, christened him Icarus. Not that he cared a screw about Greek tales, only that Icarus's father had worked to free his son and killed him in the process, and in a name as sad as that, he hoped he might be reminded of his own good luck. For it's true the thing a prospector values next to gold is chance.

His mother went along, as she did in most things, and the ol man favoured Icarus and this preference warped Laird, twisted what might've been beauty and gifts into malevolence. And the boys, with no boundaries but how far their legs could carry them, grew up feral and reckless and marauding, wilder by far than the docile beasts grazing the fields, bound to one another by a need as

relentless as wild dogs battling for rank. It's a wonder either survived, yet both came away unscathed, physically at least. Ironically,
it's Gibson who tried to shield one from the other, wearing a coat
of many scars.

"Stop piping me sewage, Gib."

Like those of his namesake, Icarus's wings are singed. He's
beautifully comic, tethered to false hopes and alcohol, unable to
heave himself up off the floor. He swears at his stumps, Lift! Lift!
with sickening devotion. Worse yet, he is handsome, handsome as
all that.

"One thing he never did was invite the entire countryside out
prospectin. He damn sure knew how to keep things quiet."

"Let's not get into the ol man."

"Good thing for you he always took your side."

"I'da thought you'da seen by now he never cared enough to take
sides."

"Right, and Laird's a priest and you never screw around on Ana."

"Listen, I don't see what you got to be bitter about. He taught
you to witch when Laird and me woulda give our eyes to have him
show us."

"Witchin's not a fuckin trade, you don't learn it, it's not somethin you sign up for, asshole. Either you got it or you don't. It wasn't
somethin he *gave* me."

He taught him to dowse when he was barely six. When Laird
and Gibson asked if he'd teach them too, the ol man sneered, no
way he could teach just any breed of dog. According to him, a
body's born with the knack. Notherwise, he told them, you might
as well bay at the moon fer all the water you'll tap underside her.

He was an ornery son-of-a-bitch sane men avoided except to
slip him a few bucks whenever a well dried up or they were considering a new tract of land. About that everyone agreed. The bastard
never failed.

It's no good flyin too high, he warned him, ya need to keep level
and not get carried away. I seen your stripe, your stripe can run
into trouble so do like I say. Don't fiddle with it, son, 'tain't no toy.

Within a week he'd taught him how to clutch an ordinary branch and mysteriously divine water miles beneath the grassy hummocks leading from the homestead into the foothills.

"With all he handed you, you oughta be a wealthy man. I sure as hell would be."

"Not a lotta wells bein dug near the Cecil."

"Shit."

The two stare at the hills, each brother locked on his own particular vista. Finally Gibson snaps out of it, remembering why he came looking for Icarus in the first place.

"Leastwise, Laird'll be a tad late. Soundin like sometime tomorrow. Seems he racked up another DUI headin out here."

———————

The second she hears his ratshit Suburban turn in, Ana heads for her room. Stops. It's off the kitchen. Too close. Laird slams the truck door and she bolts up the stairs.

Laird's a mean yellow dog. In his mind, the homestead is his and it's only a matter of time before he moves back to claim it. Come that day, some lame sheet of paper won't stop him.

Icarus snarls at Gibson, "I can't believe you told the son-of-a-bitch."

Gibson snaps back, "He's our brother, why'dya think?"

Even on the landing, she can hear him boot the back door. No matter how they rig it, Laird won't try the handle but kicks the bottom corner so the screen door buckles and bounces open. She hopes the cats have sense to hide.

Upstairs, an undulating hall separates rooms no one uses any more. The carpet gives off a musty undersmell of mice. If Gibson notices, he'll set out traps and trays of Warfarin. Never mind the cats, he'll tell her when she objects, they shoulda bein doin their job. Freeloadin little shit engines. Ana hesitates on the top step, trying to decide which door, which room. The big one at the end was Laird's, Gib had the room on the right. She should choose it, instead she takes the one nearest, Icarus's old room. She slips inside and closes the door.

It smells of him. Red clover. The room, the smallest of the three, is cramped, with angled ceilings and painted lavatory mint. One tiny window caught between the angles offers a view of an overgrown poplar, an octopus that sucks the light and smothers the room. According to Gibson, on hot summer nights Icarus slept dangling from its branches like a mountain cat. He left the house the day the ol man died, didn't pack, left his clothes, a roping saddle, a blues collection, Bessie Smith, Howlin' Wolf, even his Neil Young, his *Heart' a Gold*. He rarely returns. Once or twice a year, tops.

Icarus is lost. The world caves out from under him like a rotten floor. Hateful trick, when she closes her eyes she can't picture him. Not really. He owns a face so perfect, each feature so symmetrical, that her mind can't record it, no matter how assiduously she focuses; possibly it's the flaws memory hangs on to . . . is that where a soul breaks through?

Once when she asked him why he lived life on cruise control, he told her that he was waiting. When she asked what he was wait-ing for, he said he had the feeling that something extraordinary was going to happen to him. She laughed and told him, the only extraordinary thing he had to look forward to was a drug-related medical problem, but he shook his head and said no. You just don't see is all.

She stoops to pick up a pair of dirty jeans, as if she's in the room to collect laundry. She isn't thinking. Strange they've been here all this time. Even so, she lets them go. She shouldn't be here. Last time, Gibson found her. He didn't ask what she was doing. What could she say?

She leaves the room in a rush. She isn't crying but her face feels stained. She misses the muffled crush at the foot of the stairs, fails to perceive another body ascending. When she brushes up against him, she's expecting Gibson, convinced he's followed her. Laird leans, blocking her intentionally, and she emits a high-pitched squeak.

"Ghoul . . .?" she stammers, mispronouncing "you."

The shock thrills him. He steps closer. Laird smells of unclean underwear, pizza and transmission fluid. He puts his hand on her breast. His fingers, the colour of tobacco, are tattooed with grease.

"You can pee on my face. If you want? You want?"

"God!"

"I'd let you. I know what you like."

Ana pulls away and skitters down the stairs. Laird's wheezing jeer hounds her. She doesn't know what Laird does with women, no one talks about it. Only this time she won't tell. The other time, Gibson flew into a rage and attacked Laird while he was working on his truck and Laird spun around and threw battery acid at him. It missed his face but hit him in the chest and while he rolled on the ground to stop the burning, Laird kicked him.

On her way through the hall to her room, Ana collides with Hill coming out of the kitchen.

"Hey," he holds her to a full stop. "You okay?"

"No, no, I'm fine." She sways, almost dizzy. "Only you surprised me. I didn't hear you drive in. God knows how I missed hearing your rig . . ."

Hill grins. "I finally broke down and got the beast a new muffler." His conversation carries a faint Caribbean lilt even though he hasn't lived there since grammar school.

"I totally forgot Gibson called you . . . even so I should've guessed."

Hill and Gibson played football and hockey together in high school, and later, when they landed athletic scholarships to Mount Royal Junior College, they researched pharmaceuticals in Hill's garage. Laird hitchhiked south to enlist for covert action in Guatemala and Icarus settled into grade ten.

"Gib's lookin for his tape measure. You seen it?"

Hill doesn't know what happened, only that Ana doesn't usually get off kilter. He roughs up her hair and gives her a bear hug. She's a funny duck, Ana, nothing you can do with her but manhandle her a bit. What else works with someone so uptight?

"No, no. Only he left it in the kitchen. Over by the pantry door."

"Don't tell me he's finally gonna build you those shelves?"

Outside there's the sound of another car, the soft grumble of something British. A polite click of two doors, followed by the wild cry of a female, noise suited to a concert stadium, nothing remotely refined or operatic but boozy and hysterical.

"It's freckin freezing out here."

"There's Newt and Maggie." Ana looks up as if the bedroom wall had a window and that window looked out onto the gravel drive. Shivering alongside the Jaguar, a woman with sunset hair ricocheting off a guitarstring body summons Jesus Christ and his mother. Moonstone eyes rolling and a voice like a sander, she's dressed for Bali in a feathery halter and low-slung sarong. "Of course you'd've called her." Ana glances back at Hill. Maggie and Hill go way back. More than water under that bridge. She shrugs. "I wasn't thinking." She likes that Hill's big as a refrigerator and melt-in-your-mouth mocha fudge. A latte with soft chocolate curls. She considers telling him that Maggie is a fool, but she knows Hill knows. Marrying someone else didn't help him forget Maggie, somehow it only made it worse.

"Christ," Icarus howls. "Who called her!"

Maggie was Hill's pin-up dish in high school, and Newt's the rich lawyer she married after she got busted dealing cocaine. Maggie chronically entertains a run of lovers, but Icarus is the only one she counts.

"Come on, Sticker," Gibson jerks his head like he's getting water out of an ear. "Don't lose sight of the fact that along with Maggie comes Newt and a full-sized credit limit."

"This is totally outta hand! I shoulda never breathed a fuckin word!"

"If you weren't lookin for reinforcements and a bankroll," Gibson asks, "why did you?"

"Chalk it up to stupidity. One thing for sure, I'm outta here— me and my map are long gone."

"You won't get far alone. You know it as well as me. To do this right takes money and gear and manpower."

"Gib's right, Sticker," Hill tells him. "A guy can't tackle a project the size of this with just a pickaxe and a lame ol mule."

"It shouldn't be big as this! There's the friggin point! Things are completely outta hand. Doesn't need to be but one or two good men. Three tops. No more'n three."

"Hey," Hill says to Laird, on his way to the kitchen from upstairs.

"Hey," Laird nods, shoving past him to toss a sheaf of maps down on the table, maps he and the ol man had stashed in the attic.

Laird, when he cares enough to speak, pushes his words through the spaces between his teeth. When he's reading a man (he seldom counts much of what a woman has to say), he tosses his head back and gazes down his nose at the opponent, eyes half closed, mouth slightly ajar. He reads the man for a long time, and when he rolls his head back down, it's over; he rarely responds, preferring to keep his conclusions safely stowed with the artillery. Life to Laird is open warfare. He stalks a street like a marine slinking through a pisshole jungle, head down and turning constantly side to side, feet barely grazing the ground, hands fixed as if around a weapon, shoulders hunched for protection from what's coming as much as from the weight of the gun and ammunition. If he stops, it's to jam more tobacco under his lip or to spit. He's a light sleeper, early riser. When he talks, which is hardly ever, he drawls as if he was born in the backwoods of Georgia instead of the Alberta foothills. He still wears fatigues and camouflage pants. His only paying job (apart from gun-running and drugs) was as a mercenary in Central America and Zaire. He likes that about Africa, the lawlessness, the rampant ferocity of tribal warfare. According to Laird, the strong deserve to win. Quit postponing the inevitable, let the lion make short work of the mewling do-gooder lamb.

Icarus freezes: proverbial, predestined roadkill pinned by an oncoming beam. The rest, particularly Ana, make way for Laird, pulling over like dutiful motorists. Icarus snaps out of it, his eyes, the hazel brown of cat's eye chrysoberyl, flash with a sudden seam of light as he lopes past the others and out the back door.

————————

Despite a sky flying the colours of a Greek flag, the air smells of snow. Ordinarily this would be remarked upon, but instead they stare out at the hills, Icarus on one side of the porch, Gibson on the other, silent as the posts they're pushing against. Behind them, a crow bobs and caws, its noise closer to a two-bit power saw than a bird. If they had nothing else worming through their brains, one or the other would wing a stone at it. Instead Gibson clears his throat and rolls another cigarette.

"Look here, we're in there firmin up the plan of attack. Nailin down the details. You better trot along inside or you'll end up side-lined as per fuckin usual."

"It's my map. No way you're movin on my map."

Gibson keeps his head down but gives him a quick sideways snap. "You gotta know I fixed it in my mind fairly good." Icarus colours as his jaw works into a fist and Gibson continues, "If you're comin, you need to start pullin your weight. Seems everyone's got their ideas . . ."

"What are you doin, Gib? You got any idea?"

"Even Newt's got a plan."

"Any plan a Neuter's can't be worth a damn." Icarus starts working the sole of his boot, winding duct tape around the toe and sole to see if it will hold any better.

"Who'da guessed Newt has a pilot's licence?"

"Right, and you got your PhD."

"Turns out he does."

"Neuter can't see to zip his fly, no way he'd pass a pilot's test."

Gibson watches a chevron of geese. "Maggie said the two of them used to fly into Mexico, back when she was still doin that sort of thing. Could be he got it before his eyes went to shit, although he swears they don't worry about glasses like they used to. Plus he's got those goat-eyed contacts."

"You wanna go flyin with Neuter, be my guest. Be safer, and you'd go further, to stick a tube of dynamite between your legs and set a match to it."

"Newt's gonna parachute in supplies. There's the answer, solved."

"Newt's got a plane, does he?"

"He's workin on it."

"Shit."

"Apparently, Laird knows a guy with a Beaver."

Icarus shoots him a look. Gibson rolls his eyes and sinks them to the corner pocket to keep from grinning. "Fact is, Newt and his *wingy* ideas aren't worth a goddamn—you know it, I know it—but money's what stopped the ol man, stopped him cold every time . . . his not bein able to bankroll her right but nickel-'n'-dimin every step of the way. Here we stand a chance. Lookit, Sticker, I figure we owe it to the ol man."

Cocooned in the bedroom, Ana listens to the stereo. The *A Train* swings by. Manning the phone, she's blowing and going, organizing bulk orders of dehydrated food and camping gear, picking at her manicure and consulting mountain equipment wholesale catalogues.

Newt's set up a maquette of mountain ranges on the kitchen table. He's bunched up over it, arms knotted, coffee cold in his hand. Any second he'll hit the computer, download mining company prospectuses and *Northern Miner*'s slant on mining reserves in the vicinity of the Livingstone River.

"Hey, Hilly dilly," Maggie croons, wheeling down the corridor toward the front room, carrying a crate full of maps, haughty as a flight attendant pushing the in-flight drinks tray, "your haus frau, D . . . D . . . Dallas called to say she'll be here soon as rehearsal's finished. As if anyone's ever goin to pay to see that dyin swan dive."

Caught on the niche of Maggie's left nostril is a diamond chip, barely noticeable, more like a fleck of white dust, a holdover from other days.

In the hexagonal front room, Laird and Hill and Gibson and Icarus argue about points of entry, supplies and how much a mule can pack. Refusing to look in the direction of the other, each man talks to the floor, the walls, himself. Hill stops cracking his knuckles and studies the far side of the room, a wall of maps, poorly hung, hurriedly attached and marked with lines and pins and circles. His large shoulders lift, forming dark boulders around his ears. Hill can hoist the front end of a half-ton truck, if you need him to. "A four-wheel drive is the only answer," he says too quietly. He's irritated they're taking so long to concede.

"It's too rocky, impassable in parts," Icarus responds without shifting his concentration from the book he's reading (Brown's, a handbook on basic outdoor survival), his yawn a poor disguise for exasperation. "We need animals. No other way around it."

Hill returns to cracking his knuckles. A sound of factory pistons echoes through the room.

"We should pack what we need ourselves!" Laird's voice begins to climb. "If you got animals you got assholes askin questions, if you gotta four-wheel drive you got some nosy small town gas jockey lookin in the back and quizzin what you're doin and where you're headed—I say the fewer questions raised the better!"

Icarus stands to stretch. "Quit being so paranoid. Nobody's gonna bother with us. They'll think we're hippies headin back to the commune."

Laird rears back on his heels to study Icarus. "You think no one's gonna ask questions we start in there with mules and picks and pans, you are crazy! Outta your mind certifiable! There's gonna be questions and next thing we know they'll be traipsin along behind us."

"Minus mules and vehicles, just how are you sayin we get in?"

Newt hovers in the doorway, clearing his throat the way he will,

as though his adenoids are thin plastic bags filled with fatty liquid—
given his mother, chicken soup. "Laird's got a point."

————————

"Seein as he has to return the plane anyways, I don't see why Neuter
shouldn't hike in with you women. There's the problem solved."
Hill speaks so quietly, the rest lean like the tower of Pisa to hear
him.

"Why don't we all fly in?" Dallas stands a perfect point. "There's
the problem solved!"

Dallas resembles a young Mickey Rooney in drag. Could be the
signature Howdy-Doody keenness rooster-tailing through her
voice, or her dancer's body, ass and hips as hard as cement tubing.
She positions herself between Ana and Maggie, blatantly appraising
Maggie: the price of the amber anklet, that sleazy hot pink sarong,
certain she isn't wearing underwear, not even a wire-thin thong,
perusing the cheesy see-through top, confident, breasts as high and
rude as Maggie's can't be real, they all but sprout from the collar-
bone. Ana, she disregards. Ana doesn't belong, she should be in a
reading room in London or a café in Vienna smoking gold-tipped
cigarillos and discussing anarchy and Third World debt. She lives
in moth-eaten cashmere left over from private school, and Gib's
faded blue jeans.

"No way I'm flying with Newt." Maggie flops down on the
couch, "not now, not ever again!" Checking out Dallas's preppy little
sweater set, her toot whiddle baby doll shoes. Send in the freckin
pearls. "Love the streaks, Dallas, they make you look way younger."

"Fact of it is," Ana admits, "I'm leery about flying too."

Next to her navel, Maggie has a tattoo of a gecko about the size
of her little finger and beautifully detailed. When she's bored, she
wriggles her abs, rocking the creature back and forth, sending it
padding up and down her navel. Laird watches the gecko through
half-opened eyes, gunmetal green.

"No women!" Icarus slams his hand down on the fat arm of the fusty old chair. "Like I said straight from the get-go—no fuckin women. You get women you get problems."

"God," Dallas tells the room. "What a misogynist."

Icarus backhands her with one of his sardonic snorts. "It's nothin to do with anything but practical good sense. You put the rest of us in danger. Simple as that. The day you can drag Hill's two-hundred-pound ass out of a burning building and down a hundred-foot ladder is the day you can come taggin behind."

"Pussy," Laird says, "don't belong prospectin."

"Laird?" Maggie purrs. "Why is it, guys with the teensiest-weensiest wienies are invariably the dumb frecks down playin pocket pool?"

Maggie's itching to go. Naturally, Newt's hoping to dissuade her, working overtime, but no matter how he pleads his case, Maggie can't shake the idea of spending an entire summer in the mountains with Icarus. Anything can happen in the bush. People are thrown together, coming and going in all states of undress, bathing in the river . . . a person has to keep clean . . . taking a pee in the middle of the night—no telling who else might need to pee—some people are light sleepers, well, one guy particularly has a real problem falling asleep, especially when he's the least little bit excited, no telling but he could be out wandering most every night, all alone and away from everyone and running into another person out doing one thing or other—half dressed—no way of knowing what might happen. Thrown together. Night black as black. In those woods, those lonely, off-away-from-everyone woods. No telling.

Hill sets Laird straight. "They want to come, they can come."

Of course Dallas isn't fooled, she knows perfectly well what's running around Hill's mind. Why he's saying they can come along. Hill's got high hopes. She's no fool, she knows the man she married better than he knows himself. He thinks once they're up there, one way or another, he'll end up getting laid. Hill's been crazy about Maggie ever since he caught her showering in the football team's locker room back in high school. As if he doesn't mention that sight often enough. Dallas sees what's going down. Hill's as easy to read as a goddamn road sign.

Maggie giggles with excitement. She can't sit still, she bounces from chesterfield to chuffy armchair like a kitten on catnip. She hasn't been this keen about a project since she can't remember when. And Maggie, when she's pacing and restless, makes the world around her start to pitch and scream like the front row at a rock concert.

"It's probably true," Gibson informs Ana. "You'd be happier here. It's no picnic wanderin around the side of a mountain. Besides, someone's gotta stay and keep an eye on those chickens."

"Keep working the line, Bogie, or you'll be dishing out chicken feed instead of prospecting for it." Ana watches Maggie orbiting Icarus, intrigued by how completely he tunes her out. It's true, there are other satellites following similar laws—Maggie ignores Hill's gravitational pull just as Hill dismisses Dallas, his bit of galactic rock, while off on the outer reaches, Newt and Ana doggedly orbit, tracking, taking it all in. God, what an incestuous, small, stupid world. "It'll be crazy up there by summer's end. We'll be lucky to make it back berserk—chances are we'll end up killing each other and never make it off the mountain."

"Gib's got a point," seconds Newt. "Creature comforts count for a lot. No doubt you'll be happier here and much better off. Wouldn't you say, mein Maggie pie?"

It's Maggie in the mountains Newt's not sure about. He wants her snug in her own little bed, wondering what they're up to, worrying and bitching and making herself feel better shopping. Newt figures he's got money to spare for some serious shopping.

Hill chimes in. "So long as they keep up, they should be allowed."

Maggie objects, "Allowed? Allowed?"

"Okay, okay. You know what I mean."

Newt's a nervous pilot. The small one-engine aircraft, rented because it was cheap and available (an ancient Beaver, relegated to the illicit and bottom end, principally poaching grizzly bears), has developed intestinal spasms. Intermittently, it will groan and, for a brief surreal moment, hang suspended, leaving the passengers and pilot adrift above the range of razored peaks as unencumbered as a glider. The world below resembles an inverted shark's mouth guzzling a green lozenge, and possibly their plane.

"What's the altimeter read, Red?"

Newt wears a pair of high-tech goggles to keep from losing a contact when the hatch opens to parachute supplies and men. He ignores the barrage of cracks, and concentrates on the altimeter and the trim. The trim because, with the weight he's carrying, he needs to be aware of the Beaver's centre of gravity; the altimeter because he's pushing it with the altitude. DeHavilland didn't intend the Beaver to be a high-flyer, and this one's seen better days.

Gibson and Hill, if they aren't watching the propeller or the wings, keep a keen eye on the series of gauges. Both men have decided that when the hatch opens, Newt won't be prepared to cope with the sudden draft. Goggles or not. Silently, each one regrets riding in this plane, piloted by a man neither would allow to drive their truck. They glance over at Icarus and Laird. Laird alone seems unperturbed. Possibly flying with an blind incompetent is a lesser thrill than flying with a wounded lunatic over enemy fire.

"Time to get the show on the road."

Rolling side to side like a lumberjack riverdancing on a log, Hill makes his way back to the cargo, unclamps a crate and begins lugging it toward the hatch. Gibson begrudgingly pitches in. A distraction at least. Hill waves him aside, indicating he should work one of his own. Because the campsite is low relative to the mountain range, safely below ten thousand feet, and relatively free of dicey peaks and comparatively roomy, given the chain's congestion, Newt theoretically has time to bank and fly by without banging into a ridge. Each crate requires time for its parachute to open and, hopefully, if Newt has correctly gauged wind speed and direction along with flying speed, the crate will land on target. What are the odds? These are gambling men and accustomed to calculated risks. Newt assures his passengers he's got the whole thing computed. He tells himself not to rush, that he has all the time in the world. Of course he can't lose sight of the fuel gauge, or that each fly-by, six max, taking altitude and passenger weight and cargo into consideration, depletes fuel. Panic is no pilot's friend. Newt believes he's good at taking pressure in stride.

Hill and Gibson circle the probable outcome, a diverting if stressful exercise. Coming to terms with facing death proves hard. Harder yet is dying at the hands of a fool.

Newt flies the vibrating plane over the difficult plateau several times before he finds the confidence to begin dropping supplies. He turns to give a thumbs up. When the door opens, a hurricane force gust shoves Newt sideways and the Beaver sinks, sending the cargo heaving against its stays and threatening to come undone. The passengers, because the seats have been removed to accommodate more cargo, find themselves in the air, knocking into the plane's sides and ceiling and other jostled men. Newt hollers, lunging for the halfmoon stick to right the craft. The passengers are silent, each too busy with an inner monologue to bother much with vulgar small talk.

"Bombs away," shouts Laird.

Hill and Gibson pause to study Laird leaning into the opening, barely hanging on, apathetic as a postman facing a strong head wind, about to charge across the open air like it was a field of blowing snow.

Icarus crouches well back, gnawing a thumbnail, devising a way to tumble out of the plane backward. He doesn't mind doing it so much as having to look—facing it is the problem.

"Goof!" Laird snarls. "Where in hell are you going? I was on my fuckin way. Someone needs to be on site."

The draft from the open door sucks up most of Newt's reply. Metal and men shouting at each other drums out the rest.

". . . drop supplies first."

"Keep on target, Neuter, if you know what's good for you."

Newt shouts again into the din. "Supplies first!"

With the pilot's attention diverted, the plane veers, sending Hill into more crates and Icarus. Both men swear at Newt and each other. Braced like a downhill skier inside the door, Laird waits for Newt to take another stab at it. As a mercenary, Laird made a hundred jumps, and now, because he's universally despised, no one dissuades him from jumping first. Before Newt gives him the sign, he jumps.

Newt screams, "Not till I say."

Gibson hollers back, "If we wait for you, most of the gear will end up at the bottom of the mountain."

"You never flew a fucking plane!" Hill tells him.

"Closest he came to flyin was drinkin martinis upfront in business class."

The plane lurches out of a spiral and into another hard turn and once again they fall against each other like bowling pins. This time the abuse adds to the bounce of the machine.

It's the jutting rocks Newt worries about clipping; he hasn't bothered mentioning he's rusty . . . saving face, really. He enjoys the prestige afforded a pilot, the way in conversation people give him certain things, but he's let it slide . . . money, time, the usual reasons for allowing any skill to skid, a trade he decided against, one of a multitude of things he might have done, should have done, perhaps, but didn't.

Hill and Gibson begin dropping cargo. In six consecutive passes they manage to see that some of it hits target. They tell each other that the percentage of crates that miss are par for the course.

"We can hope they contain Newt's bogus scientific widgetry and not anything we'll need."

"That last one that missed was our fuckin chainsaws and the generator!"

"We won't need chainsaws," Newt shouts back at them. "Besides we got hacksaws and hatchets up the ying yang."

Hill and Gibson jump one after the other, and make it look like they've been doing it for years—beginner's luck.

Finally Icarus, afraid of heights, plummets, nervous, suspicious, waiting to the last and making Newt do another turn before toppling from the plane like a child falling from a teeter-totter, trying to collect himself to correct his descent and yanking the cord too soon. He lands in a pile of crates, tumbling into another set and rolling straight toward the edge of the cuesta, enough to give Newt heart failure. He stops in time and shakes himself and waves Newt home (although he doubts he'll make it) while Hill and Gibson work free of their chutes and stumble over to help. Laird couldn't care less, he's already emptying crates. Newt equipped the expedition with every gadget the mountain equipment emporium offered, and Laird intends to claim the best of it first.

"I need my head read! Waltzing around some goddamn cliff with a fifty-pound pack!"

2

Ana jerks the padded frame of her high-end pack to ease her sacroiliac. Straggling behind her, Dallas and Maggie bitch under their collective breath. Maggie is the colour of fall leaves, her face swollen from exertion—following her is a nasty run of language gone afoul.

"We shoulda never agreed to hike in. We shoulda demanded to be flown in like the rest of the freckin little princes."

"You were the one who said you'd never again fly with Newt," Ana reminds Maggie, "not after the last trip you two took to Oaxaca." Ana isn't a risk-taker. Jumping out of a plane is a sure way to break a leg or worse. But Ana doesn't favour rock climbing much more. She hadn't expected the trail would be so hard, or long, or high. Gibson, while he hadn't lied, definitely kept her in the dark. Possibly his idea of a joke.

"Can you see the freckin top yet?"

"There is no top," Dallas answers, her voice as mean as the rock she grips. "It's a myth to keep us from murdering the little shits."

The flat pan of the mountain's face is steep and smooth and the faint bighorn trail fades treacherously into towering granite obelisks. Increasingly the small footholds are farther apart, fingers grip the surface, faces press against the sun-hot stone while toe and foot work to fix another rung. It's quiet but for a capricious trickle of gravel coming out from under, ahead or behind, followed by a curse, and quiet. Now and then an alpine shrub crouches in a split rock, dried sufficiently to come away from the matrix. Odd it hasn't, stranger still it grew. Behind, the sky is bright enough to paralyze, dangerous then at this height. Beyond their rib it's impossible to see how far they've climbed, no velvety glimpse wavers enticingly below. The curve of the slope, the way the rocks jut, cuts off the world. Nothing exists beyond the ledge on which the support foot hesitates and the space in which the hand pats out a fresh hold.

Newt stops to wait for Ana. Silence reverberates with the congested hum of an ear pressed against an empty cup.

"Don't worry, it's not much further. We're almost there."

"Don't bullshit me!" Ana reaches for a stick to drag herself to the next negligible crinkle. She wavers, her mind reeling drunkenly from exhaustion, and slips, catches a stalk, clings for a second, feeling it give way in her grip, homeless alpine and Ana suspended for a brief uncertain time, then both sliding in a swift fall. Bracing himself against the wall, Newt, misshapen from monitor and keyboard, barely a week free from office briefs and summations and computer games, reaches down a carpal-syndrome arm to catch her by the wrist. She's pissed and wants to go back down, whichever route.

From the top, the view stretches fifty, a hundred miles. Blue-violet in the distance, a cliché, but no less beautiful because the haze is hacker's violet daubed straight from the tube, nothing can catch the smoky way it lies upon the hills, rolling, or the way it meets the river, the silken shade covering the mossy bed of trees, or drifts to sky, or goes on from there, forever. That is untouchable, beyond the stain of description, of small or vast cliché, it *is*. It stops. No matter what thought or stroke of paint or prefab building brushes it, it is beyond. It takes the tired and mundane and transforms them in a glance. That's what power places do, that's why other nations called them sacred, they are the world beyond contamination, beyond destruction, no matter how many tour buses or hotels or subdivisions spread like warts over top, the power endures untouched, seizes ions and shakes them out, whisks away the wrinkles of the tarnished soul and connects it to the space beyond the heavens.

Their camp is high upon an alpine cuesta pinned to a craggy fence of dangerous rocks that stops the hardy flocculent grass and obstructs the view of anything but taller peaks and sky. Behind the strip of expensive tents and hastily rigged tables and clustered colonies of stout white boxes stands a cage of rocks, confirming the terrace is but a nick in the numinous range. Cutting between the barbarous stones, strategic ambages uncoil in twining tributaries down around a small clear tarn, a ravine, along a creek valley and deep into the interior rib cage.

When evening's bloodbath finally finishes, the grassy rind becomes oddly larger, seeming to go on like an innuendo fading into a black portière. Their fire is a mean spearhead in the darkness pointing to the others in the dome.

The air smells of tents and packs glowing newly in the dark. Maggie gazes at the fire until her eyes smart and transcribe an orange schooner, burning on a plastic Fellini sea. Although she isn't looking at him, she watches Icarus. Maggie married Newt *after*. Even in high school, Hill was so much filler, an excuse, a way to spend time out at the ranch. Icarus is the ninety-eight percent, the nothing holding all the rest together.

"Asshole." Maggie sighs.

In the dark, Icarus, limping yet, paces between the tents and fire and when he stops for half a second to catch his breath, to think what goes where and why it isn't working, he gazes at the sky moving too quickly. He wants the show to stay, but even the moon, wobbly and bashed, has slipped higher, gibbous and faded, hardly worth watching.

"This time next year we'll be rich as thieves."

———

Third day in, Hill brings down an old bull elk. He fixes the rack, a damn nice size, over his tent. But no matter how he marinates or fries and fricassees the cuts of bull elk, it's tough as gardening gloves.

"God, Hill," Maggie tells him, pitching her serving back in the pan, "I'd as soon wear it as eat it." And she wanders off toward her tent to get ready for bed, peeling off her clothes as she goes. Aware Icarus has left to wash up down by the freezing lake, she won't be far behind. Dallas decides to follow Maggie, never let her out of her sight is the plan. "Wait up, I'll go down with you. It's always good to have a little company when it's dark as this." Hill smiles to himself. "Yeah," he says, "Maggie's been known to have trouble finding her way back in the dark."

To break the monotony of elk, there's rabbit stew and grilled lake trout with a side order of pan-fried frog's legs. It's true the cold lake and creek feeding into it brim with browns and rainbow trout and Dolly Vardens and the troupe bury the campfire with small sweet-tasting fish. Maggie's already getting more than a little sick of fish. Fortunately they parachuted in a substantial supply of canned goods, reams of rice and beans and mainstay grains (great for those who like oatmeal and beans day after day), along with coffee and pasta, broken to bits, and apples and oranges, bruised and mushy, a few trays of jealously guarded canned fruit, and crates and crates of dehydrated camping food, inedible and unfilling and untouched.

Nights are cooler than they'd like, a good reason to linger fireside. It's routine for Laird and Icarus and Gibson to stay up half the night poring over maps, quarrelling. The point of contention isn't new, the same unresolved point arises again and again. Where to begin their search? Exactly which mountainside, which river valley? They continually circle this question, some warming their hands on it, others spitting sidelong into the conflagration.

Icarus tells Gibson, "You need to borrow a pair a Neuter's glasses you think that's a river. It's a creek. Any blind fool can see as much. What we're lookin for is a river!"

"Admit you're wrong for once, why don't you?"

"What? Don't you guys ever sleep?" Maggie staggers out of her tent, half asleep, to wander around the campfire on her way to pee. "I'm curious just when you boys are planning on goin to bed?"

Laird spies with his gunmetal eyes, Maggie shivering and twitching and bending down to rub her legs, with nothing on under the T-shirt outside of some jewellery around an ankle and a couple three toe rings. Icarus snarls at her, "What in hell are you doin paradin around in perfume? Patchouli brings bugs faster than if you smeared yourself in fish roe."

"Freck off, asshole!"

Maggie heads for the woods. Under her breath, she's blasting him. Fairly standard stuff, a DVD she routinely plays. Love! Oh boy, she could tell him a whole lot more. Forget the piss poets prattle on about, what rot, and the other thing, love—it doesn't biodegrade. Stroll through the gutter or a geriatric ward of a long-term facility and you'll see, the vessel might be shot to hell with radiation or crack but love blooms on. A stunner all right, if a field of screamin yellow dandelions can be construed as beautiful, certainly to the infected, it's a host of freckin daffodils.

Make no mistake, it's the blood, the driving universal force, not some show of flowers. Once it's got hold, it doesn't let go. Love is— that's all. The ribbons you tie around it, the trunk you shove it into, that changes, not love. If you're bitten, you're malarial for life. Don't freckin celebrate! If you consider yourself lucky to be in love, wait, love'll teach you different. Romantic as fire and wax. Come closer, the arsehole whispers, you're not nearly close enough. There's a shred remaining. Let me hold that too.

She pauses as if to light another cigarette or pour another drink. Love isn't a mystery or a drugstore panacea, some universal aspirin for the heart and soul. Love is all there is, beyond oxygen, beyond hydrogen, as mysterious, as complex, as deadly simple. Take my word! It doesn't break down, worse than freckin plutonium—what is the universe but black?

Next morning, it's another lazy day. Altitude sharpens the early heat. Dallas and Maggie, skin pimpled, desert their tents, meet, silent and surly, at the firepit to nibble cold, oily elk steaks and burnt packaged pan fries, give them up and pour coffee from the pot hanging from a bent coat hanger over a dying bed of smoke and climb to a higher, flatter rock, already hot. Steam curls from it like a standing iron.

They are above the clouds. It's no longer disorienting but normal to look down on suds of white and above at primary blue. Below them, cotton towelling bumps against the rocks and bounces slowly free. A few higher strands of bleached soap scum cling to the sides and stay.

Months back, deep in January's coffin, Newt, caught in a long checkout line, read in one of the pseudoscience journals drugstores sell that traces of mineral deposits turn up in bee pollen and honey. It was the final piece, all he needed to put his scheme in motion. He drove in a blind rush to tell Hill and Gibson exactly what he'd discovered and what it meant!

"Gold!" he shouted, waving the article in their faces. "Gold shows up in bee pollen! It's as easy as analyzing a pot of honey! One look and we'll know where we need to start. The precise location. It couldn't be easier. The bees—the goddamn beautiful bees— flying from one happy mountain valley to another will do our work for us! We won't have to do a thing but look in a microscope! It's too goddamn perfect to believe!"

Convinced he was the one to set a rigorous scientific standard, Newt appointed himself officer in charge of the honey brigade, and no one else objected.

"I'm ready for the next batch," he snaps across at Ana, stagger- ing down the path, exhausted under the weight of her pack. "Chop chop!" Beside him, in a sumo squat, are two equally expensive microscopes, downside crate left are avenues of glass slides and honeycombs, individually tagged with his distinctively fussy hand- writing.

"I suppose we ought to station a few hives further afield, you know, broaden our scope." Ana pauses, realizing she has no idea what she's just said.

Newt twists his head stiffly to make eye contact, nudging back the flap of his foreign legion kepi with his shoulder. "You're not getting discouraged? Not when we're this close!" his tone one that coachmen use to goad heavy-hoofed, overworked beasts to slave on.

"Discouraged isn't the word I'd put to it."

Ana considers flinging the remaining samples over the cliff. She stops herself in time; it's not Newt she's angry with, but the other four men gathered like sultans in front of their tents. The tension between the four has worsened. It will deteriorate further, these sorts of grievances invariably do. She's tried talking to Gibson but he refuses to listen. No, working with Newt, distracted by his scheme, harebrained or not, is the best way to keep from going stark raving mad.

"Forget it!"

Icarus's voice fractures the quiet mountain morning, distant spires return it missing the anger, a hollow chime, broken and badly cloned, noisy all the same.

"No way it's as far south as we've been looking." Icarus jabs a long knubbly stick at one map and the next, pointing out gradations to Laird. "Might as well try Hawaii next for all the good it'll do." He's a creature of intuitions and this time he knows he's right.

The ground in front of the tents is quilted with forestry maps, most a pale mint green, some a sepia tone, others so heavily marked that now charcoal and graphite dominate. Gibson, usually the most difficult to convince, paces back and forth, visiting map after map, confident an idea he hasn't hatched can't be worth a damn. "Could be Sticker's gotta point, we been over'n over that south slope."

Laird unrolls another set of maps. "Even you have to admit it needs to be scouted out!" His voice low as a slow-burning fuse.

"It's been scouted out," Icarus tells him.

Gibson stops pacing. "Might make sense to try lookin west by northwest. Common sense tells us that much. Be what the ol man'd do."

"You pair'a Cub Scouts know hikin'n fishin and stokin a piss-poor campfire. Me, I know prospectin. The ol man took me every trip. Two a you tagged along a couple three times but me'n the ol man lived prospectin."

"You're not the only one that knows about prospectin gold," Icarus fires back, clutching his divining rod—his expertise, his contribution.

"We're on top of it! It's all but kicking us in the balls." Laird crouches over a map like an animal settling down on a fresh kill. "This southern slope—we need to get this southern slope under our belt. Whadya know about workin a grid? We're workin a grid here."

"It's got nothin to do with workin a goddamn grid. Goddamn nothin on that southwest slope but elk droppings and grizzly turds!"

"You tellin me I don't know what I'm talkin about?" Laird, jaw fixed, rises to stand across from Icarus as if they've entered a ring and are waiting for the bell to sound.

"No way it's hell'n gone further south."

"If I say it's south—it's south!" Laird holds his anger level as a hammer poised to drop.

"I don't intend wastin another day goin over that goddamn south western slope one more effin time!"

Laird goes for Icarus, Icarus wriggles free, and they face off. In the backdrop the wind ruffles a few leaves the wrong way.

"Hang on." Hill, weight straightening one leg, his expression glazed (he's heard it all before), leans back to watch Dallas and Maggie suntanning, their bodies greased rivers silvered in the sun, Maggie's pubic hair shiny as a stack of pennies. "Why not let our green beret run another check on the south slope he's so damn sure, and the rest of us move on to the next ridge?"

"Bingo!" Icarus swings his divining rod. "Us three and Betsy here'll head out on the other ridge, see if we don't come up with somethin today."

"We do it, we do it together!" Laird decides.

They head out, maps, picks and pans as well, protruding from their packs like sticks from a geisha's knot, backs bent from the weight, the sun lost on their matted hair and private disputes.

"You guys are fucked," Dallas shouts down at them.

"It's gold, sugar, pure and simple." Laird charges ahead, determined to set a killer pace.

"It's nothin to do with gold," she yells back.

"God's got plans for you . . ." Maggie calls after them as they disappear behind the jagged jaw of rocks. "Dementia!"

———

Midday, Newt and Ana hike to a hive located four miles southwest of camp, at the bottom of a pretty mountain coulee. Tipping along the rocky alpine bank, the hive resembles a robot, deserted, R2D2 left to guard the slope while Bruce Dern goes increasingly berserk.

"Don't take all day," he barks back at her, dipping side to side from the weight of the heavy metal case.

Overhead, a long-tailed hawk passes a tall black spruce, wheels and stops upon a naked branch, high and pointing toward the sun. The sky, a quiet blue, takes Ana away. A paler shade outlines the tree and hawk, they appear black and cuneiform, magnets fixed to a blue door, one she enters without a second thought.

"If she would simply do what I ask," he moans, following an old sheep trail down the coulee, "trust in me—that's what it comes down to, trust. I don't suppose," he sighs, continuing to muddle across the grassy bank, "she ever really has."

Ana isn't listening now he's turned his thoughts to Maggie, a depth his tank can never fathom, but continually circles from the surface. Silence expands in the sultry heat, provoking suspicions and spells. Ana finds it intoxicating to imagine the many hearts weaving a potion of both.

"I don't suppose I have to tell you she and Icarus are . . ."

"Old friends, Newt, leave it at that."

Behind him on the trail, she gazes on a stony plain spilling poppies and shabby fireweed. The path narrows, continuing down the rocky slope into a ravine. Fast water fighting with the bank of honed boulders infects the air with noise rich enough to taste.

"I'm realistic, maybe a little too, is the thing."

"Realistic," she reminds him, "is the name of generic tape decks and AM car radios."

On the way back they stop in an exiguous meadow to enjoy a cheap lunch of dehydrated goat cheese and a mean scrap of soda bread. Newt recklessly unzips his white beekeeper's suit past the crotch. His hand rests there, drawing comfort from the rubbery feeling. On the limey stretch of grass he is a pristine grub supine on a meadow plate. His expensive glasses reflect the harsh light making it impossible for her to see his eyes. The distorted view emerges post-modern, severe and pleasantly deconstructed.

His nose is large. When he swings it around, he does so with pride. "Have you," he clears his throat, "ever considered leaving Gibson? Beats me how you hooked up with him in the first place. You aren't half bad looking, and besides, looks aren't everything. Who knows, you might do better."

His smile is worse than his voice, which has a haunting quality difficult to place, a burr that doesn't fail to catch. Easy to imagine it on the car radio selling Oldsmobiles, possibly pizza. Impossible to place such a voice in a darkened room, working through ebullient candlelight, plunging hot and gasping down a powdered neck. A voice better suited to the gavel and auction block or a high-powered bench.

Smoothly reaching out to brush the frayed hem of her blue jeans, he beams over his Ray-Bans. In the sun his eyes are bloodshot, plastic fractured with red, reminding her of an advertisement for garbage bags, an albino flogging cling wrap.

"What makes you want money so much," she asks, brushing him away, "that you willingly dress up in a plastic bag and fondle bee shit?"

He laughs, a vacuum sucking a close corner. "I don't know why the rest don't like you, I find you surprisingly droll."

————————

Sunshine basking on cinnabar hair. Maggie pads her foot in the fast creek that feeds into the ravine, her head resting on a knee. She's drowsy with heat and the sleepy sounds beyond, the hush of the woods growing behind her and the monotonous rush of water. Nearby, a woodpecker taps endlessly, a dark bird scrabbles, hidden under low matted bushes. Far away there is a swooping hawk. On a snapping sound she jumps, her hair floating back exposing a body painfully pale. She listens, then after long seconds her head drops again to her knee.

Under cover of deep growth, Hill watches her, savouring her wait, the arc of her neck reflecting light like a mirror. "Been waitin long?" he asks. She turns, then looks away. Still he sees her colour.

"You're late, arsehole!"

"I was on time, sat on this same rock, and you, sweet thing, were late."

"Sorry, cowboy, I was early."

White dreams parade across the water, near enough to touch. Staring at the rocky bed and small darting fish, she considers leaving. He crouches beside her, whispering along the dark side of her nape, "Don't lie, Maggie, you don't do it as well as I'd like."

Much as Maggie soaks in the sun, she never toasts but remains a ghastly white. In the splendour of late afternoon, her face is a river of its own, one he doesn't like to read. When he hears her voice without seeing her, he imagines she is vulnerable. Her voice is her hook, how many times has he told her that? She has a surprising laugh, hoarse and old. Hill envisions a lonely midlife crisis slumped on a broken bench staring glassy-eyed past her absinthe whenever Maggie laughs. He wishes she wouldn't.

Once, years ago, she told him that she'd never been unhappy. I've been frustrated, frustrated certainly, but nothing more . . . maybe a little lost, at loose ends, sometimes, you know, when I'm between jobs or something, but no, I can't say I've ever been unhappy, not really, you know, not like you . . . nothing like you. I don't let things get me down. I'm beyond that shit. And he told her, You're the sorriest woman I know.

Some days, when he's gone off alone, perhaps hiking through the woods, a day that's sunny or at least mild, on such a day he persuades himself he is free. That's when he hasn't seen her for a space of time. When he's close, as he is now, he is convinced he'll never get shut of her.

She rolls on her side, an elegant unwinding beside him. Her feet are small and not well arched. Unlike his wife's acutely arched workhorse feet, callused and bruised from dancing on point, Maggie's are plush, softened cushions, painted toenails and pumiced pinkened heels, rich creams and oils rubbed and rubbed, all the same undeniably flat. Hill studies the ankles, perversely shapely in their bonelessness. He thinks of deboned poultry in the market, the way the skin sleeps on the flesh. She touches his hand, hers hot from the sun, his cool, almost numb from the weight of his body. She smiles, her too large too thin lips flattening into that horrible victory-laced sneer.

In direct sunlight the moonstones fade away, leaving her eyes blank empty pages, seeming to flip languidly in the breeze of routine blinking. He tells her, "I thought I'd never ditch her. Between the heat and the dope she finally crashed."

"She's exhausted. Every time I go pee at night I bump into her. One thing I'll say for your D . . . D . . . Dallas, she's a wonderful light sleeper." She sprawls like a harem dancer, rocking the gecko rhythmically as a castanet. "But, silly Hilly, whatever possessed you to marry the trowel?"

Years ago Hill was alone on a 747 to India, making a break for it. He'd asked Maggie to come and she'd refused. Minutes before take-off she sent him a message to disembark . . . and he did. She only wanted to see if he would.

He gave up on her after that, moved in with Dallas and told himself he was a happy man. A man'd be a fool not to appreciate a woman as sensible as Dallas, a few years older than the rest of them and with a body wiry as a chainlink fence. He isn't sure how Maggie came back into his life. He doesn't want to remember, but Maggie knows. She can't abide losing anything.

It goes back to Icarus. Everything else is Nytol to nullify the fact Icarus doesn't care for her but fucks her when it's convenient . . . *convenient* . . . his word. I told you not to, was what he said last time he left. Not to what? she yelled at his back, but he never answered. Icarus never would though, would he?

She pushes Hill down, forcing her face into his. She isn't pretty, even she knows that. It's something else with her, some savage skulking along the outer reaches of her smile and body temperature. In photographs and mirrors she comes across ugly, but nothing captures the other thing, the power or heat.

Rounding their way back to camp, tired and sore, Newt and Ana catch sight of the others fishing for supper. There's no sign of Hill or Maggie. And hurrying to inquire where they are, Newt stumbles off the ridge leading down to the lake, plummeting straight into it. Gibson and Icarus shake their heads in disbelief. "He's a sinker," hoots Gibson, smacking his leg, not even sorry Newt may've scared away some fish. "Neuter's a goddamn sinker, wouldn't ya know." Ana drops the samples to swim in after him. Because he's a poor swimmer with a fear of deep water and a body mass inclined to sinking, the rescue takes longer than it needs to and is more comic.

"Shit," Laird drawls. "I seen rocks stay afloat longer."

After midnight Gibson and Ana return to the small cold lake. It's the only spot around. Ana watches moonlight stipple the black water blue, mosque and turret blue, streaks carrying a shimmer of Persian onion bulbs. She's working her thoughts away from the obvious, all the hearts and rivers she'd rather sail down. The night is dull newsprint black.

"We need to jettison Laird."

"Not fuckin likely," said in the voice he reserves for ordering another round.

Where's the point in trying to persuade Gibson? For Gib, listening amounts to a brief time out, regulation, an interval allowing seconds to fast-forward through his menu of daydreams and ruminations. Gibson listens with half a mind—while one half records, occasionally managing a quick replay or some pretty fancy editing, the other half channel-surfs. Beyond that, his hearing is acute, a first-rate instrument.

"Brother or not, you shouldn't've asked him along. I warned you. We both know what he's like."

"It's a little late in the game to be pullin Laird. Besides, the world's full of Lairds, nothing but Lairds. Why give him a second thought? Without a negative, where's the point plugging in?"

Gibson's a marmalade alley cat sneaking through the heating ducts or drifting in with the mail, crabby and curdled, his face spoiled from midnight skirmishes, ears jagged as broken-off bottles. It's all desire and wanting. Even when he's hoping to go slow, he can't halt the hurry-up hunger slipping through his pores, a queer smell, sharp, immutable. If only his knees weren't so buggered from football. And his back's acting up, one too many low friggin blows.

"Take me to bed." His eyes are half closed and puffy.

"I'm not just ready." She knows he needs a few more cigarettes before he'll settle. She leans back to study the moon and tells him Laird reminds her of something gone bad, some slimy mess way at the back of the fridge.

An owl circles over and over the empty field of water. Gibson waves his arms at the sky. Approaching summer, the sky is black and fibrous as hodden, stars shiver brightly through their cold web. Orion dodging the dog star. He sings up at them. He's not happy, it's not that kind of song.

Finally he takes hold of her as if to pull her out of the way of an oncoming car. They are alone, there is nothing out there but clouds of bugs and night birds and black thick enough to stack.

"There's no gold here," he tells her, as though it's a revelation, as if it's a freshly discovered puncture. "It's true," he repeats to convince himself, "there's no gold here."

Laird, all bones and lean good looks, shoves his back against a razor-skinned spruce and stares at Icarus.

Icarus stares back. "I'm tellin you once'n for all there's nothin here, nowheres near close! We been over every speck not once but twenty times—day in day out—and there's nothin!" He pounds the heel of his boot into the hard dry ground, loosening a smell of drought.

"Could be more!" Hill tosses out. "More'n likely be nearer thirty times we scouted this strip! Can anybody tell me why we're back doin this southwestern slope? I figured we'd all agreed."

"Only reason I bothered comin this last time was to show Laird once'n for all and be done!"

They're six miles southwest of camp, docked on a steep rocky ramp. Having crossed a valley, evergreen and rough with spindly high elevation spruce and bush, some new growth turning a pale lemon lime from heat exhaustion in the unduly dry spring and, after doggedly struggling up the facing slope, as far as any of them want to climb today, they've come to rest, hungry and thinking about heading back, dully watching a lazy herd of elk wander along the valley bed, feeding and walking on, a dozen or more. Hill and Laird contemplate picking off the bull. Each measures the rack and considers the frailty of expensive high-powered rifles. Further, there are splendid glimpses of a nullah, which from this height runs to deep cyan, and far beyond the valley climb more mountains, ragged and frightening, no one really notices, yet whenever Icarus glances at them, his chest tightens. They are all that thrills him, possibly the only thing that ever has.

"I feel it," he says, almost under his breath. "It's there, I know it," and he points at the river lying in a distant northeasterly valley like a fuzzy mauve caterpillar in a bed of fresh leaves. "It's in that direction there! Why the fuck won't you listen—I know what I'm talking about. Over there's gold, gold . . ."

"The only hit of yellow inside'a that river is bear piss," snarls Laird. "Could be elk shit. Longside some goat shit'n sheep . . ."

"I'm tellin you, it's there. I can feel it." His eyes shine with certainty.

Laird digs his toe into the short grass, browned to gold from drought and winterburn but struggling to green again. The wind arrives, as it always does by late afternoon, and blows his sandy hair into his eyes then out, and swats last year's empty germens into the ground. "You're always feelin somethin or other. You're a regular psychic circus show, you are."

The air stinks of sticky resin, the tinder tincture a forest vents after months of hot weather (strange in May), where every blade and needle reeks of thirst and dust and every tree is related to those January cadavers, brittle green and falling in broken sheets of sharpened pins. Where is the breath of spring, the heady stench of moulting earth and sap?

Seeded like clumsy flowers over the grassy mountain pitch, the others wait as though anticipating some great paw to come and swipe them off. Arm wrapped round a sharp rock's throat to keep from sliding away, Ana closes her eyes but is too tired to sleep. Inside she's screaming, Damn, damn.

Icarus moves the divining rod as if to put it under wraps. "Close as it is," aiming his chin toward the northeasterly twist of river, "it's stupid not to look."

"Ceptin, Sticky Icky, we'd be lookin in the wrong fuckin direction!"

Maggie picks at last year's dead grass. "You're only frustrated, Laird." She gives up the fistful of scorched grass to the wind and scrolls onto her back to watch the clouds small as toiling tractors. "It's been hard on you bein this long away from wood alcohol."

Icarus snorts, he rarely shares a laugh. Laughter is an intimacy for him more difficult than sex.

Given Maggie's penchant for romancing the mundane, Icarus is as mysterious as the Great Pyramid, entrance hidden, with an arduous climb up to the heart of the tomb, emptied and ruined, robbed long before. For this and the rest of Icarus's woes, she blames Laird, and if, as drugstore psychologists suggest, sibling order cuts the pattern of a life, perhaps it can be put down to something as sweeping as that, for the family is unhappy and sibling rivalry plays its bitter part.

Laird frees the hood of his butane, simultaneously thumbnailing it, sending a heavenly blue torch snaking in the air like he'd trained it to stand on its tail. Lazy as a vendor fanning flies, he glides his free hand over the flare. After a few idle passes, he cups the palm on top of the tower, donning a monk-like grin and staring sleepily at Ana. A smell, almost sweet, wafts through the air. Mesmerized, Newt and Maggie and Dallas watch him. The others turn away. They've seen him do this before. From his eyes, he appears to be enjoying it, a meditation exercise he routinely performs for cocktail waitresses and cops. Not a muscle flinches. He fixes his hand until the flame peters out. The smile also gutters as he dips sideways to plant the incendiary device against the ankle of Icarus's boot. "I've about had my fill of you," he tells him, renailing the spindle, blowtorching the raggedy hem of Icarus's blue jeans. Too late Icarus jumps back, kicking the thing out of Laird's hand and slapping the leg of his Levi's to knock down the blaze.

The two brothers circle, counter and clockwise, a pattern they routinely set, stalking and being stalked, hunter and hunted, each step killing the ground separating them softly.

What was it with Cain and Abel? Why would a kind, all-seeing God abandon one son to such obvious and seemingly pointless danger? Where is biblical justice when the guilty son survives and trundles on to prosper, not in the slightest hobbled by guilt, but possessing an efficiency enviable in a centurion or a butcher? Did God need one brother to die, as though employing some dramatic foreshadowing for another, later-born son, not in order to save some from sin, as it would later play, but to establish an order where destruction plays as big a part as creation? A world where the depths of volcanic overflow form the very basis of husbandry and life? Where good and evil and every shade between are essential, where nothing is completely understood but necessary, and the minions of each are left to fend for themselves?

Laird drives his fist into the side of Icarus's head. Icarus staggers, and although he can't focus clearly, deflects Laird's oncoming strike with his right forearm while launching a left scud to the troche between Laird's eyes. Both men repeat the same worn-out lines, how quickly, how precisely they will kill the other arsehole.

"Stop it! Will you stop?" Newt pulls himself up, shouting, "I've got news!" Mindful he may have left his entry too late, he yells to compensate for lost ground. Leaning to pitch each word. "For Christ's sake—will you listen?—I've found traces of gold in a sample out of hive thirteen, the far hive, the one west of the ravine! Not far from here! Further south southwest!"

Neither man wants to stop. They haven't the slightest interest in Newt or anything he might have to say, yet they do begin to slow, the punches weaken, their bodies wind down as though they are electronic fripperies Newt's yanked the plug on. The word "gold" reaches beyond the simple recesses of hatred and jealousy, deep in the subterranean tunnels of their collective unconscious.

"I haven't finished running all the tests. But things appear promising." His arms, winging oars on either side, blur. "It's definitely promising!"

Icarus hangs like a drunken mule, Laird's fists drop to his side heavy as dual wrecker balls, jobless and ill at ease. A collective "Huh?" translate duh? Then Laird steps in front of him, "Why'd you wait so long to say?" The wrecker balls ease back to chest level.

"I don't know . . . I wanted to surprise you I guess. You know, save it for the absolute perfect moment." Smiling broadly, happy for any response, eager to stretch his few moments of power and influence.

Laird kicks at the dried-out grass with the steel toe of his boot, and tells him quietly, "You're startin to piss me off, big time." Laird's voice is too calm. Newt should know that.

Gibson takes a deep breath and exhales, "Could be this means Laird's right after all, Sticker. Looks like we might need to give the south slope another goin over."

"Fuck off!"

Icarus heads across the slope leading toward a better view of the river and the place he believes they should begin to prospect. When he gets like this, he doesn't walk but takes the ground in bloody blocks.

"Hang on, Icarus," Newt shouts after him. "Did you hear me! Hold on, will you! I said I found traces!" This voice brash and animated as a comic-strip rooster. "I said traces!"

Icarus holds up a finger. It stamps the air for a brief moment, some ancient key, freeing a hive he's holding deep inside to blow in the wind and float back over them; if only it was black oil or tar wafting back to shore instead of swarming frustration.

Newt studies the hand and finger suspended in the air, he could be a tourist admiring an ornament hanging in a foreign garden, until Icarus takes back the hand and continues along the couloir and out of sight and Newt snaps back to life. "Why won't you listen?" If only he had hair enough to pull.

Unable to decide whether to follow and drag him back or stay and send someone else, Newt stumbles into Laird, and quickly turns to catch another glimpse of the empty trail. There's a murky obduracy in Laird that puts him off. Those grenade-green eyes. He yells "Wait" at the gravid rocks, runs halfway and back and halfway again, repeating his news as if barking into a crushing wind or at profoundly deaf children.

Icarus is alone at last. From the bluff he looks down on the river valley. Midway through the scumble of freshly painted green, a crippled fox sniffs out a burrow, teaching her kits to hunt rabbits. In the quiet behind him, bush tits venture from their wicker cage, chatting busily to each other. Bush tits are unusual, the peculiar early heat may have thrown them off course. He doesn't give it much thought.

Far along the riverbank, Icarus sees, or thinks he sees, a shape. However, when he fixes his binoculars on it, there's nothing there, nothing out of the ordinary. No sooner does he turn away than he senses it again, a figure, possibly a woman, yet when turns back to look, there's only the mountain valley, empty as ever.

Gibson intrudes on Icarus. "I said I'd come and tell you," he mumbles finally.

Icarus continues gazing at the valley.

"Newt claims he's found traces of gold in the pollen. Minute traces. According to him we're right on top of it."

Icarus turns, allowing Gibson to glimpse his profile.

"Newt thinks we oughta give the southwest side a real goin over."

"Why won't you listen, Gib?"

"We need a little more to go on than another of your hunches."

"That's not you talkin."

"Look, it's bound to be a bit like luck. Sometimes you run hot, other times you're cold. Why can't you see, you're runnin cold?"

"I'm on, Gib. Spot on. I'm tellin you. Take my word."

Gibson looks away, he's angry enough. "Newt and Laird are started over on it now. I said I'd come and get you."

"It's not by the friggin creek or the friggin west side or any-wheres down south—there's the reason the traces were goddamn minute!"

When the young bear approaches the lake, Ana doesn't scream for help. She doesn't move or make a flurry of noise to frighten it away. She follows none of the free and sensible advice park rangers have handed her for years. Instead she waits quietly while the young bear, unaware of her, ambles pigeon-toed toward her stony seat near the water's edge.

3

A one-winter bear, its sunken sides and demarcated ribs betray the poor time it's had fending for itself. All the same, the bear is beautiful—she never anticipated that. She envisioned bears as coarse and blundering but, even starving, its coat possesses a deep sheen, the face dusted with a softness reserved for pandas or koalas, its plastic orange nose nearer to a toy than anything real or dangerous.

It's closer now, some twenty feet away. She fights a desire to call it over so she can tweak its rubbery snout, convinced that if she did, it would toot a cute clown honk or possibly begin to dance. Somewhere in this dither of toystore fun, she decides to keep the bear. It obviously needs looking after, and it's time she took on a pet. Although she's never wanted just any sort of pet, she recognizes this remarkable playmate is the perfect answer.

The bear shifts nearer the water's lip, and she culls various names. A name is important. She must have a way of calling it. She fixes on the bear. Come Tundra . . . Moskova! Here, Kiev!

Vaguely aware of something in the air, the bear stands on its hind feet and sniffs, holding its front paws next to its chest and lifting them out around its head, shifting side to side, looking this way and that. In this rotating way, it finally finds her.

The bear appears uncertain what to do. Towering on its hind legs, it debates whether it should run or attack. The head rolls a bit. The eyes open wider, while the mouth appears to want to roar or speak.

She whispers sweet meaningless phrases as if to a small child lost and frightened. The words have a calming effect. Tension eases. The bear, when it stops, doesn't face her but an uncommon lightness it catches along the brow of rocks. The scent and play of shadow and reflection are new.

Laird waits, hidden in a reef of rocks overlooking the small lake. He followed Ana to watch her skinny-dip. Voyeurism is a practice he cultivated as a child, watching the bull or stallion work, or his mother sneaking to a loft with one of the hired hands. Ana has a fine pair of tits. Worth scouting out. Without a second thought, without warning, he raises his twelve-gauge pump shotgun and takes aim. When he's within range he never misses. Near as this the contest is one-sided. Still a man's obliged to grab pleasure wherever he can.

Ana, sensing something, stands, clasping her hands to her throat. The lakeshore is silent. Voltaic calm levels the air. A minor crack. Hardly worth noting. Still the sound sends her running, unfurling her arms out around her head, both hands opening and closing, searching this way and that. In her wambling, she finds Laird, and the reason the bear has dropped along the water's edge like an over-sized baseball glove. Lunging first to comfort the bear and veering to charge Laird, her head wobbles as if to come away while the eyes and mouth widen to roar.

The evening air is fragrant with the stench.

Laird rigged a pulley to a good tall pine to hang the young bear to gut and skin and sun-dry and Newt sawed off a haslet to roast with a sauce of red clover and wild dandelion leaves and a side dish of dehydrated chili con carne. The camp smells of game searing and beneath that another aroma, cold and oddly metallic, the lingering scent of an abattoir.

Dallas circles a washbasin. She's lost her left contact. She yells at the rest to keep away, afraid they may step on it. She's mad they're not helping, she yells about that too.

Maggie hisses under her breath, "Dumb bitch."

"Goddamn, I can't see a thing!"

"It's on the side of the washbasin! I can see it from here in the light. Only an idjit wears contacts in the bush. Newt knows that much."

A herd of wapiti forage the far slope, nothing but a few specks. Even in this fading light, Maggie can pick out horn lengths, queer markings, sex. It's impossible for her to imagine life in a fog. The dependency unsettles her.

Oh, the scene is homely. Caribou moss, dried to mould-coloured cornflakes, crumbles underfoot and black moss droops in dusty webs, silken suppleness beaten down in the rawhide sun, nothing more than false beards now, brittle whiskers hanging from shrunken limbs or furfuraceous trunks. Nothing to take and hold. Another skid-row Santa hangin out.

Dallas rolls the contact over her tongue, pops it back in her eye and returns to the business of wiping the back of her legs with a rag. Mosquitoes surround her in an oily aura. Behind them the wind moves a door flap softly against the front of a tent. The sucking sound fills the air.

"I'll be done in a second, then you can have it."

Maggie'll go for a freezing swim before she'll muck around in a pan of grey slop water, dead as cement.

"Funny though?" Dallas gives Maggie a lick-my-boot grin. "You going off like that—again. Without saying? Here, in the wild, it's only common sense to say. After the last time, I thought we all agreed? Anything could happen."

"I waved at Ana on her way to swim. I thought she'd tell you if she got back before me."

"By the time Ana got back you were the last thing on her mind."

"I don't suppose I could've known that."

"Perhaps you weren't alone? Makes sense you wouldn't be worried if you were meeting someone?"

Newt stops to listen, and Maggie smiles at Dallas, completely unperturbed.

Grieving for the bear distances Ana from the others. They are aliens she's encountering for the first time. Dallas is a hard woman, but her life is hard. How could life be otherwise when the one you love loves someone else? Dallas and Newt share this. Yet both married knowing. Neither was deceived. In Dallas, the side that might have gravitated to tenderness if she'd found herself loved has atrophied. And Newt, a gentle (if obnoxious) man, wastes away trying to beguile a woman who never turns to him without wishing he was someone else. Strange, neither is a romantic. Both are pragmatists. Yet they live for love, on hope of it. What have they gained, these pragmatists? A house, a Jaguar, a partner of sorts, impedimenta interring the certainty of never being loved. This certainty is their security. Perhaps their only one. Ana watches the pair, confident any similitude is superficial. Security and means are nothing to her, she turned her back on both some time ago.

"Potatoes are ready," hollers Newt, rolling the praties, dusted black and powdery as hundred-year-old eggs, free of the fire, gingerly poking them with a stick as if to make sure they are dead. The potatoes are a jealously guarded delicacy. Dallas uses a stiff leather glove to lift the tin kettle of chili from the flames and set it on a nearby rock. The smell of roasting bear brings another torrent of black flies.

"None for me!"

Newt carves generous slices of meat onto a waiting pentagon of tin pentacles (even Newt pauses to interpret the portent of fortuitous prosperity). To keep them warm and free of flies, he tethers each beneath a bending drag of smoke.

"I told you—none for me," Ana shouts at him. "No way I'm eating that poor sweet bear."

Suddenly Hill is behind them. His thin shirt, run with dark wings of sweat, hangs weighted with a day's futility while his face hides behind a growth of grime and dirt. Only his eyes are bright red taillights glowing in the dark.

Maggie winks at him. "We've been wondering what'd become of you. Dallas here has been fretting you might have been so all alone."

Hill leans over the roasting spit, too tired to do more than sniff at it. The fog of bugs, suddenly more interested in the stink of over-heated blood than barbecued black bear, surround him in a dusty quivering drape.

"Sticker's gone off on his own. No tellin when he'll be back."

Newt hands Hill the extra plate of meat. "You want to know what his problem is, I'll tell you what his problem is—Icarus thinks he's smarter than the rest of us! Like a law degree means nothing!"

Hill shrugs. He isn't going to say. "I gotta feelin he'd just as soon we left him go."

When he kisses Dallas, he stops. Her lips feel like saltines about to break away in his mouth, reminding him he's thirsty and miles from a long cold one. He glances over at Maggie.

Maggie looks away, thinking of Icarus. Memories are break-throughs only in pain. Odd, isn't it, how events engrave so differently one heart or another. Where Icarus never recalls a fleeting glance, Maggie battles to forget each moment, Vermeer-clear and indelible, pervasive as Prussian blue on fine linen, the way he looks with sleep playing down his lashes, to keep it safely stowed under the seat in front of her. Inevitably it leaks free.

Sometimes love doesn't offer any other choice. Despite what self-help books and counsellors preach, love is beyond all that free-will malarkey. In some wretched cases it has no connection but to the recombinant ropes of feeling leading from one to another, binding, and all that. What else holds any meaning? What else exists? Life outside the ropes is a terminal. Endless and empty.

Once Maggie told Icarus, probably drunk out of her mind, it doesn't matter, she meant it anyway—even now she believes it to be true—that he is dead. Despite being warm-blooded and pausing now and then to grab another breath, he has departed, not simply a few selected nonvital trivial parts, such as some dance-hall gambler missing heart and/or balls and stumbling through a line of coke and/or beer and a rash of boring steps—but dead dead. She's never figured out how he is alive yet dead or how it came to be, but simply understands it's some dangerous quirk of fate. Perhaps the price a phoenix pays—to rise up from ashes, the bird must turn to ash. Sometimes she understands the dead dead are placed alongside the living dead (. . . her!) to make them experience the pain of breathing, and through breath return to life. That's all she does, nothing more, simply breathe. The razored grains of oxygen, the dazzled heavy molecules of dioxide and carbon, in and out. Only that. She feels it now. Each breath.

"He won't be much longer, it's nearly dark, he'll be back . . ." This said softly to herself, but overheard by Newt and Hill and Ana.

The crepuscular sky has cleared, one last great wave of burning yellow washing slowly out. There's a hush of pending frost. As the sun stumbles and falls, the moon fades up on the far side, blue as water. Spring's old moon, half there, assigned to herald bad weather, it's forgotten its place in a senile grin and totters indecorously young, visiting the shameless serenity of dotage, a whisper of its other mislaid self.

In the light Maggie appears as blue as the moon, waiting for the stars. There in the folds of clouds a splinter of light sneaks through, beckoning, faint as a distant porch light. The marbled moon faces approaching darkness, confused as an Alzheimer's patient gazing on a tray of tiny brightly coloured pills. Yes, yes, benign and beautiful peace.

———

Maggie and Dallas swim in the icy tarn. Rather than washing dishes, they run, clumsy retrievers, into the mountain water and out again, their shrieks clapping through the stand of peaks, to sun and, once

dry and hot, race back in, unwilling to accept that the inviting lake
is impervious to anything so capricious as sunlight.

South southwest. Down along a ravine's gentle outer crust,
Newt, with the solemnity of an orthodox priest, waves his smudge
pot over the flat head of the hive, clinging to the spiny side like a
cheerfully penitent drunk to a long and badly bent streetlamp. He's
unsettled and defensive. He hasn't been able, under the scrutiny of
the others, to replicate his findings. And while he toils, Ana, Gibson
and Hill struggle through the scorching afternoon collecting soil
samples from the sheer inner thigh of the ravine. Their bickering
has finally subsided, each exhausted to a point beyond caring. Nothing disturbs the air around them now but a buoyant canopy of flies
following the current of their exasperation.

Hunger calls the group in from the hills. They slog back like
sun-dried bordercollies bringing home the herd. Camp is pretty
much as they left it, unwashed pans and plates wait where they
were set down, the same half-eaten fish and bones, uninviting after
so long in the sun, give the air a fragrance and a deluge of bugs.
Worn out from working on their tans, Maggie and Dallas are reluctant to quit their nap. Maggie calls sleepily from the tent to Newt,
"Bring me some when it's ready. And a little tea, please, but not too
much sugar, Newtie." Disenchanted, the others prepare something
that resembles food, and waiting for it to warm, go for a time,
almost an hour, without speaking or arguing. They barely glance up
when the latecomers approach camp.

They're walking shoulder to shoulder, but it's clear Laird and
Icarus have spent the day at each other's throats, the way their shirts
swing open, free of buttons, forming bunches along the neck and
chest, like the gathers cotton takes when yanked by a fist working to
hoist sack and tonnage free of gravity and into another fist. Although
neither face wears a bruise more serious than the usual accumula-
tion of dents after a day in the bush, both men are smouldering.

The argument hinges on who can read a map, nothing more
grave than that. Icarus insists, having found it (whether hidden in a
used Bible as he claims or dragged, as Laird asserts, like a scared

rabbit from a rib cage of broken dreams and sad delusions lodged somewhere in the back of his primordial fucking skull), he's convinced he's best qualified to decode the squiggles on the page. According to each, it's plain and simple.

"Can't read a map's his problem." Laird craves a shot of solvent, something clear and strong as paint thinner. Little will reach him now outside of alcohol or drugs or taking and freeing a neck as methodically as he might a champagne cork.

As soon as the others, hunched over their dish, appraise the damage, entirely minor, their heads fall, like a flock descending over a mud flat, to continue eating. It's the same old argument. On and on the same. No one needs to think about it, it's there in every eye. Despite his beguiling guise (possibly that's why he's beguiling?)—he's mad—Icarus is mad! Crazy as a toot!

Lattices of complex paradigms blister Icarus's bloodshot corneas. He's sick to death of talking. His gait is thrown off—evidently one leg has shrivelled. Suddenly he is roaring, silence broken in a spume of volume. "It's not some fuckin creek! What? those old buggers couldn't tell the difference? They made it far as this not knowin the difference between a river and a creek? You think that, you're more fucked than I thought!"

Hill glances up from his tray. "A creek's a lot more likely to turn yellow. Even you gotta see that. Like the story goes, the stream they worked ran yellow from the gold."

"That creek's blue as the South Pacific!" shrieks Icarus.

The map is badly drawn, on that they agree. What the others (Laird and Gibson primarily) interpret as a mean creek switching lazily between the bony ankles of a ravine, is actually, according to Icarus, intended to describe a river. This river, the very one the creek feeds, is on the other side, miles away from where they've set up camp. Miles in the opposite direction of this fucking southwest ravine. The very river he continually points at, jumping up and down, screaming as though to God, IT'S THE MOTHERFUCK-ING RIVER, in order to direct their attention to it. Regrettably, the area between their camp and the river (where Icarus wants them to relocate) is difficult, cut with treacherous sheer mountain passes, rarely explored. This may explain why the others are eager to avoid it and invent reasons why the lost mine can't possibly be on the other side of such unfriendly terrain. Especially since the first prospectors were old. This enrages Icarus. He isn't polite, he calls them stupid and worse. He rants and festers and finally explodes. There can be no resolution but his. It's as obvious as it is straightforward, the Lost Lemon Mine is hidden deep in the stony ramps rubbing the heels of the river.

"This here's a dead end," he explodes again. "Where on the map is there a ravine? Answer me that? There's no ravine!"

Clearly, they read the map differently. He's tried to explain the ravine is a mend on the map, nothing more. They've confused a mend in the paper, the result of the reckless way the page was torn in half and glued together, badly, to signify a ravine.

"It's a river! The old farts couldn't draw!"

Through logic and deduction, the rest are convinced each piece of the puzzle fits. Newt says he'll stake his fortune on it. Fed up and cracking his knuckles to keep from pasting Icarus one, Laird tells him, "No way those old farts woulda made it over those passes to the river. No how—no way! Besides, they took in mules. No way animals, no matter how surefooted, woulda made it."

Gibson flicks his cigarette into the fire. "Besides, it's a ravine, you can tell from the way it opens. You can't read a drawn line is your problem. You lack visual perception."

"You need fuckin braille!"

"You so sure you're right, asshole," Laird thumbs the air, "head out on your own! Nobody stoppin you!"

———————

Icarus leaves base camp early, long before dawn, determined to reach the river valley by nightfall. Unfortunately he encounters such boroughs of rock, he slogs for the better part of three full days before reaching the divide marking halfway.

Here he meets a treacherous rock face beyond his ability. He ought to turn back; pure stubbornness prevents him. Twice he slips, clinging to the rock's slick denture by will-power alone. He simply will not fall. Each time his footing goes out from under him, he clutches thin air until he locates some handful of oxygen, happy to cradle one foot while his other boot works the siding as though revving his motorcycle. What little rock isn't solid tumbles out from under him like loose change, trumpeting the jazzy depths of their protracted fall. At the summit, reason and vision fishtail, encouraging him stupidly to glance back down. The view is ludicrous. From the acute slant of the facing, he realizes he ought to be dead. Perspicacity leaves him vertiginous and he crouches on the edge for a long time, unable to free his gaze, contemplating God and fate and luck, those things that swim around a mind dizzied by its own unaccountable good fortune.

Unsteady on his legs, staggering drunkenly, he forces himself onward. Unfortunately, at the next turn he reaches a chasm, not wide so much as viciously deep. This time he doesn't gaze down the abyss but senses it from the frightening faraway rush of wind swooshing through the bottom narrows, a chilling noise that makes him think of great snapping bullwhips. He doesn't want to deal with this. Every rational, sensible fibre haggles to go back, and he would if the cliff and its tall skyscraper scarp weren't so fresh. His only consolation is that Laird isn't here to watch him panic. Asshole, anyway.

He contemplates the rope for some minutes, gathering strength and stupidity enough to pitch it to the other side. The crampon appears ridiculously inadequate. The store clerk at the cut-rate mountain co-op assured him it would be just the thing. Don't leave home without it, the store jerk warned him. Icarus regrets buying it, regrets bringing it along; if he hadn't, he'd be forced to retreat. Supine at his feet, claws up resembling a skinny mutt playing dead, he recognizes the tool for what it is, some improbable prop from a stage version of *Moby Dick*. A toy never meant to work. Fucking piece of shit.

Niggling arguments and qualms not easily assuaged churn this
way and that, leaving him agitated in a mechanical way. How many
times will chance pluck his ass free? Surely chance, if she's a lady,
prefers to space each rescue into a harmonious bouquet or wreath
(depending on a body's destiny) rather than bunch the spray
together in an unattractive clump? Or does luck, as rounders and
gamblers allege, run in streaks? Garlands, no doubt, for some.
Not necessarily his. Perhaps his has run out, or twisted unhappily
around some vulnerable part? It is the next natural assumption.

Before he knows what he's doing, he picks up the rope. An
inner voice repeats, Do it, just fucking get on! He fights a sensation
of being trampled, a fleet of jogging shoes and a marathon of legs
crushing past.

Once he secures the hook, he yanks the rope, testing it again and
again, tightening or readjusting his grip. Several times he pauses
to stare at nothing but the air as though listening for something,
possibly the snap of bullwhips practising in the pass below. Finally,
when he can delay no longer, he lets himself drop clumsily over
the side. It happens quickly then. The rope gives way under his
weight, silently yet decidedly, and he instantly struggles to turn
back. Unable to loosen his hands, fearing when he lets go he will fall
too fast to ever reclaim a hold, his feet work to grab the edge. He
feels like an ape swinging from a vine. AHHaahAHH, this way and
that, big toes big plungers working to suction onto anything. Only
upside down, with one foot braced against the rock face while
the other flails along the sagging rope, prototype of any broken
windmill, he realizes it's a false scare. The rope will hold, having
found its natural state of tension appropriate somehow, slack though
it is. Strangely this means nothing, his mind is no longer capable of
metaphysical (comical or profound) or universal reasoning, although
ironically his limbs resemble a universal joint more closely than
ever before, he thinks of nothing but *feels* the falling depth. It rings
musically through him.

He begins again, pulling himself across, hand over hand, exhilarated with each act, releasing one hand to search out a new hold—

starship hand! His skinny body dangles, lamely swinging from the
exertion of holding his weight with the one hand as the other fer-
rets out each fresh hold. Failed funambulist, he feels the breeze,
a breeze he barely noticed before, riffling his shirt and along the
exposed back and abdomen. Yes, there is the recurring feeling of
the ape again. Oh, dreary thought, dreary day.

The thing is wider than he perceived, standing safely on the
ledge. He feels it now—misjudgment, its implications. Regrets, an
assortment of curses sweep moodily past.

He repeats a different litany, a song that bubbles up without
touching the conscious mind, absorbed with tasks enough: wind
and velocity or weight and gravity, tedious textbook nonsense.
One thing, one recombinant embedded in the DNA, never lost, is
his fear of heights. The rope makes a strange noise, and then of
course it slips. This much he should have anticipated, but still it's a
surprise. He freezes, suspended like a starched shirt from a droopy
line, the wind pestering his midsection, a joker with a feather. He is
a child tied for torture. He's in the middle. He's made it as far as
that. It strikes him that he's invariably in the middle, that wretched
station too far from either bank. Tautological business. He must
move on, one way or the other. Time will force the issue, he simply
isn't strong enough to hang on forever. Suddenly, as if on cue, the
rope gives way again. Time, he considers once more, time.

When he makes it to the other side, he works to free the rope,
not an easy task, a bother of business, shivering and yanking the
cord, all the while dancing as though he's a vacillating suicide along
the edge of the chasm, an edge not at all secure but susceptible
to gravity's fast line, impatient to break away and fall to its lover's
depths, waiting for some minor aggravation, such as the sort he's
inflicting, swearing like a pirate, bobbing and jerking in a fury to lift
anchor and steal ship and be free.

Of all the Christly things he might be doing in this Christly life!
Oh, he can swear. He'd really shout if he wasn't concerned about
the dynamics of sound and displacement. Although he's never
studied physics, life's tossed him a share of indelible lessons on

tail-spinning gravity. What he can fit into a lethal tirade under his breath, he does.

Exhaustion arrives before dark and he collapses and sleeps. He awakes hungry and with a terrible thirst and devours the little he has before setting out through a tangle of rocks and undergrowth that soaks up miles and another afternoon. Finally free, he has a fairly easy stretch for the next day and a half hiking along an over-grown dew line. His sixth day out, he makes his way along a narrow kame leading to the final peak. He slides on his ass as if riding a toy sled down the ravelling gravel slope to reach the valley bed.

Crumbling sun dazzles the exhausted man. Indifferent to the river's sequined skin, he concentrates on a crib of citron stones. Water lapping his legs, Icarus drags rocks from their bed. Per-versely, when he lifts one cobble free, the stones, bright as tinny lemon lights, brown in his palm to slag.

The river runs slower here, pauses to catch its breath before rounding the flattened bend, where it gathers up its falbala to negotiate the nearby narrows. Dragonflies, quiet in their work, hover over shallow pools trapped along the stony bunk. The river valley resonates with its own particular quiet. Herds of elk and bighorn feed along greener distant slopes. Frogs stop. And start. The air is lazy, or something else, tranquil perhaps, the slippery platform before sleep arrives or departs.

The river's music seeps through. And here where the river sings—all rivers do but some congested intersections obliterate the music while others rise above the babel to fill the world—he settles quietly to listen. *It's here.* The words shiver silently around him, beautifully, like birch leaves shaken by the wind. He repeats them to convince himself, unsettled by a falseness in his voice, cer-tainty overturned by hope. But it's more than simply hope.

He's a range of premonitions and intuitions. The top of his head, that enormous rotating dish, begins to transmit and feed. His vision blurs, wavers in and out of focus. Wham, the heart stops, and begins again double time. He can't breathe. It's impossible to hear over the hammering in his head. And the wind, God, some kinda cyclone's come up. Paralyzed, scared out of his mind, know-ing he might die, he's hurtling through space, catapulted, breaking apart. Smack into the fact, the irrefutable, undeniable truth— *this is it*.

Somewhere in this seductive valley the mine is hidden, some-where in the thick tree-covered rock. He's more certain of this than he is of the existence of a base camp or the others arguing around a supper fire. This sensation, this interior galaxy of feeling, is stronger than reality. Reality is humdrum, stippled with the occasional joke or better than average bit of sex, but nothing in reality touches this.

In the murk of pre-dawn, base camp reminds
Icarus of a suburb sleeping. It only needs the
regulated hiss of automatic sprinkler systems, a
thunk of paper pitched against a door. It's deeply
quiet here, without a wind, before the birds. He
heads directly to Gibson's tent, intent on the task of
waking him. Gibson's a heavy sleeper. It goes back to childhood, knowing how to rouse him: wrap a hand around his mouth
and hold him down, and wait. When he begins to surface, Gibson
fights; even in a dead sleep, he'll put up a battle. The trick is to
maintain a hold on him and avoid taking a hit. Once he feels him
stir, Icarus yanks him from the sleeping bag, straining to pin his
arms behind his back and shove him through the tent's flaps into the
bracing chill; let it finish the job for him.

"We're wastin a day arguing."

"A day? It's the middle of the night." Half asleep, stumbling
free of Icarus and sleep, Gibson sways, trying to get used to being
awake. His fists, missing their target, boomerang back against his
body.

"It's there all right—right where I said it'd be. Get your boots
on, we need to pack up and break camp."

"Get that goddamn flashlight outta my eyes! I'm goin back
to bed."

"I'm tellin you I found it and you're goin back to bed?"

"Grizzlies travel mountain passes by night." Gibson works on a
kink in his lower back. "And sane men leave em to it."

"We're wastin time. We gotta organize our gear."

"Listen, you got so much friggin energy, how about grabbin a
rod and catchin some breakfast? Wake me when she's done."

4

"Fishin? Fishin? We gotta get packed and outta here. We can't be fartin around fishin."

Laird slides out of the dark with the air of a man who's been awake for hours doing God knows. "You're full of shit. No way you'd come back empty-handed, not if you'da found her."

"I found her all right!"

"One thing I know is you found bugger-all."

"You know I'm right." Icarus sweeps the campground with his flashlight like a fireman with a short hose. "You know it! The ol man knew it! Everybody knows I don't say a thing is there if it ain't!"

"Show us your meatball, Chef Boy-ar-dee."

"All right, maybe I can't tell you what happened—not exactly—not so it'll make sense." Icarus focuses on Gibson. "Alls I can say is, as much as you trust me to find water—as much as that—trust me on this—I know I'm right."

Gibson grinds the heels of his hands into his eye sockets. "Surely you brought us a little more than that to run on?"

Dawn arrives and fizzles out. Socked in, morning's light grimaces behind cotton wool, small and circular and green, an eye too swollen to open. Their wrangling echoes through the nearby spires as though the day were bright and free of compressed batting.

"God," Maggie whines, staggering out of her tent. "The food situation is making me mental. Fish, fish and more freckin fish. And don't talk to me about rice and beans—just don't!" Maggie doesn't want to slip any further into the mountains. Bottom line, her midnight excursions aren't netting the desired quarry, the game trailing her out for a three o'clock pee are Dallas or Laird or, now and again, Hill. "I've had my fill of altitude and rocks! I want to go home! I'm craving pizza . . . I can see it floatin in front of me."

"Didn't I say we'd screw around all day?"

"Hey, Magpie." Hill wakes up like a kid. "How's about I whip up some pancakes?"

"I hate pancakes."

"Last night I had such a dream!" He charges around making

everyone pancakes, talking a streak. "A mother to end all dreams! I woke up tastin metal in my mouth. Still can a bit. But it was that real, I woke up believing I was still inside the middle of it. Inside the mine. I'm dead serious. I found the mine—located the entrance, smack where Sticker said, longside a river. I knew in the dream Sticker had said . . ."

"That was no dream! That's what happened! You were dreamin my actual honest-to-God trip! It spilled straight outta my genuine life and down into your dormant dreamin brain. It was that powerful! No way this is coincidence! Not something this important! Your tapping into me actually locating the mine and it comin out in your dream is an omen! An honest-to-God sign."

"Omen?" Hill's head turns.

"This here's one of those times when life hits a Bermuda Triangle!"

"My dream was a Bermuda Triangle?"

Gibson props his chin in his palm, "Next, I suppose you're goin to be tellin us what our dreams mean? Suppose we can look forward to that."

"What it means is goddamn obvious. The Lost Lemon Mine is where I said. Maybe now you'll start listenin to me."

"Next, you'll be tellin us what we're dreamin before we dream it."

"Gib, fate's workin here, we turn our backs on it, could be we miss our chance. Any fool can see it's starin us in the face. Alls we gotta do is reach out and grab it."

But Gibson doesn't intend to deter the expedition, simply send it on its way without him. "Ultimately," he tells Ana, and his plate of mushy pancakes and dried apple and fried fish, "when it comes right down to it, it doesn't matter a good goddamn which strip of rock we spend the day lifting or peeking behind, either way we'll come away broke and tired and fucked."

"After so many dead ends, it's only natural to feel disillusioned." Ana starts cleaning up. "But this mood will pass. Same as it always does."

Ana is having difficulty. The dream, despite her desire to believe in it, amounts to pure campfire suggestion, the warp Boy Scouts weave of goblins threading through a shadowy bush. Regardless, she'll follow Icarus, not because of the dream, or because logically they need to search the river and surrounding slopes (after all, it's no more than common sense to search every possible cranny before admitting defeat), but ultimately her desire to please Icarus is her overriding reason. It's up to her to bring Maggie and Gibson around. And when the rest are convinced, Laird will be forced to follow.

Confident they won't be gone more than a week, they elect to travel light, minimum hassle, everyone's ready for a break, even though they'll be trekking through dense terrain, there's a holiday atmosphere, a let's-get-the-show-on-the-road ferment, and more attention goes into packing fishing and hunting gear than seriously moving camp.

Maggie and Hill leave the group to wander on their own. On long treks it's standard for this to happen near the beginning, while the trail remains easy and familiar. Laird and Icarus preoccupy themselves with pace and battling for the lead, this too is very ordinary. Without Hill, Gibson usually slips back to walk with Ana. They rarely talk but hike on, relaxed, stopping often to take in a bird or a fleeting glimpse of distant sheep or other transients— or simply to read the stunning spread of mountain peaks.

"Anyone would think Newt and Dallas are married, the way they take each other down."

"Yeah," Gibson laughs, slipping an arm around her, "a boxed fucking set."

Ahead of them, Dallas and Newt can hear fragments of the conversation between Gibson and Ana. But it's disjointed, without context, and they aren't listening. "I don't see what guys see in her? She's got such small pointy teeth."

"If Hill can't keep his zipper . . ."

"I don't blame Hill," Dallas divulges. "I mean, it's not like he can reason much beyond his goddamn crotch. Hill's a guy, one hundred percent. The exact opposite of you."

Her face bothers Newt beyond words. Its expression of unrestrained disdain, reflecting what she thinks of him, his mind, his good looks or lack thereof, enrages him. Adding to his angst is a warbled blind of jealousy. It's because of this he speeds up to get free of her and all that he might like to do.

Dallas, perhaps from years of performing on the stage in everything from musicals to half-time spectacles to *Giselle* and *Swan Lake* (when she formed a company and launched the shows herself), has learned to read the mood of a house. This safety feature, this internal red light is flashing now, some generic symbol on the dashboard of her mind's eye blinking on and off, a small niggling beep chirping on and on. Her stage instincts urge a quick exit: hit the dressing room, bolt the door, refuse all unexpected bouquets. But Dallas elects not to back down. It's clear Newt needs a lesson or two.

"Could be that's the problem. You being such a wuss."

"Look," he says, too quietly—Maggie, if she weren't so far ahead, *God knows where doing God knows what*, would understand what this tone implies, that the line is drawn—"I think you've said enough."

Dallas catches up to him, wearing a lopsided grimace, her upper lip curled seductively back, as though lifted by the wind, a preposterous zephyr uncovering not only an inflamed gum line in need of a dental hygienist's pick, but a treatise on the unlikelihood of her ever having said enough!

"If you kept better tabs on her . . ."

"Me! Why don't you try giving the man sex more than once a month and maybe he'll refrain from seducing other men's wives?"

Dallas lifts her arm smoothly, as though executing a cloying movement from the dying moments of *Swan Lake*. Like many similar flutterings, appearances can be deceptive; behind the grace and simulated vulnerability lies a steely strength waiting to connect.

When it strikes his jaw, the other wing flutters briefly and follows beautifully behind, masterfully clouting the windpipe. Newt wavers, rattling like a pot carelessly set down, and folds, toppling in a hurried drop, knees crushing on a wreck of rock. The rest, his torso, tips over then, ringing still, to let the head settle against another slab of rock, all the while the mouth sucks and sucks and cannot find the air.

Newt envisions an impotent pasha beating his wives and realizes this is what he wants, he wants to beat the living shit out of her. If he could. Her stamina strikes him as macabre. She should have been a prize fighter, he sees it clearly now. A fucking George Chuvalo on his hands.

"Don't hurt his face," hoots Gibson.

Newt's head's a little fuzzy. He narrows his gaze on Gibson. Yes, he decides, I'll have to kill him too, then turns, awkwardly, back to Dallas. It's not finished yet. If only the top of his head didn't pound, a ringing, moronic melody.

"Dallas," Ana intervenes, "why take it out on Newtie? You two should stick together instead of tearing at each other's throats."

Oh, la-di-da. She's never liked Ana—right from the start she had a feeling about Ana. No sooner had Hill introduced her to his good buddy Gibson and his good-for-nothing brothers and their slew of slutty girlfriends and she knew there was something fishy about Ana. Could see it in her eyes, the way she stares down her long Prussian nose, high and mighty, better than everyone, snooty fucking bitch.

"La-di-da, you're no better off than the rest of us. Gib's worst of all."

"If you're coming—come!" Gibson hollers back to Ana. He's in a tear to reach the cliff and begin the climb to catch Laird. "Boot it, babe! This ain't the time to fall behind! They're startin to kick ass."

"Wait," Ana calls to him, and returns to helping Newt to his feet. "Maybe if I look for a walking stick? It may help?" Newt erases the suggestion with a flick, "I'm fine," and dusting himself off, valiantly limps along beside her. "Really."

Having cleared the summit, Icarus slips out of sight. Laird, barely visible, is a small squiggle on the sheer rock face. Splayed against a smooth slab, a flattened bug, he works to find a foothold and struggle onward. Limbs, slapping out a hold, appear broken and worthless.

————————

Ana is afraid to cross the chasm. She gibbers on about its depth and the yawning width of the span, the probable number of feet involved, remarking on the frailty of the fascia and underpinning on either side, the ramifications of erosion, the probability of such an ill-supported lip giving way under impact, the degrees suscepti-ble, the minimum force required. She envisions herself trying and failing and falling. She sees this vividly. The immediate and deliber-ate drop. The image coats every calculation.

"I'll go first."

"Gib, I don't see what your going first has to do with anything?" She shouts this at him even though he is standing right there. "Whether you're on this side or the other won't matter a damn, it certainly won't affect whether or not I fall!"

"I won't let you fall."

The group has collected in a slack knot some feet back of the clough. Most have slipped off their packs to rest, drinking from their water bottles and smoking. They are tired from the climb, and three days of hard trekking. It was much further than any map suggested. And much harder. They have argued about these dis-crepancies. Who recommended the reams of worthless maps, who insisted they had a friend who worked for Forestry and could get them rejects for nothing, who persuaded the group to set up camp so far from anything anyway, and who exactly decided to check out the valley. Oh, yeah, and who thought up the whole thing in the first place. Hill and Dallas are still arguing. Newt and Maggie, finished for a while, backs sharply turned from one another, smoul-der under a blackened canopy of silence. Everyone is hoping the bitter peace will last. Without having to carry Newt's insistent chittering, the wind feels almost soothing.

Icarus, tired of playing defence, doesn't wait with the rest but leans sloppily against a dead pine not far away from Ana. She waits for him to say something. In the interval, Dallas takes over. Accustomed to performing grand leaps, Dallas tells her, "Forget the rope and spring across. It's no big deal. It can't be more than ten or fifteen feet. Okay, sixteen."

In this light, the rope floating on thin air disappears. It is so fine a thread. A foolish use of hemp, a tightrope.

"Don't worry," Gibson reassures her once again. "I'll go first so when you cross, if you lose your grip, alls you'll have to do is reach across and grab onto me. I won't let you fall, I promise."

She sees herself missing his outstretched arms, possibly slipping straight through them as she would a safety net with a gaping hole, and there would be nothing he could do to save her then.

"Look, how about I tie a rope around your waist?" He says this jokingly, half expecting her to laugh. When she doesn't, he can't think what to do but continue on with the idea. "I'll secure the other end around my waist so when you cross you'll be attached to me. Alls you'll have to do is make sure it's secure around your waist."

She stands well back of the edge yet she can hear the water running like a distant sea against the rocks. She is frozen here. The wind will never stop.

"I can't do it! I'm going back!"

Maggie and Newt stand behind Ana. The three collect, silently.

"Why," Ana asks, "can't we make a rope bridge? I really don't see why not?"

"Besides," Maggie notes, "if we find anything we'll need a bridge to get it back out."

"We won't find shit," Gibson tells her, and resumes rearranging the packs, putting the heavier ones aside to be bucketed across. The lighter ones the men, including Newt and Dallas, will ferry on their backs.

"There's not enough rope," Hill informs them calmly, hoping it will slide past, that no one (specifically Dallas or Laird) will follow the observation with more smartass remarks intended to frighten as much as amuse.

"It's not that wide," Icarus says, "it's deep but not that wide."

"I'm afraid of heights."

"Yes . . . so am I."

Dallas, bored, reclines against a rock, "We can't screw around all day. Not unless we wanna do it in the dark."

Gibson slides his arm around Ana. His voice can be surprisingly soft, as it is now, the voice, if he'd ever had a child, he might've used to help mend a bruise. "Sweetheart, you don't want to give up now, do you?"

"Yes, I do."

Icarus takes her hand. "I'll carry you across before I'll let you do that."

"Then we'll both fall."

"I won't fall."

She lets herself lean into him. She doesn't want to move. Icarus smells like clover, no matter how hot or tired, he smells of white clover.

Finally, Gibson and Hill decide to haul a few fallen logs to bridge the span. They stand the taller one and let the timber topple to the other bank. It shudders and, not reaching far enough, sticks out like a childish wooden tongue, then dips and falls, turning several times and disappearing, banging against the sides and eventually crashing loudly into some distant run of water. Neither looks at Ana; they turn and walk back into the stand of trees to drag out another, longer log. This time they send Icarus across to help position it on the opposite side. It lands, rolling for a while before settling, then they set the next one. Both men are exhausted, sweating badly. Their anger has made them very strong.

Laird rolls another cigarette, "That'll only make it harder to jump across. Besides, no telling what the extra weight will do to the edge. It's probably not strong enough to support it is what I think."

"The point is," Hill tells him, hoping to sweep over the last remark, "that no one'll have to jump."

Unconvinced, Ana stares at the fallen conifers. She hasn't any confidence in them. After all, it's not like they're nailed down. And Laird is undoubtedly right about the increased stress.

Maggie concurs. "It doesn't look any safer."

Newt turns his back on the sorry bridge and looks back at the way they came. "It's not."

Halfway across, Ana freezes on all fours. She clings to the log as if it is her lover and she is paralyzed by a searing climax. Gibson and Icarus wait on one side, arms outstretched and ready, bodies canting toward her as though she is the sun, while the rest, back where Ana wishes she was standing still, loiter, restless and bored, anxious also that she might fall. She is awkward in her clumsy crawl, it will be a miracle if she doesn't tip and in an ungainly rush miss gripping the side or grab unfortunately late. Besides, the logs are not solid but roll like lazy dreamers bumping against each other in the night. No one wants to watch her fall, no one wants to clamber down the chasm to reach her broken body, and they aren't sure they could simply leave her. Some indulge in dioramas involving the police and legal obligations, while others see a vast stretch of futility, the bother of breaking camp and explaining to outsiders why they came and how they ended up here, in such an effin bind. Each in time decides, if it happens, to wait downstream for the body, or whatever broken bits remain, to collect in some tranquil holding zone. And Ana, seized as she is, knows this is what the rest have individually decided. When she recoups strength to continue, the rocks come at her, chase her like wolves and the waving starts once more, and reality below, its river and wild crevice, shifts positions, dancing beneath her until she isn't sure where the river is, or if there's more than one. It's no longer clear if she is clenching the log, for the log is invisible, finally clear as glass. She is in space, floating freely, disconnected from the life support.

"Don't look down!" Gibson yells.

Dallas shouts, "Hurry up, I'm coming behind you."

Until this moment, she liked Dallas.

"Don't rush!" Hill takes Dallas by the shoulders, intending to restrain her if necessary. "We're not in such a rush," he whispers, "we need to spend the next ten years scraping what's left of her off the rocks." And shouts to Ana, "Take all the time you need. You're doin great."

"If you want I'll come get you?" Gibson offers.

She finds her voice. "NO!"

She isn't sure the logs can withstand more than one at a time. Or the ground supporting both logs and traffic. It comes down to stress, how much pressure the spoiled lumber and sorry patch of ground will bear. Wouldn't you know, the wind kicks up. Oh, if she had nerve to swear.

Dallas shoves Hill's arm away. "If we don't hurry up, we might as well camp here!"

"No point goin on at all." Laird takes a toke from his joint. "We might as well head back now."

Until this instant, getting back hadn't occurred to her. The game sinks in slowly. Returning days later, exhausted, to face this same chasm, these same decomposing logs and having to cross back over the chasm, weaker, sapped and probably starving, possibly near dark. She vows never again. She'll grow wings and fly before she will find herself stranded on a toothpick in the middle of a mountain abyss, no matter how shallow.

When she opens her eyes, she is mortified to discover Gibson grinning down at her. And her anger recedes into self-recrimination. "There," Gibson takes her arm and grabs her waist to haul her next to him, on good safe ground. "Alls you needed was to take your mind off it. Amazing the miles a fit of temper will cover."

———

The air around the river unwinds quietly, not even their heavy breathing stains it. For a quarter of an hour they lie upon the rocky mattress dipping their faces in and out of the freezing river. Anxious to glimpse beneath its surface, behind the well-laid maze, as though the furry stones are cards waiting to be read. Cool, numb with relief, they roll onto their backs to study the clouds. There is a bird somewhere that won't stop calling, its cry drifts through the calm like a harried mother in a mall summoning her child.

Clouds tumble across the surface scales, pausing for a brief second as though cottonwood wool blown along a tarmac, quickly plucked away by a gnawing breeze to stop again somewhere further down. Beneath the clouds, their couch of rocks appears dark and very plain. Beige and other sombre variations of brown untouched by any celebratory hint of gold, only green or black or grey. Uncannily the same.

They become quietly absorbed in the examination of each other's wildly skinned rumps and napes, silent as assiduous apes grooming one another. Icarus wades into the water. No one cares what he's doing. It seems entirely natural to glance up through the dull light and observe him, thigh deep in freezing mountain water, plucking bits of gravel from the river's floor. Weeks ago Gibson might have joined in. No longer.

"Even if we find traces here . . ." Maggie watches the rest pitch tents and collect firewood and prepare to boil packets of organically flavoured vermiculite. "Fat lot of good it'll do us. I mean we'll have to haul it out, won't we, how are we going to do that without a major hassle? What, we carry sacks out on our backs? I mean how heavy is a sackful of rocks? It's a little more than I signed up for."

"Relax." Gibson takes a break from chopping kindling. "We aren't gonna find shit. Icarus just wanted Newt to have a chance to fish this part of the river before we take him back home to his fancy clients and golf cart."

Icarus wades out of the water to find the stick he's hidden at the bottom of his pack. "We start first thing. Before sun-up." The late day air is sweet with the scent of fast-moving water. "I can taste it. It's here, all around us. More gold than maharajahs own.'

He rests the divining rod between his knees like a set of reins he's allowed to drop. Head bowed, he concentrates on freeing his mind of everything but the stick, willing the wood to inch its way inside until nothing separates branch and skin.

Divining is seemingly no more complicated than a peaceful promenade across a field, following a twig. The magic isn't in the stick, its power has nothing to do with seasoned or green wood, a new fork is as adept as an old one. No, it's some mystery emanating through the ground, air, into the branch, and pair of hands following it. Its secret lodges somewhere in the keyboard of quarks and infinitesimal quantum fields that jimmy open the imagination, the stuff that fires the cosmos. There. There is the world of the diviner.

First a charge to signal the stick (and through the twig, the ground and universe) that there is an expectation, a call, a ringing, an imaginary press and release, press and release. A channel swings open. Serenity seeps in, and in the dreamy pier between breaths the message arrives. Allowing the message to infiltrate is a delicate business; desire gums up the works. The art rests in letting go and allowing some *other* to permeate.

How does the balm of water miles beneath the ground stray like scent through earth and stone to crack the surface like the first plane attempting the sound barrier? Somehow it manages, and, breaking through clay and granite, reaches the stick with strength left to penetrate the wood. From there it climbs the fork, travelling between the atoms, through them, who knows, and finally passes from the stick (but it can't be easier than breaking ground or sound) and once through must reach the hand, must not dissipate but break the skin, enter without leaving a mark like smooth lotion sinking through the epidermis, dermis, marrow, blood, to sail faster than thought through arm and brain into the realm of cognition. Small wonder science puzzles at the possibility. Sublime miracle, it works.

Dawn brings a chill. Across from him slump Maggie and Dallas, cramped and hunched on a log that is still moist from heavy dew and morning river fog. They ignore the tricky wind slapping smoke in their faces and out then back again like a cumbersome tail wagging in front of them; each electing not to move but wait, like patient puppies for the bigger dog to have its fun and be gone.

From the ridge drifts a round of song, possibly sparrows but beautiful in the fresh morning sun. Down by the river, Newt and Ana wash the breakfast dishes, rubbing sandy gravel into the slimy oatmeal charred in volcanic crusts to the blackened bottom of the only large pot, alternately digging at it with Swiss army knives or an array of flat and pointed sticks, scouring, heaping on more sand, finally frustrated, handing it back to the other skivvy. Both are silent, angry. In spite of knowing they should leave the cleaning up, that eventually the others will pick up after themselves, neither can allow the mess to fall as far as that and remain slaves to an intrinsic fastidiousness. It's this creek of frustration feeding their bitterness.

Gibson hunkers next to the packs, rearranging the overstuffed gullets and bulging pockets, removing flat tin pans and pails, returning them in another order, swearing for a time before beginning again. Close by the queue of tents, Hill huddles in a shepherd's hook, studying a length of map; he leans back to check another, smaller chart and returns to the larger one. His concentration is so deep he doesn't hear Gibson shouting at him, asking if he's finished so he can pack the goddamn maps!

A couple short miles from camp, the rapids drown every other sound, a wild carwash roar puncturing the air. Something in the fierceness of the tumult is industrial, clamourous, the din and echo found in automotive plants, generated by the force of the fast-moving water suddenly choking beneath a fallen tower of rocks that unexpectedly takes the river by the throat.

Icarus isn't sure why he's made them come this way, he hadn't planned to. Yesterday afternoon, squatting in the freezing river picking up stones, he'd assumed they'd ford the river this morning and wander like hungry herons along the shallow shore and hurst. It made sense to take a good long look at the opposite side—get it out of the way right off the bat. Besides, he'd generously decided, everyone's in need of a little holiday. But this morning when he took up the rod, he knew, he finally knew, and even then the furcate stick told him it was time to begin, and he listened. After all, he wanted to be told.

Ana observes him following the stick and laughs. "You're like an old dowager with a ouija board. Don't try and make us believe you aren't moving it."

"Fuck off."

He knows even if they don't. Freeing his eyes from the rocky path leading into the broken wall of rocks, he searches the sheer cliffside. It would be easier scrambling along the slack-jawed gravel detour than clambering up the high and slippery heap of rocks choking the river. Still the stick doesn't turn to entice him away from the stony trail but pulls him further up into it.

"What I'd like to know," Newt queries, following some distance behind and fiddling with his eyeglasses (broken in a fall, the left temple's come away from the adhesive tape holding it), "is how precisely a piece of dead wood intended to locate water can be right smack beside a fucking torrent and ignore it, the very predilection it's alleged to gravitate toward, and yet nonchalantly disdain, to steer us straight to the fucking pot of gold? It doesn't make much sense! You have to agree, it raises questions—even given that we believe a twisted stick can find water—even given that   questions arise! Talk about mixed messages! Exactly how does a twig distinguish between water and gold? I mean to say, Newton had his difficulties! Would someone care to explain it to me? Granted, I'm a Philistine, a novice at these things, these finer metaphysical points, but possibly one of you enlightened apostles could illuminate me? How it works? Precisely?"

His words mix with the rush of the river. Broken, they make less sense. Regardless, they've all thought as much. Newt invariably expounds at length on what the rest have decided days before in four words or less. No one bothers to glance back at him. Wet with the spray of rapids, they struggle silently up the looming fist of rocks strangling the squalling river, any grumbling lost in all the other noise.

Grouped, backs turned like windworn stumps along the crest of rocks, they hunker conferring, scanning the view below. Apparently the maps are inaccurate. Each and every one. Laird, Gibson,

Hill and Newt find this particularly unsettling. Granted, it isn't altogether new, the maps are not infallible, over the weeks they've come across a host of discrepancies, but this lapse is of a different magnitude, a mistake of greater significance, with far-reaching implications. They unroll the maps between them, positioning their backs to the spray in a vain attempt to keep the paper dry as they lean to study their charts, eager to discover it's a case of careless skimming. They want the maps to be true.

Yesterday, atop the thin lip of the last great slope, contemplating their impending slide down its steep runway, they were unable to see as far as this. They'd expected the river, as the maps indicate, to continue curling narrowly and swiftly between the sheer mountain cliffs—this wide-open alpine meadow is a surprise. Uncharted. Not one of the forestry or industry sheets marks a meadow, or for that, a field. Although it isn't large, it's large enough and very beautiful, protected the way it is. The river, after the fall, flattens out again, meanders in a lazy sprawl.

"Oh, dear," Maggie sighs. "Why all the fuss?"

"One of the maps shoulda got it right!" Dallas backhands the air. "I mean from a plane a blind man couldn't miss seeing it, could he? It's the size of a goddamn football field. I don't see how you lot flying around dropping off supplies and sussing out the area missed seeing it! It boggles the mind!"

"It's simple," Icarus tells her. "When we did a fly-by and took a boo, it wasn't here, sweet pea!"

"Right!" Dallas returns to her stretching routine. "What you're really saying is, you were scared shitless of jumping and weren't concentrating on much outside of that!"

The five men exchange silent glances. No one saw this field, and if they had to, they'd swear it couldn't be there. They are unsettled and quiet. Things aren't making sense. No way all of them could have missed seeing it, in spite of being nervous and distracted. When they think back, they know it wasn't there. It was exactly as the map describes.

"What do you expect?" Maggie chides, without bothering to consult any of their pretty charts. "That's why I never read a map, they're always wrong. I can't believe you didn't know that much. Honestly, Newt, what sort of freckin barrister believes everything he reads?"

It takes some work to manoeuvre down the wall of distended rock. The boulders aren't steep but their gravid roundness, exacerbated by a glassy surface, makes them very dangerous and every one finds it tricky to grip the winebarrel bellies. The rounded bottom half isn't laddered with rungs of smaller stepping stones but defended by a moat of jagged spires, which are cunningly stationed to prevent anyone from balancing on a spiny minaret and vaulting beyond the long run of stakes without suffering some injury. It takes time for them silently to accept they have no choice and, clinging to the slick stone balloon, worm their way toward the craggy tush. It looks too easy. Laird, opting to go ahead and help (expecting to cop a few cheap feels) leads the way, and the rest slither down in turns. The group is preoccupied, too diverted to complain. No matter how painstaking they are, each one twists an ankle or scrapes a shin, and it isn't until they balance safely on the bottom pins and flat ground is within easy jumping distance that Newt resumes his rant, as though some oaf has foolishly hit play. Miraculously, when he trips on the spiky ridge he doesn't hurt himself. While the others envision blood and broken bones, he shakes himself and walks on, talking still.

From the moment Icarus touches the grassy field, he feels it. It's as if the world turns to celluloid, not a heavy acetate but a flimsy plastic sheet, shining still, that lifts as easily as sandwich wrap torn and tossed away, and underneath, in the second it lifts, he glimpses, for a brief prolonged moment, an underworld. There isn't time to identify, not accurately, what it is before it vanishes, leaving the lingering conviction that he's glimpsed something uncommon, even in dreams.

5

He remembers colours. And people. Whether a settlement or another world, he cannot say for sure. They are gathered on the meadow, a great crowd, as if the green was a mall or stadium, a place where crowds collect. He can't think where he's ever seen such a throng. Not really large so much as strange. Yes, and large, too.

He decides he shouldn't tell the others. They aren't likely to understand but simply to use it against him, another weapon in the case proving he's not only crazy but a cretin too. Rubbing his shins and head, and trying to think, he wanders in a groggy circle some distance from the stones and further into the green. He's shaky and unprepared to talk to anyone. No, and the ringing in his ears, that's the other thing.

Ana lets her head fall between her knees. Oddly, she also can't stop the buzzing in her ears. It's giving her a headache.

While he studies the alpine meadow, Gibson unconsciously rubs her back and explains to Hill that she freaked on the rocks, while he repeats a litany of *You were great, babe, just great,* in a gentle purring voice. The field has his undivided attention. As he studies it, his rubbing grows increasingly absorbed and rough. She doesn't object. She likes it, the roughness helps her forget her ears and their awful ringing.

Newt pauses in mid-sentence, breathless, suddenly struck, his expression one of implicit wonder, as though an unknown trickster had tossed a bucket of ice water in his face, and while his breath floats somewhere between his lungs and throat, his eyes hold the happy moment of surprise before the shock registers, before he realizes he is both wet and cold. Instantly he unstraps his pack and scrambles into the meadow with his arms spread, once again a young boy pretending to be an airplane. Surely he must be making a noise, motoring his lips together in a dreadful sputter. He isn't, of course. He's yelling at the top of his lungs about the beauty of the place, and what's wrong with the rest of them. Why don't they join in, why can't they appreciate life as he does? How is it he's the only one with joy enough to give his heart to life?

"Come on, you assholes!"

Intent on expressing the moment, he cartwheels, and the first one, because of the long run, works. He fishes through the air in a handicapped star, spinning haphazardly and docking on a crumbling tine; irrepressible, he leaps up, screaming, fists flying, to swerve back to see who is watching. Predictably, the swerving one way and the other and back again unbalances him and when he dives into the next one he spills onto the back of his neck. Too sore to think, he unrolls and pulls himself up and throws himself into yet another. Slower, of course, painfully unsteady, his vision strangely blurred. There now, he's lost his glasses and charges wildly, as if he'd dropped his head also, and yells for Maggie to come quick and help.

Hill hangs back, resting against a dry rock face, arms braided in a long and sloppy knot, surveying the meadow. Even the grass is different from the hardy, scruffy breed typical at this altitude. Possibly the proximity of water, perhaps the sheltering cliffs, too, have nurtured it? Odd, though. If he didn't know better he might imagine he wasn't actually this far up but down a ways, a good long ways. The difference in vegetation makes him uneasy. Hill likes things to follow a predictable path. He's a one-and-one-makes-two kinda fire ranger. When one and one rebel, he frets. In the sharp sun, his eyes narrow to darts as he scans the green board for predictable signs of life. Things aren't right, he knows that much.

In the middle of the meadow, Newt gives up on his glasses (when Maggie didn't come rushing to help, he decided to wait and let her find them later) and, throwing his arms in the air, he leaps stiffly across the lush grass as though riding a pogo stick. His wild screaming has slowed. He's tired. And sore. And losing more than breath.

Hill wants him to shut up. He'd like everyone to be very quiet. Right now he needs to hear what the meadow has to say for itself. He scouts the trees along the far crust of green where the trees begin and the cliffs abruptly end. There isn't a bird, no sound or sight of one, but with Newt carrying on the way he will, it's no bloody surprise.

"We should move camp here," Maggie stretches, sunning herself from a smooth dry rock behind Hill. "It's way nicer."

"No," Icarus says. "Not here."

Hill doesn't know why but he agrees. "No," he tells her, "we're fine where we are." And he leans back to rest his head against her thigh.

Ana bends over again, ungainly as a studious child learning to tie her shoes, and suddenly and without reason, vomits. No one moves to help her. Gibson gazes at the foaming sea green pool near his boot. With his hand resting still on the small of her back, he had felt the retching arrive and build, had felt it travel slowly through her, but hadn't understood what it was. Why would he?

"God," he finally manages, "are you okay, babe, or what?"

She continues to hang, doubled over. If it didn't hurt so much, she'd shake her head. Abruptly she retches again.

Between them, Hill and Gibson decide what the trouble is. It's the heat and the altitude, combined with the climb and descent and an unreasonable fear of heights. Ana mechanically agrees, she can't think what else it might be. Before she can pull herself up, she retches again, gagging and shuddering badly.

Laird suggests she fuck off somewhere else away from him, to puke. He tells Gibson, "Leave her puke her guts out—you'n me need to case the meadow and far cliffs." Suddenly everyone wants to begin moving, instinctively agreeing there is no time to waste. Gibson pats her back as though it's a book being shelved. "You'll be fine," he says, working his arms free of the straps of his pack and dropping it next to her. "Alls you need is to clear your beautiful head and rest. You stay here, maybe find some shade."

Predictably, Maggie and Dallas volunteer to stay behind to watch over her. Both are strangely tired. "Don't worry," Dallas yawns, "we'll make sure she rests."

Lost in the middle of the green searching for his glasses, Newt shouts for everyone to come and help and then much louder for everyone to stay away or they'll step on them sure as hell. No one hears him.

Laird points his chin at Icarus. "He's probably got what she's got."

Hill agrees. "Probably the water. First thing I noticed. The water's a little off, don't you remember me sayin?"

"It's got nothin to do with the goddamn water." Gibson rolls his eyes.

"The lake's clean, I know that much."

"Those two are always a little sickly," Laird explains. "Only natural it'd hit them first."

Gibson jabs a thumb at Newt. "If there was somethin wrong with the water, our canary would be pushin up daises, not pickin them."

Curling into a tight question mark, Ana settles on a collection of fleece and Gore-Tex. She could almost sleep, if her head didn't hurt.

From the shade of rocks, Icarus watches them hiking toward the rim of trees, taking the wrong direction entirely. He doesn't bother calling to tell them they're wasting their time. He's glad to be alone. His head is buzzing badly, as if a lawnmower were shearing the back of his head.

It begins again. First the edges lift, ripple slightly as in a breeze, yet the day is quiet, there is no draft, much as Icarus might like one. Regardless, the bottom edge of the world as he imagines it gently wavers. When it lifts, the buzzing stops. In one swift, painful rip, a bandage yanked away, the scene finally emerges.

At first the faces appear to be familiar, perhaps the others dressed in costumes, but naked, wearing only feathers and bits of leather. Some carry long spears, others haul heavy baskets or children. Their bodies are painted, some in handsome geometric designs, most in free and fluid patterns, all somewhat psychedelic.

Soon the features are no longer familiar but exotic. The hair is short and blunt and dark and the skin tanned or swarthy. The faces stare at him without emotion, except for a mild sense of surprise at seeing him seeing them.

This is it then! he realizes. They are accustomed to floating next to him, unnoticed. Clearly, they're at ease with him, the only novelty arises from his seeing them. This, apparently, has never happened before.

He clings to the branch, afraid to let it go but aware he couldn't anyway, the current is too strong. The jaws that lock him are stronger than life's flimsy hinges. They will hold him now until it's finished.

The thing he can't get over is how much the faces resemble everyone he knows. He can't shake feeling they are in some odd way related. Their dress stops him for an instant, but in the next moment he forgets and concentrates on the faces, when again the differences reappear to stop him short. He hovers in this confusion for some moments. Finally one of them moves. Her eyes.

Some fifty or more are gathered on the meadow, engaged in simple chores. Obviously the meadow is their front yard. Along the cliffs, at a dangerous height and well along the sharpest side, they've constructed great cubes which they've somehow fixed to the walls. These retreats aren't crude dugouts or pre-fab boxes attached to existing caves, artlessly expanded, but solid habitats built squarely into the cliffs, vaguely Tibetan, vaguely Chinese or

Japanese, slightly reminiscent of the Navajo or Hopi but entirely their own. Washed white, possibly with lime or chalk from nearby cliffs, the apartments are painted with geometric designs like the patterns painted over some bodies. They reach the dwellings through a series of impressive ladders and ropes, which might be swiftly drawn up. He surveys the dwellings. Difficult to build at such a height. No simple matter, hauling woven buckets of clay and sand and water up a rope some hundred, two hundred feet. Braiding such a rope is another matter.

The meadow then is their park. He studies it once more. A smattering of women collect water by the river. Further along the shore a band of men quietly net fish, while inside the green a party of old women smoke trout. Children dart about playing with dogs and a young cougar they are teasing with sticks. The cougar appears to enjoy winning the game.

This is not a glimpse of an old world. This is not a flashback into a settlement that existed aeons ago and was massacred on this very spot. These are not ghosts or homely spooks haunting their terrible grave. He's read of such things, a clairvoyant suddenly stumbling upon a battlefield and witnessing the annihilation. This is very different. These people are alive, here and now, and smoking trout in the middle of the meadow when not two minutes before it was empty save for Newt blindly searching for his glasses.

If they are alive, as he knows they are, how can the two worlds occupy the same space at the same time? Questions begin to pour in, yet his mind is blank. How is it he slipped through? Could he have fallen into it at any time, anywhere, or is it something to do with this particular ground? Some strange component, perhaps an inexplicable mix of quadrature and constellations?

They can see him, of that there is little doubt. Moreover, they're acquainted with his world, if displeased, preferring to avoid it as motorists avoid a congested autobahn. Surprised now to be observed, for it's new for them, they appear accustomed to living alongside his reality without detection.

How does it work, one on top of the other, why don't they collide? What separates and keeps them separated? And what made him suddenly aware of it?

He may be hallucinating. With this in mind, he searches the green for sight of Newt. If he can find Newt searching for his glasses, something will make sense, although again he has no idea what.

There he is! Right in the middle of a smoke pit, completely unaware of it, of anything. Preoccupied, Newt doesn't feel the smoke, he isn't hot, he doesn't feel the embers under his feet, they aren't burning the soles of his expensive hiking boots, he sees grass green as plastic shamrocks, and even that's a blur, and nothing else. Not a glimmer of the double-exposed world filters through. There, he's spotted his glasses square in the middle of the ashes! One earpiece is missing. He bends again to search for that. He's swearing. Icarus can hear him over the squeals of the children chasing the cougar, its young piercing cries mixing with the trail of profanity.

It's unsettling, knowing what a thing is not, yet possessing no idea what it is. That it is, there can be no doubt. How did he escape noticing an entire village wandering the green in front of him? Right next to him, a woman stands so near he could, if he wanted, reach out and touch her hand, and this is the first he's noticed? But could he touch her? Would he feel it, would she? Her eyes are dark as anything he's known, the black that reflects every other colour, like a starling in full sun.

Along the fringe, Gibson, Hill and Laird wander, unsuspecting, nearing the trees bordering the rim of cliffs, completely oblivious to the upper story dwellings, staring straight up at the crags, utterly blind to the apartments, wasting their time instead of investigating the sides for possible openings, entrances, hidden caves, glints of gold, that sort of thing, going so far as to stop to point out cave after cave and entirely missing the patchwork of overhanging bungalows.

It may be, as Hill's suggested, that he's contracted some lethal microbe from the water? These visions may be a result of it. What other explanation is there? Only that he's passed out, comatose, suffering an out-of-body delirium or worse.

They don't appear very interested in him. Where at first they were amazed he could see them, their interest quickly fades and returns to life as usual, as though he isn't there! Perhaps they realize he's impotent.

If he speaks, will his words register here or in the other reality, his reality? Will the others lounging in the sun or Newt hunting for the lost earpiece of his glasses hear him, or will his words be locked in this new world? Perhaps they'll drift through both? But where is he actually? In this foreign one, or his own, or fallen somewhere between the two?

No sooner does he attempt to utter a simple phrase than he realizes his voice is frozen shut. He can't say for certain if he's even blinking, although he must be, his eyes aren't dry or irritated. And he's breathing, or he imagines that he is, although he can't move his hand up to check his pulse or put it near his mouth to feel his breath. Yet he must be breathing. Only he can't feel his heart beating. Has he had a stroke?

Another thing, he can't hear, or yes he can, he can hear them, he simply can't understand what they're saying. It isn't that they speak a foreign language. They use a different frequency. Everything goes by at such a speed he can't filter meaning from the noise, he simply can't decipher it. The effect muddles his mind. His brain racing to decode sounds aches from the effort and his mind's screen jiggles like a scrambled television channel.

The women, he decides, are especially beautiful. And it's the women he'd like most to listen to. Their difference excites him. Self-contained, so much themselves, they appear remarkably free in a way absolutely foreign to him. While it's true they appear disconnected, it is more than simple detachment, because, oddly enough, they are simultaneously utterly connected, aware of the world in a way he cannot fathom. They seem capable of seeing the air, as they see him, as if he is no more than some uninteresting colour or gas floating through the atmosphere. They give the impression of seeing deep into the elements of the very water, the sky, capable of understanding, but not intellectually, of actually becoming one with life around them. Yet separate.

These ideas are as alien to him as the sounds the women make, the way they speak. His head reels in a new way, a way he has never supposed possible, not as it happens from alcohol or drugs or illness but during a battle that challenges the warp and weft that tie things together, the pilings holding it up.

They must belong to some First Nations tribe, although from their costume he has no idea which one. It is not common to the area. Nothing he's casually encountered in *National Geographic* or a textbook or on a jaunt through a local museum, but out of place.

They are naked but for a few feathers and the feathers are very old, some might say shabby, obviously collected from birds unknown here (or if they flourished here once, gone now or extinct). Much too bright, garish almost, even in their faded condition. There is the way the women carry their children in woven slings that is foreign, common to parts of South America or Asia. And then the baskets the men store the smoked fish in. They are unlike baskets he's seen produced by local Natives, which are tightly woven and fine and smooth, where these are loose and made from an odd, thick, broad-leafed grass. He can't think what kind, or where at this altitude he might find such grass. Everything strikes him as odd, yet he is overwhelmed by the easy regulated cadence of the encampment, its intrinsic order. Every action appears so well thought out, each article, from the long elegant curve of the spoons the women use to baste honey over the smoking fish to the spits for meat and carved smoking racks, is well constructed, utilitarian but artful, the two joined beautifully as is common in Egyptian or Chinese antiquities. Nothing here is rushed, all the rough edges long ago discarded. Everything is given time and reflection. Simple industry works through the park in a simple way like water over rocks.

The entire episode unfolds in less than twenty seconds.

"What's the matter? You look like shit!"

He recognizes Maggie's voice. No doubt he's staring straight at her, and he does vaguely register her face (those wretched vulpine eyes) but he doesn't, not really, he's not seeing much of anything. Not now.

They've gone. He can't grasp it, the fact refuses to sink in. Yet when he focuses on the common, they are not there! Incredibly, they are not there!

"Come, lie down next to me." Maggie's voice is sweeter than usual, strangely concerned with something outside of herself.

He continues looking to the park. Newt no longer runs willy-nilly over the meadow but has wandered into the conifers in search of the others. Newt calls them, shouts various peculiar names in various directions. They do not answer. Everything is normal. The smoke pit has disappeared, the drying racks have vanished, everything has been strangely erased, even the beautiful women. Their eyes. Black and oily.

"Yes," Icarus says, surprised that his voice has returned, that it didn't disappear along with the rest, and aware that it sounds odd. "I'm not well," he admits after a while.

"Here, you need some water. You're dehydrated is what."

He shakes his head. He doesn't want anything. It's still too soon.

They pull him down, Ana makes room for him next to her on the dock of jackets. She's feeling slightly better. The ringing's stopped, leaving in its wake a headache. One of those wormy sinus portamenti.

Dallas puts her hand on his forehead. "You've got a fever. You've definitely got a fever."

"No," Ana corrects her, "it's the difference in the air here. It's so thin. You need to stay still," she tells him. "Here, take some of the jackets and lie down next to me. You need to keep warm."

"They've picked up a bug or something," Maggie whispers to Dallas, and the two stare at the pair, sharp-eyed health inspectors.

"It's the water! We need to stop drinking the water." Dallas empties her water bottle onto the ground. "Not without boiling it first. Hill says it's full of laguardia or something—sounds like that New York airport."

For the long crawl back over the swollen stones to the riverside campsite, Ana is barely conscious. The episode dims, like a drunken rave evaporating in the wake of headache and nausea, gone with the trays of ashes and empties. Strangely though, as she approaches the halfway mark, or thereabouts, she feels better. The migraine and vertigo disappear and Icarus recovers as well. She notices it in the way he begins to haul himself up the rocks. He passes her, charging to the front to challenge Laird's lead. "Everything's back to normal," she murmurs.

The campsite feels queer. In their absence something has trespassed, possibly a cat or a bear rummaging for food. Even though there are no apparent signs, the air strums an unnerving twang.

"Will someone grab hold of this?" It's stated as neither a question nor a request, and apparently not the first appeal, but given in a tone that implies the last of many. Ana looks around, as though just waking from a long nap. Bent awkwardly beside a blazing campfire, Dallas clenches a heavy canvas sack of water which she apparently intends to pour into a small, somewhat precarious, pot. The problem as she sees it is to transfer liquid into the tippy pot without spilling half of it. "Will one or the other of you zombies grab hold of it!"

There's only Maggie with two free hands, but Dallas can't seriously believe Maggie will help.

Not far from the fire are stacks of twigs and branches as trim as jungle huts. Newt scavenged and chopped the wood and as he runs lamely down to the river to fill more jugs, he curses the sorry lot of them, pissed that Gibson didn't pack more pots and pans, pails and bottles. "What were you thinking?" he shouts at him, launching into a fresh tirade on the dangers of contaminated water, what they can expect, the pain they can look forward to, the side effects and long-term impact!

Laird moves to punch him in the face. He's drawing back to aim when Hill smacks him, not hard, but hard enough, square on the shoulder, to knock sense into him. Hill's on Newt's side—after all, they both believe there is definitely something funky about the water. Hill's been plunging firepit stones into the pails to jump-start the time it takes mountain water to boil.

Hill tells Laird, "Seein as you're not motivated to haul water, why not leave those that are to do a job?"

"Fairies and old women boil water."

"Not all of us are immune to every gnarly kinda microbe. Not all of us spent half our life inside a jungle drunk tank."

Laird skulks across the shallow part of the river to the opposite shore to have a look around, maybe snare a jackrabbit for dinner (shoot shit outta a few scrub trees while he's at it). He's sick of fish. Sick of a lot of things. Don't they know. Behind him the sun spills coinage every which way.

Ana stops gutting grayling and joins Dallas by the fire. While she holds the pot under the pail and Dallas slowly pours, they swear at one another. "This pot's way too small!" Dallas roars, convinced somehow that Ana is responsible for the kettle's size.

"Hey?" Ana jumps back. "I wasn't ready! You've soaked my jeans and boots. It'll be hours till they dry."

"What kind of cretin holds a pot so close as that?"

Hill wanders further upstream, wading out to an esker, a gravelly wafer sinking into a jam-splattered river. In the late sun, he's a fly-fishing logo, reel rolling in song, rod buggywhipping a fine line, scribbling, lofting, coming down on the river's bruised rind. Raindrops of no-see-ums bull's-eye the skin; they're swarming around him, bandaging his head with their loose-fitting gauze, unwinding and tightening, but he doesn't care, silent and fishing. What matters but that?

Icarus tells Dallas, "It's not the goddamn water!"

The rest continue picking bones from the first course. Fish heads and fins form reefs on the plates.

"What else then?" she tosses her bones into the fire. "Answer me that!"

The supper air smells of seared flesh, wrapping the evening in

backwoods contentment. Laird squats comfortably beside the spit
he's rigged up, slowly turning one end. Tears of fat dance on the
embers and sizzle as Maggie slathers Newt's honey over the bur-
nished hare with a flat stick she found by the river.

Icarus pokes at the fish heads and bones he's tossed in the fire.
How did it happen that Laird jerry-rigged a similar spit or Maggie
thought to smother honey glaze over the carcass? What are the
chances? How many times a day, a night, do the worlds collide?

In the distance an owl begins to hunt. Stars will soon burn
through the milky tea sky. The fireside clan, gathered patiently, wait
for the hare to be divided between them. Gibson takes his turn
rotating the spit, fiddling with the skewer to keep it from sticking.
The head of the animal is a small knot of wood, ebon from the
flames, burnt bronze and sleek as a Syrian artifact, a running shape
extended beyond limit, deer-like but not, no leporine life left in the
elegantly worn haft of either a spear or a stick.

"For once I gotta admit, Sticker's probably right," Gibson drawls,
removing the animal from the spit to apportion. Divided, the hare
is a mystery. How could so little come from so canny and swift a
whole?

"If it's not the water, what is it? You're so smart, Gib, you tell
me." Abruptly it's dark and when Dallas smiles, she looks like a
toothless street sweeper in Bombay. It's the play of the fire on her
cheekbones and nose, like a candle guttering within a skull; even
so, everyone looks away.

"Gimme a break! It's the wa . . . water!" Newt has difficulty
forming the words. "Leave it at that! What?" he stammers, "you
want me to set up a lab and prove it once and for all?"

"Threats won't help, Neuter." Gibson quietly helps himself to a
few morsels left on Ana's plate.

They all wish there was something to drink besides boiled water
and Labrador tea, serum to wash away the tantalizing bite of rabbit,
too evenly divided. Laird deliberates on the complexities of rigging
up a still, the palatability of spruce bark or pine resin, the likeli-
hood of either tasting close to retsina.

Maggie slouches against the side of Hill's log, allowing her blanket to fall open. That old trick. Her moon-dusted body too bright to look at works anyway. Her eyes in the firelight affect him the same as ever. He can't be near her for long, not this close. He leans back, picking his teeth the way he will with his hunting knife, slowly bending forward to rest his arms on his knees and spit into the fire, pissed at feeling hungry all over again.

Icarus studies the inky wind-drawn treetops, working to catch sight of the in-between world floating over his. More than that, he's free-falling, dropping headlong through space into a pair of black opal eyes.

Icarus heads toward his tent, the dome set off from the rest, back in a world of its own, getting weirder and weirder, flaunting a series of geometric designs painted around the sides and feathers pasted down the front flap.

Ana follows. On her sleepy trek toward her tent, she lets out a shrill gasp. Nearby in the sooty shadows there is something, a figure moving, and suddenly there is another flare of yellow light, startling in the fuliginous night.

"Whoa." Icarus freezes.

"Holy shit, it's a cat!" Hill whispers loudly, finally seeing the shape slinking through the bush.

Laird leans, picking up his 30.06. "I see it." But when he goes to aim, the animal has gone.

––––––––––

The field remains, exactly as before, much larger than a football stadium. Again the maps are laid out and reexamined. Again the heads bob down and up and down again and shake, imperceptibly, for no amount of force can convey their dismay.

When they reach the park, Icarus takes the green by inches. His concentration is shot, communication between the branch and ground is lost, not a trace of electricity surges, not even the subliminal droning common to computers and cell phones or malfunctioning freezers. The twig remains a twig, devoid of current or magic.

Maggie smiles at him. "You look about ready to scream." He's rarely out of her sight.

"Nothin I'd as soon scream at as you!"

"Why," she asks, softly, "can't you be a little sweet to me?"

He glances at her for the first time in weeks. "You know damn well, Magpie." And he turns to investigate the far woods.

The rest drag behind, wishing they were home in the backyard with a beer and a barbecue. For an instant Ana can smell the spicy burgers, the freshly mown grass, can see bowls of potato salad, cobs of corn waiting to be shucked.

Newt, lagging further behind, stumbles, sending his armload of water bottles propelling down around him. He rolls as if stricken with severe gastric pain, pawing the air, his clothes. In the confusion, his foreign legion kepi turns itself backways round, converting him to a devout Taliban wife.

"It's that damn repellent." Gibson never has a problem with black-flies or mosquitoes, and can't understand anyone that does. "That shit attracts bugs faster than a drag queen's French perfume."

"It's body temperature!" he yells, working madly to stuff his pants into his socks. "I've read reports!"

"Probably got his period," Gibson tells Hill. "I heard they can tell."

"You're not funny, Gib. I don't know why you try." And he takes out the Deet and rubs his hands and face with more lotion.

"Reports hold that shit's lethal, what with the ozone and all. Somethin about the way the UVB mixes with the plastic container and the pesticides increases estrogen levels resulting in pattern baldness and low sperm counts."

When Icarus reaches the trees the wind starts, slowly lifting from the ground like mist, turning the sheet of grass in its hands as if opening a book, and he thinks, good, this is good, and keeps walking toward the trees.

While Gibson and Laird argue about which path to take, Icarus is well into the stand of alder. The direction he's chosen doesn't make any sense. It leads to a thicket of dense bush and, judging from the growth, straight to a bog.

"That dawg don't hunt," Newt tells Laird, expecting him to laugh, expecting him to at least share a conspiratorial grin—what's the point of clichés if not for that? But Laird gives him the finger and storms after Icarus. Clearly he has to take charge or they'll spend the best part of the day lost and looking for all manner of bullshit but gold.

"We're here for one thing." Laird picks up the pace. "Don't let's forget it."

In the distance, Icarus pauses. Around him, quiet, skinny trunks, scaly and miserable, the size of hockey sticks, convey a sense of defeat. This feeling is heightened by moss dried to pucks, sprouting a few half-dead mushrooms, withered noses stuck in the air like spectators from the winning side. Spruce needles blight the moss like blood-rusted compresses dropped on a locker room floor, leaving him feeling raw and unwell and wishing it wasn't half-time.

He slumps down in the middle of the woods for no reason but his legs collapse out from under him and his mind slams against invisible boards. As he sits quietly to recover his strength, it begins again. Women appear in the trees next to him, one especially. If a few males also appeared, or the children and the cougar or the old hags gutting fish, if any of them made a shadowy appearance, he might be inclined to believe it could be something other than a mirage but his wanting it to be her, and her appearing, as if at his bidding, convinces him the episode can only be a cheesy, tantalizing hallucination.

He shakes his head, imitating a man dislodging a wood tick from deep within his inner ear, and sinks further, feeling soiled and disreputable and thoroughly ridiculous, as though he'd ordered an inflatable doll, and the mailcarrier, holding the rimpled brown package (broken open in transit), watches him sign for it, smiling.

It's time he took a hard long look at himself. Fact is he's concocting pornographic delusions of women. Fact is he's no better than some bozo wanking into a napkin in a tittie bar. Laird's little brother. What's left but soiled overcoats and a cock, sloppy as an elephant's hose, dangling between his knees while he skulks hookers' toilets hoping for a good time? Laird's fate now suddenly his.

She has a dog with her, a mutt of a dog, spotted yellow and white, some unfortunate cross, with the usual big sappy eyes and a pink bubble-gum tongue that won't stay tucked but slides out the spent elastic-band grin like a slippery shirttail. When the mutt sniffs his hand, he remembers he doesn't like dogs.

Hold on, he felt that.

Before he manages to stand, she settles next to him and he freeze-dries, stiff as a moose in a lobby. It's okay because he can see her on his periphery and she is beautiful. He hadn't imagined that. She whispers something in his ear. Unfortunately he can't understand a word, same old same old. Once in a while he catches a syllable, a shard flying off a consonant, and he considers asking her to slow down but he likes the sound of her voice too much to interrupt—besides he can't pry open his jaw.

It doesn't matter. Doesn't matter that he's staring straight into the sea of skinny trees rather than her fine eyes because he can see her regardless, and that, although it doesn't make sense, is plenty.

Then right in front of him, in the middle of the scrawny staves, another group of women abruptly appear, absorbed with their chores, collecting firewood and deadfall. It's as if they've been there all along and his monitor has finally tuned in and turned on.

How is it, he wants to ask her, that we live with the same set of trees, under the same set of friggin clouds but we never collide? Why don't you, he needs to ask, and regrets that he cannot, use a different set of trees, a different kind of sky? How come we work on the same set, yet never confuse our props or lines? By the way, how is it I can feel your mutt slobbering all over my hand and I can't speak to you? Don't mind my asking, but things are a little fucking fuzzy.

Hazy figures hover in the background, blurred and out of focus, only a smattering of old women and toddlers are clearly fixed and near. This strikes him as arbitrary. On the distant green, barely visible from here, a few older children play tag and a few head of horses graze, tails flicking as steadily as hands on a clock.

What happens to the horses, the mutt or the poor cougar or the fish some old crones are frying? The stink of the fry? Why don't they linger in the picture as do the trees? What makes some particles slip through while others stay on one side or the other? If I handed you a cup of java, could you drink it?

His questions run across his mind like a screen translating the libretto but finally tire and die out. A tranquillity settles over the scene that could put him to sleep, further convincing him that he's dreaming, but he doesn't care. Dreaming or conscious no longer matters.

Finally he can understand her! As though some uninvited house guest forgot and left the receiver knob on another setting, VCR or CD, and suddenly switched it back to tuner.

"Go away."

That's what she is saying!

"Leave! At once!"

Her voice is soft. Only he can't believe she's asking him to leave. Perhaps not asking so much as commanding. Is she crazy?

She repeats it again—it's conceivable they are the only words she knows. The old women collecting firewood continue culling fallen boughs, but he knows they're listening and in their hearts they're also advising him to leave. Their voices, solemn yet as musical as a Greek chorus, drape the air like black crepe. It's awful now and mournfully loud.

For Christ's sake is all he can think.

She doesn't move, even so her eyes come around in front of him and float above his own.

For Christ's sake is all he can think.

Black and oily, these eyes don't hang back but pour inside. Then instantly she's gone, stealing his breath, taking it with her and leaving him falling through space with earth a good drop away.

Standing squarely in front of him, bolstering a runt spruce tree, Gibson drawls, "You keep shoutin, asshole, I'll help em haul you away! No doubt about it, you're fit to be tied."

"Can't you see he's not well?" Maggie's whisper is the cloth she'd like to daub along his lips.

"Where'd you find the dog?" Ana bends to pet its velvety snout. "Hello, angel," she coos to the dog. "Where'd you come from anyway, you sweet old thing?"

Icarus forgets feeling sick and turns to look at the mutt. In spite of disliking dogs he reaches out to pet it. The dog smiles at him and back at Ana. Its wagging tail clubs her knees.

"Funny," she nuzzles the animal's long silken ears, "finding you here out in the middle of nowhere. Did your people leave you, precious, or are you lost?"

Funny, Icarus thinks, funny? Funny ain't the half. How does a dog slip, like a rabbit down a hole, from one world to another? And be solid enough to bend down and pet, and the dog and Ana both experience it? Like it's real. She's not just seeing it, she's kissing it on the snout and the dog's getting off, its tail's whirring like a propeller. Gibson joins in petting the dog, and decides, "A dog this fat and happy belongs to someone."

"Nearest highway's a good eighty miles back," Hill reminds him. "Nobody's camped out this way and no dog's gonna hike in eighty miles and arrive here porked up as him."

"That's just great! Someone's got here ahead of us!" Newt braces the small of his back to study the cliffs, certain they are the traitors hiding the enemy.

"Nobody's here," Laird tells him.

"Surely," Maggie says, "we'd've noticed a campfire, dark as it gets?"

"As often as you're up at night, either you or your fan club woulda seen it," Icarus searches the woods.

Hill says, "One or the other of us woulda spotted smoke during the day, clear as it's been."

"Like I said, I woulda noticed." Laird scans the skyline.

Gibson agrees. "There'd be the usual bag of fat-free tortilla chips or empty bottles of Perrier and Tsing Tao or Dos Equis longside a condom."

"How do you explain a perfectly well-cared-for dog?" Dallas stares at the dog angrily, as if it's the dog's fault for being fat and happy.

"God knows." Maggie shrugs. "Probably living on gophers or garter snake eggs."

"No way he's been living on lizards." Ana points at the dog. "This dog belongs to someone. One look'll tell you. He isn't matted, I can't see any ticks; another thing he's not the least skittish."

Continuing to rub the dog's ears, digging deep inside so the dog groans and rolls its eyes back with pleasure, Gibson drills Icarus. "Whereabouts you say you found him anyways?"

He considers the question, working to fix the events in his mind, determined to remember exactly when he first spotted the dog. Yes, he admits to himself, I'm groggy, my head hasn't cleared. "The wind in the trees," he mumbles aloud, suddenly aware that makes as much sense as anything else. And he wishes he owned the energy to point.

Everyone stops bickering; each wearing the same oh-shit-here-we-go-again sneer, some flavoured with alarm, while two or three faces approach anger. Laird refers to a universal mother and other random gods, something he's inclined to do when he's contemplating altering another man's jawline.

Icarus knows he's said a stupid thing, and he'd like to correct it but, much as he wants to stop spewing gibberish and begin to speak sensibly, he's simply not in control.

"Wind in the trees . . . there's nothin as pretty as wind in a tree."

Laird kicks the ground and Gibson rolls his head the way he does when he's waiting to order another round and the waitress has disappeared out the side door for a toke with the band and Hill gazes off at the cliffs working his knuckles and chewing the side of his lip and Ana and Maggie hover around him, busy birds, flapping, cooing demulcent words as though he's a young nestling fallen from an aerie, consulting each other, the sky, the dog, asking what they should do? What would he like?

Maggie wishes she'd rented more tearjerkers, convinced that somewhere in the cloudy footage of Bette Davis or Merle Oberon flickers a moment, a scene in a sanatorium or out on a battlefield where the long-suffering heroine rescues the fallen hero. She can picture the scene, she knows how it's supposed to go, the part where he slowly drags himself out of his coma, gazes deeply into her eyes, and comes to realize (finally!) through the stupor of pain that she's the one that saved his life, their eyes moisten, the camera pulls out of focus and they fall deeply in love. Music or some familiar sickening sound floods the senses, strings or something she wouldn't ordinarily like, a song composed for such a rendezvous and inappropriate elsewhere, designed exclusively for dour bedsits, surgical wards and other heavily shelled encampments. Maggie knows how the scene reads, she simply hasn't nailed her lines.

"Where'd the dog bugger off to?" Gibson studies the trees and cliffside for the dog.

"He was just here." Ana is too concerned about Icarus to look for some dog, no matter how cute. "He's got to be around. It's not like there's a lot of places for him to go."

"Dog! Here, boy! Come! Atta boy! Dog!"

"He doesn't understand English," Icarus murmurs faintly.

Hill, scanning the trees, the cliffs, narrows his eyes. "Oh," he sneers. "Not many of us here fluent in caninese or mongrelese so's he'll have to manage here with dawg or dumb fuck!"

"You won't find him. Obviously they remembered they forgot him and they slipped back and nabbed him."

Hill stops then—does a long slow pan back to Icarus. "Mind tellin me who forgot him?" he asks, gently, as if he's talking to a bit-shy yearling or a shoat he's coaxing into a crate.

Gibson studies the ground. At first he thought he'd look for some tracks, maybe track the dog that way, but there weren't any prints, not that he could see anyway, and when he heard Icarus, he stopped cold. It dawns on him that in spite of everything he likes

Icarus, enough that he doesn't want to watch him lose his mind. It occurs to him that's what's happening. Icarus is losing his mind. There's no other way of putting it. Facts are facts and best faced head on.

"There he is!" Maggie points off to one side. "Musta caught scent of a rabbit or some other game."

Along a tussock of dried snuffy grass, clinging like worn-out hands to a rusting base of cliff, the dog, sejant and pleased, watches them as if he's on duty, his tongue falling and curling, drawing back to collect yet more saliva and falling again, unfurling longer each time, spooling drool to mires on either side.

"It doesn't make sense. They musta sent him back."

"Here, boy," calls Gibson, choosing to ignore Icarus, to ignore what he's saying, at least for the time being. It could pass, whatever it is, things do. "Atta boy! Good dog!"

The dog doesn't move.

"He hears me okay, happy where he is, is all. He'll come when he gets a notion. Bordercollies got a mind of their own. Anyone who knows the first thing about dogs knows that."

"Bordercollies do what they're told," Dallas informs him. "Looks like a two-bit shepherd spaniel cross."

"Looks to me like he wants to show us something," observes Ana.

Dallas sets her straight. "Life's not some episode on goddamn *Rin-Tin-Tin*!"

The wind picks up. It snatches Newt's kepi, and in the air it becomes a winged sail. When it snags on a dead upper branch, the ship reels one way and another, alternately gazing longingly at the sea of sky it hoped to cruise and skeptically back along the sorry pass that carried it here.

Icarus probes the trees. The noise in the uppermost branches unsettles him. "The trees . . ." he murmurs again. It's all he can manage in way of a warning, but he speaks so softly no one listens.

Ana jumps up, pointing at the churning spires. "There *is* something in the trees! Look how dark they're getting!"

No one glances up. "It's Newt's dippy hat." Gibson keeps his back to the woods and its queer flagging light, absorbed with Icarus and what's happening to him.

"No," she says, beneath her breath, "you should look."

The light is playing tricks, flickering from olive to malachite. The way, moments before a tornado or hurricane, the atmosphere ferments, concurrently dark and light, as if it's in a hurry and unable to decide. It swerves again. A banana-green wash, the sick shade of shit, sweeps surreptitiously over the scene. The wind works cables around ankles and necks and the air brings an odour not easily placed, offensive and pleasant, one thing and the other or both all at once, heavy as a wall falling, no holding it back.

The grass takes a queer turn of green, wet and shiny as fresh-slathered paint or cheap patent shoes and the sky contorts as if punched from behind. Grisly arcades tear open and pour with raw light, long lasers painful to watch, and the wind takes down the trees causing the alder to weep. Leaves, newborn green, fly through the air in serrated hearts and spades, beginning a bizarre game of chance.

Most of the tribe are down by the river, hauling brimming seine nets to shore. Crews stationed along the banks busily empty the catch, hammering the heads of still squirming fish with smooth jadeite cleavers. Further along, others gut the doughy bellies as if slicing dinner rolls, leaving children to collect beaded ropes of viscera to feed skulking dogs. Young girls wash bones for old women to use as needles, and old women store candied roe in special bowls for the feast later that night.

Leafy herbs dry on flat rocks, laid in no pattern but tidily scattered safe from the spray. Racks span the length of the bank and far into the green. Their design is a good one, easily assembled, rapidly taken down. Fish curing over bony bars hang like grey and pink socks in the sun.

Young children watch their siblings learning to manage the nets. Transfixed. A few of the youngest, old enough to run, chase flies and wasps from the fish and trot steadily to keep the dogs and magpies away from the rest. Smoke fills the air with the smell of something delicious. In the middle of the green, a small clutch of crippled-up crones roast a young animal, a colt or a fawn. While they tend the meat, they mend broken nets and gossip. The words and broken old fingers circle between them as calmly as flies.

Over the day is a feeling of joy; surely it must be a feast or a wedding, the way everyone smiles and visits while they work, for the air bustles with anticipation.

It's too much for an ordinary mind to decipher, nevertheless, they scramble to interrupt the phenomenon. And cannot. Sound comes, garbled and distant, as if far out to sea, waves of laughter breaking through clearly and fading out sharply.

Children dash across the green this way and that, younger children clamber up the ladders, jump back down. In front of them, toddlers and old women mill about, sniggering and stuffing their work-reddened fists deep into their grimacing faces. There is a rushing, building, charging, blown in blasts one way, another. The uppermost branches lean and wheel so rapidly they circle the sky as if spun by a spoon. Shaking cleaves through the air and ground. Like wind in the trees.

They are seen! This is the terrible day!

Within a blink it vanishes: some invisible wizard claps his hands and the scene evaporates, sans lingering scent or vaporous haze. It simply and magically disappears.

––––––––

They hunker under the ashen cliffs for a long stupid time, grey, half-dead oysters soaking on a half shell of lime, shucked and raw, incognizant of chef or broiler or tongue.

When the hologram went poof, it scattered a bewildering calm, a lovely potion, leaving them drowsy as babes in a hammock, suspended, without a care in the world. Too much too quickly and nerves short-circuit. Flooded, the over-loaded breakers blow, shut down completely, simply stop routing data through the cranial circuitry. Years from now this late spring afternoon may play back a blur of dead air and blank tape, possibly a smear of green, nothing more tangible than a nagging insinuation. Something happened, for sure.

Later, probably hours, they straggle up, tottering and sore and wishing it wasn't so far, heave-hoing their heads as though through a noose to wend their way out of the darkening woods, across the rich green, and up over the round slippery stones back to their sorry camp, happy suddenly that it dozes far on the desolate side of wherever the hell they've just been.

Hill, it turns out, isn't up to fishing. Fact is, he hasn't the snap to do much but slump, granite-heavy head propped in those baseball-mitt paws, pondering the pitiful smoke screen, waiting for story-book answers or warm, toasty explanations. The fire is dying. Newt built it for Christ's sake, no wonder it coughs up white hunks of smoke and nothing like heat. Ordinarily, by sundown Hill's chopped wood for the night, built a fire to last and hauled water for dinner and dishes and pails for the women to bathe in and in the time it takes the rodent or raven or pan of rainbowed fish to fry, he maps out the following day's itinerary. Not tonight, forget it, forget fishing or snaring rabbits, this evening he's not hungry and he can't remember ever feeling less like himself.

Gibson pokes at the logs, tickling them with a bony stick. Perhaps by making the flames dance up he might read something in the sparks. Across from him, Ana and Newt tear open packets of chili and salisbury steak and hang sick as drunks beside the wheezing smoke waiting for the pot of ice water to come to a boil.

Finally it's dark. Somehow that helps. No one glances at the night sky, what's the point? There's nothing new there, certainly no answers they'll decipher, simply more of the same, insoluble puzzles. They've been through it before. Tonight they don't want a glimpse of worlds beyond, not even a provocative glimmer, at least not for a time—they've had enough for a while. Easy answers are what's wanted, nothing more complicated than a game of bingo in a nursing home shortly before tea. A metronome, a great steady tick followed by a grand heroic tock. The one clinging fast to the fixed and predictable tail of the other. Nothing outside of that. They are prepared to let the other (the magical, and occasionally sought after by foolhardy innocents, other) slide away now, preferring to hunker, as they are, by the fire as if on an infinitesimal raft, abandoned and drifting through space, going nowhere, fated to bob further and further into the deep unknown, without words or images, blind and speechless and startlingly old, desperately wanting to hang on to the small feeble wish that at last and at least, they are safe.

The feeling persists while they eat. It neither improves nor dissipates. The dried packets, now swollen and strange, served as a cold fecal goo dropped with difficulty on each tin plate, taste of dioxin-bleached chipboard and, notwithstanding the labels boasting of organic and gourmet and taste-bud delight, the gruel reeks of pesticides and chemical plants, and paradoxically each chewy mouthful remains indelibly, incredibly, impossibly flat. Although no one has the energy to attack the packages slowly burning to black vespiary leaves alongside the clots of untouched, flame resistant fodder, they know they've never tasted anything so foul.

It's implicitly agreed they've seen something, although no one has a glimmer of what. Nothing floats through their minds. They remain hollow, scraped and emptied bowls, waiting in a sorry line to be refilled. Questions wait also, accumulating slowly. Every nerve end is writhing, working in its way for some connection, feeling as a worm must once it's been inexplicably sliced by some strange large wedge of steel rolling through grass and away.

God! God!

Although they've never called out to him/it/her before in quite this way, presently, each with an emptied heart and in time does precisely that. Surely it's the last stone to turn? What other is left? What, indeed, but to bleat and bleat again into the intransigent dark.

Silence suits the night. On that they agree. Possibly they've never agreed on more. They ask no questions because the mere thought of answers frightens them. They wait for a great comforting hand to come gently in the night and massage them. Only that it's so long in coming unnerves them.

Gradually things sink in. They're bound to though, aren't they? It's true things seldom stay put, no matter how much one might prefer that they did. They continue like the stars and moon to roll forever somewhere.

Status quo then is another myth they feel implode. Unpleasantly deep in their very blue very private Tahitian sea, relativity's puffball bursting.

Slowly, slowly it penetrates. Yes, they've witnessed the unusual. It's safe to assume most have no inkling such a possibility exists. Ah, possibilities, yes, given what's occurred, what else does life offer? More, certainly. Possibility suddenly emerges as a word of white-hole magnitude. An appropriate shudder follows the revelation. They all, granted some slower than others, arrive at this berth.

Imagine the miracle of a trailer park emptying after a flood, good ol boys abandoning their overturned tin cans to belly up to the levee, swearing they've never seen the like; Joe Bob and Cooter, experience hanging from their belts in pink fibreglass rolls, can't think why the flood waters chose their trailer, their truck, can't fathom why life wilfully levelled all they'd assumed was fixed. No matter, Joe Bob and Cooter will blindly ignore the accidental and precarious will of the world, they'll hunker down and dig in and dedicatedly rebuild on the flood plain. Such fodder founds colonies, fuels wars, and will carry humanity like cockroaches and rats through environmental or nuclear holocaust or into the frontier outposts of deep space.

Who can explain why, when good sense would urge them to leave, they do not? Abandon ship! Run for your lives! Surely such tunes automatically accompany scenes reminiscent of these? What is this inexplicable need to stay put? Why hunker down? Why gamble? After all else has fled, what thing is hope to persuade the heart to cling to nothing . . . not even air?

In some essential way the possibility of escape never presents itself. Once Joe Bob and Cooter or Laird and Newt witness the flood waters recede, nothing else is relevant or required. Recession is the only reassurance necessary for the conscious mind to kick in and allow memory to do what it does best, fade. The mind then begins to rewind and erase. Normalcy prevails! The mirage disappeared, that vital fact, that critical piece is all that's required to drown out unrest.

Newt begins with a protracted disquisition on shared hallucinations, listing, as though each idea is staggering news, the various causes and standard conclusions of such merged mirages, citing only the obvious and minor (convinced everyone's had enough of the major and subtle). According to Newt, the holograms (for he insists they were beautiful projections, although he never offers a cursory explanation to cover how or why) are patently harmless, impotent flickerings, illusions of light, mere moving pictures, albeit unusual and unnerving, but nothing permanent. He insists they take his word that the chimeras were a collective whimsy of their minds to be brushed aside and forgotten.

Maggie disagrees. It's obvious in the way she pushes her boot's toe into the ground, the sudden intensity, that she's frightened. She begins, slowly at first, to draw her ideas around her, seeming to turn them one way and the other like weathered objects she's recently hauled indoors, as if she expects whatever is hiding inside to come scurrying out.

"No," she remarks, quietly. "I don't think so."

The rest, staring at nothing, thinking of much less, wish for silence much more than for answers, perhaps for peace or a great gentle hand to lead them through the disquieting dark.

"I remember reading of similar things. There are a few documented sightings—it's known amongst archaeologists."

"Archaeologists!" Newt scoffs. "How can we take what they say seriously? After frying in the sun fondling caryatids, it's no surprise they see things! I'd hardly call the observations of a group suffering sensory deprivation and heat exhaustion entirely credible!"

"But it happens!" She cups the air. "They'll be on a dig when suddenly the entire ruin comes to life! It's been documented! It's a fact! The site appears to them as it was! Just as we witnessed this afternoon!"

"Group hysteria, exactly what I've been saying. What makes you suppose group dreams are rare?"

"I think it's more than that," Icarus mumbles. "You haven't quite nailed it."

But when Maggie turns to him expectantly, he falls silent. He can't explain and his words feel odd. He sinks back into a silent comfort zone.

"Yes," recalls Ana. "Wasn't there a famous case where a researcher witnessed an entire battle? Somewhere, I can't remember if it was the Civil War or some Indian massacre—I keep thinking Wounded Knee, maybe Little Bighorn?"

"That's nothing," Maggie tells her. "I have a friend," she says, turning to Hill. "You know, Sarah Schultes, it happened to her." When he looks uncertain, she tells him, "You've heard her talking about it! She brings it up every time she gets stoned. Anyway," she waves him aside and returns to Ana. "Sarah Schultes was in France, an old palace or something, a museum I think, wandering through the garden or courtyard, it doesn't matter, but in the blink of an eye she was transported back to the seventeenth century. Holding her guidebook, she was suddenly surrounded by an abbey of nuns dressed in the queerest habits and hoods, weirder than any she'd seen. Only she saw them walking around, these nuns! Heard them singing and chanting. And there were bells, there'd have to be, wouldn't there, and god knows what—nothing was close to the same. Even the songbirds were different. Turns out, when she snapped out of it, the guide was telling the group that it used to be an abbey in the seventeenth century! And when she researched it later in the library, the habits the nuns wore in that abbey were exactly the same as the ones she'd seen. Now how would she've known that—no way she could've imagined it! Not something she didn't know? I mean how can you imagine something you've never seen?"

"Yeah," Hill nods. "Right. I remember hearin that story."

"Right." Gibson relaxes back against the log. "That makes sense. A glimpse back in time."

"Like *The Twilight Zone*?" Ana raises both brows and hums the ubiquitous soundtrack. "Or that film—what was it—you know where Helen Mirren, no, more like Greta Scacchi, whoever, plays some scrawny middle-aged dowager blithely touring Versailles and suddenly the path takes a queer turn and she ends up back at Louis's court?"

"That's what it was." Gibson bobs his head. "Pretty much explains it."

Icarus murmurs, "I don't know."

His hesitancy causes Newt to consider the proposition, shaking his head skeptically. "I suppose," he grumbles, unconvinced. "A flashback?" (Conceded to simply keep abreast.) "Group phenomenon again." (Pointed out to maintain ground.)

"Only we all saw it," Maggie holds. "It wasn't our freckin imagination. It happened. There's the difference."

"Time travel," whispers Hill, as though trying to explain it to himself. And in a louder, surer voice, "Some weird drop zone. I don't know how a thing like that would work. In order to accept that, you'd have to know time travelled a straight line, that there was a past. I don't know," he says shaking his head, "it's not altogether straight ahead. Time, once you start thinkin about it, gets tricky as hell."

"Exactly right!" cries Newt, seizing on the idea, one he's convinced he knows a great deal more about than the rest. "I think we can safely say," and he grins at Icarus, "that group hallucinations are the same phenomenon whether witnessed by archaeologists or you and me or Sartre stranded in the Sahara or Napoleon in a Russian blizzard, nothing more than a combined illusion or mirage! Nothing mysterious. Entire caravans wandering across the desert will imagine an oasis. It's standard, an unavoidable given. They all swear it's real! This was the same thing, is all I'm saying. We're saying the same thing. It's nothing real. It was a mirage. We've been alone and isolated for too long. What the expression *bushed* refers to in fact."

"No way I'm saying it was a mirage!" Maggie tosses another twig onto the dwindling fire. "It happened—we witnessed the past. Those people weren't figments of our imagination, or some queer way the light moved. They were real! We saw straight into their life. It's clear they used to live here! They inhabited this place and were probably slaughtered by soldiers or settlers, maybe even our ancestors, a hundred or more years ago. We saw them as clearly as if they were alive today! That's the miracle of it!"

"I don't suppose it matters," sighs Hill, "because we'll never know one way or the other, will we?"

"I read somewhere," Icarus mutters, arguing with himself, "that some physicists are beginning to think dark matter is the gravitational pull of a parallel universe. . . ."

Newt settles to repair his glasses, wrapping a wad of adhesive tape around the hinge. "Either way, what are the chances of seeing anything like it again? It was a once-in-a-lifetime phenomenon! We'll spend the rest of our lives like those old farts in wheelchairs recounting the Great War. This," he tells Maggie sagaciously, "is the highlight of our pitiful lives! Our great war!"

Maggie tells him, as she so often does, that he's fucked, and limits herself to one small hit from the passing joint, a taste to help with the sex later. She'll need help, that much is clear.

"No," Icarus tells them. "There are times when life hits a bump. Bam. And quick as that nothin's the way it was. That's what's happened here."

Dumping the dregs of the Labrador tea onto the fire, Laird says, "It happened—so what! Where's the problem, it's not like it hurt us. Take it for what it was—nothing more funky than a good hit of blow."

————————

The next morning they sidle around each other like convicts in a small but electrically wired exercise pen. No one slept worth a damn, they look like death-row cellmates, skin tone and corneas a similar grey wall.

Newt's lost his glasses again, plus he's got a migraine (which he blames on last night's chili and salisbury steak—even though the labels say organic, no way they aren't pumped with nitrates; he can always tell).

Way back in the cliffs the birds are bargaining, have been for a while. God knows what they're hawking. Their noise doesn't suit the day's bad mood, the sun sagaciously remains hidden behind its ratty duvet, even the bugs have taken the hint and wait in a low-moving plane on the other side of the river like punks casing a 7-Eleven.

Down by the river, Icarus gazes at his reflection. Narcissus swooning on gravel, his reflection floats like platinum foil. He went there an hour ago intending to brush his teeth. Splayed on the bank, desire's desiccated bones, he might as well be dried and stuffed and carted off, a rack of sorts fit for brollies and hive-inducing scarves. It's his dreams he can't shake, vicious little soldiers stormtroop his veins like vagrant Nazis, occupying his neurons, and he can't switch them off. They play on like a television gone berserk, running *The Night Porter* again and again. Of course he isn't gazing at his own pretty face in the water, he's lost, remembering hers. Those starry black eyes, unfathomable, pervade each empty part until he responds solely to her, to thoughts, remembrances of her.

The river laps the levee. Watch. Here as you fall.

Another quarter of an hour passes. Fireside, the water reaches a cranky boil, half a dozen foil packets float on the froth, jostling angrily into one another, threatening to break open and spill their sulphurous innards if it happens again. Too wiped to lean over and haul out a packet of exsiccated eggs and bacon, the group huddles, staring at the roiling pot like drunks locked on a dryer in an all-night laundromat.

Camp life rumbles dully along, barely a blackfly tussles through the gluey breath, when unexpectedly Ana bursts from her tent, half naked and screaming full strength. The scream fades lower, then louder, in and out, annoyingly close to a siren. It's that kind of fucking day.

Laird and Newt glance at her briefly, bored and wishing she'd stop. Newt's headache is worse, Laird's is hanging on about the same. Besides, no one can make sense of what she's saying, her words are garbled and lost. She shouts in short puffy bursts, sprints to the campfire, thrashes her arms, howls a bit, huffs, retreats halfway to the tent, returns to the fire, pointing and yelling, occasionally remembering to hold her shirt closed. Newt and Laird understand she's naked under the shirt. It flies open each time she flings her arms to point at them or the tent. One thing, Ana's got a fine set of tits, but it's early for that.

"Get a grip!" Dallas rolls her head.

"Your top's open," Maggie tells her, staring dully over the rim of her mug. She's exhausted, as if coming off acid. "I think you've lost weight." Her voice is sleepy still, what's more her throat's sore.

"There's bugs the size of rats loose in my tent! Oh, my God! Come quick!" When she throws herself against Gibson, the shirt falls off her shoulders. "Christ, Gib, do something! Did you hear me or what? There's giant bugs flyin around inside our tent!"

Before asking what sort of wild flying insects, he rights the shirt (one of his) and buttons it up. Her eyes are wide and stoned. "Okay," he says, "start at the beginning." His voice is a flat parody of a private dick. Robert Mitchum playing Marlowe.

"It's okay." Icarus walks toward her—he isn't holding out his hand, it only seems to her that he is, it's the odd way he's carrying his toothbrush. "It's okay. They won't hurt you."

"Who won't hurt her?" Gibson asks, suddenly mad. He'd like to hit him. He realizes it's what he's wanted all along. This whole damn thing is Icarus's fault. Finally everything is clear.

"How can you be sure?" she asks Icarus.

"They've been comin and goin all night."

She nods, ambivalent, unclear what reassurance can be derived from discovering giant insects have used her tent as an airstrip while she slept soundly. More like out cold.

"Put yourself in their position. They don't want to upset us any more than we already are, but they have to get on with their lives. Same as we do. Aren't we all trying to do just that?"

She shrugs negligibly, scarcely willing to concede they may have a life to get on with. "Why should I be in their way?"

Icarus sighs. He can't think how else to explain it. "We can't expect them to control our seein them, no more than we can control their seein us. We wouldn't want them to exercise that sort of control, would we? No, it's better this way, both of us unable to control what the other side sees."

"It is?" Ana remains unconvinced it is true that one side hasn't the power to control the other. She'll reserve this for a later debate.

Gibson feels like hitting him again. "Don't worry," turning to investigate their tent, "I'll take care of whatever it is." The hope of smashing something, soon, energizes him.

"It's too early for this shit!" When Laird gets mad he grows several inches, gains twenty pounds, sometimes more, depending. Coming to life, he snarls at Icarus, "Okay, bright ass, you know so much, you tell me what's happening!"

"They want us to leave."

"Fuck em!" Laird shrugs.

"*Fuck them!*" Gibson shouts, surprising himself. Until this very second he'd settled on leaving. First order of business: tear the tent apart, beat the shit outta whatever, throw what he can in a pack and get the hell out. Just this morning he told Ana to get her head behind hiking back over the chasm, because like it or not they were clearing out, if it meant dragging her kicking and screaming every step of the way. Now, for no reason, he decides to stay. She stares at him; he never makes sense, not ever.

"The important thing to remember," Newt drones quietly, like a monk repeating interminable prayers, "is that nothing out of the ordinary is happening." He paces in a circle, pointing his nose to the ground as though by keeping it fixed he'll best track whatever it is he's lost sight of.

"What's that?" Gibson asks him.

He glances up, slightly cross-eyed. "Nothing's happening, don't worry."

"Newt," Gibson speaks slowly as though he's disciplining a child missing all but the reptilian stem of his cranial cavity, "Newt, something *is* happening. That much should be clear even to you! *Something is happening!*"

Newt sinks back, watching him from over the hump of his shoulders. "There's no need to shout." He limps to a safer corner, unable to comprehend what's gotten into everyone or why they insist on taking it out on him.

When Gibson opens the tent, he expects it's empty. "There's nothing here," he yells back to Ana, and yanks open the flap, permitting the rest to see past him and well into the tent.

"Yes," Maggie whispers, "there is. There behind you."

She's by herself this time, squatting quietly on the sleeping bag as though she's peeing in the woods. In her hand rests a small stone shaped like a divining rod, similar to a ginseng root, vaguely describing a man or at least the human form. Seeing it, Ana realizes the stone turning through the air might appear to be a bat or a giant moth or a spearhead.

The stone looks like two men or one, depending on the way she holds it. She faces the far wall of the tent with her head raised as though she's a defendant facing the bench. Much as he'd like to approach her, Icarus cannot take his eyes from the stone.

Slowly her body drifts apart, worn out and gradually dying, small pixels gliding further and further apart, each infinitesimal dot expanding to its own separate world until the infinitesimal galaxy is no longer visible in this one. For a long time a heavy greyness remains, a forgotten blanket of iron filings. The air floats in a similar soupy way. Eventually that leaves as well, and there is nothing.

Afterward they stand dully side by side, fixed, like cement statuary. Perhaps a quarter of an hour passes, possibly more. Time again is irrelevant.

There's no help for Icarus, he's transfixed by the stone abandoned in the middle of Gibson's bedroll. Did she leave it, perhaps as
a parting gift? (Hope is the opiate of fools.) When Icarus thinks of
her, his body gives way. From his first fractured glimpse of her, she
claimed him, staked his heart as carelessly as a prospector working a
spent ridge. Once he feels Laird's corvine eyes perch on the stone,
Icarus hurriedly explains to him that she's forgotten it. This makes
sense to Icarus. After all, she forgot the dog. He decides she must be
absent-minded.

Laird snatches it, something in the colour triggers his curiosity.

"She'll be back for it. It's not ours."

Laird rubs it between his fingers, wipes it against his shirt, and
holds it to the light. When he takes it outside, they all see it then.

"Gold!" Maggie whispers. "Gold!" The fact shivers through
them. Each dry leaf and stone vibrates with the news. Gold! In the
sun it shimmers softly, old in the way of museum gold. It is a pipe,
beautifully carved in the shape of a man, the legs twined apart like a
woman in love, only the head is that of a jaguar or some other handsome cat.

"God, but it's beautiful!"

The pipe is no mirage but some other conundrum, as she must
have been, for even Disneyland's magnificent holograms don't dis-
tribute gifts, particularly golden trinkets. Not ones you can keep.

"Gold!" they each repeat again and again. "Gold!"

Laird cradles the pipe in his palm as though it's a hatchling, barely
alive, while the rest hold their breath and gaze at it, afraid if they
blink it will disappear (possibly into one of Laird's many pockets).
Under their breath, they repeat *God*, or *gold*, until the two words
meld into one.

The cliffs, the river, the starving woods fidgeting along the edge
of the lush green, clamour and beckon and no eye glances idly
around but when their sight drifts to any cove or cliff, they think,
gold, and, is it there?

No one considers the darkening sky, or flapping tarps of ravens
and marauding blackbirds hurrying for cover from thunder rolling

down between the mountains in great terrifying blows. Strangely, no one sees the jagged electric spears advancing. Only the ravens, flying daggers across the black, caw, Why, why, what can it mean?

———————

It rains for days, turning the campsite's gravel bed into a sponge. When the river swamps the rocky vale, they are forced to haul their soggy bedding to higher ground, yet the torrent, unwilling to give way, continues pelting down, as if attempting to erase every trace of the intruders from rock, tree and time.

Afterward, nothing is the same. A trip to the river means a chance to pan for gold, to study the gravel digging into their knees; an expedition into the cliffs or along the rocks to the waterfall is an opportunity. No one hangs behind or dawdles. They want to divide into a million clones to search every cranny and stone. No one is tired. Their faces are distorted by a fever uglier than malaria, nothing sexy. Devoid of Peggy Lee's sultry heavy-lidded craving, their heat wears no appealing tatter, nothing save raw, stinking excrement, hideous to any uncontaminated eye. They train no other thought but gold. It fills them. Their bones are filigreed with reefs of gold. Golden rivers glut their minds, flood every conduit, their very blood runs with dreams of gold, powering their hearts and souls and cranial canals.

Icarus follows behind, a mute ass plummeting into an abyss, asking why: Why, discovering that she's forgotten the golden pipe, doesn't she rescue it, as she did the dog? Surely if she wants to get rid of me, she knows better than to leave gold lying around? She must have guessed the impact it would have! She must see that about me!

Then in a terrible rush, while struggling to catch up and stumbling over rocks and falling back, it becomes suddenly clear to him. It's *fated*. Life, dreams and destiny are inescapable. While the others charge ahead, dazzled by the golden ornament and the need to find another, this thought settles in an inexorable and odious pattern at his feet like dance steps painted on a studio floor, easily read, easily followed and clearly and irrevocably fixed. Nothing can alter it. There can be no going back—no safe return.

————

The obvious hasn't occurred to him—leaving the pipe was a terrible mistake. She was distracted, it happens to everyone, even those living in some other world. She had no intention of leaving it. She would as soon have left her heart. He doesn't understand.

She hadn't meant to be seen. It wasn't her doing! She can't control when they see her. Most of the time she passes unnoticed. They walk straight through her. Over top. She has no idea what made that morning different.

The elders are furious. They know what's been lost. They know it cannot be retrieved. Worse, the intruders haven't the vaguest idea what it is that they've found. And Aluna, didn't she send the thunder loud enough to drown them? Isn't thunder the guardian of gold? Pray to Aluna that she will protect them from Youngerbrother.

Youngerbrother has returned. Even in this last hiding place, he has found them again.

Part Two

ICARUS

*In the beginning there was sea and darkness. Then
Aluna, the Great Mother, created the nine worlds: all
that was, is, or will ever be.*

1

*Aluna created Elderbrother, and set him free in the
fifth world, this world, with its five floating realities. For
a long golden stretch, the fifth world was tranquil and Elderbrother and his progeny loved Aluna perfectly. But Aluna required
chaos and brought Youngerbrother to live with them. Where Elderbrother
was light, Youngerbrother was dark, and where Elderbrother was full,
Youngerbrother was empty, and the fifth world changed overnight.*

Alone in his cave, the paye (a master shaman) smokes roots by
the fire. Namsoul, which means jaguar devourer, stops to chew the
blueball, a mushroom the colour of pale delphiniums. Riding the
blueball, Namsoul will fly to the Milky Way, Aluna's vagina. It's
there he'll confer with paye of the other worlds, hoping to learn
why Aluna has allowed Youngerbrother to see them. Until now
Youngerbrother has been oblivious to the realities floating alongside the conspicuous one. This has been Elderbrother's advantage.

First the inside of the cave fills with feathers. It's very comfortable to be surrounded by gusts of beautifully soft feathers. Brilliant
and many-coloured in the firelight, they float around him, small as
distant boats, thickening with each slow paisleyed swirl until they
block out his hands, the walls and fire, leaving only feathers. Namsoul isn't mystified, he knows what they are. Their beauty doesn't
distract him. It's comfortable because it is as it should be. He takes
another bite from the blueball, chewing it deliberately. He knows
what he's doing.

At birth a paye is taken from his mother and kept in a cave, tended there by an older dying paye, fed special milk laced with particular herbs and juices and tasting only certain powerful plants from childhood on. For twenty years Namsoul never saw the sun but knew the world solely by the light of the moon. Mink-coated shapes in furry distances, smudged, blurry heaps of bush, leaves dark in his hand, void of acute green or gold, only torpid licks of colour, yet the scent of each species marks every pore, leather soft or powdery or crackling into broken, jagged saucers. He's never known a woman or a friend. He fasts. In this way he understands many things. Where anyone can learn the properties and habits of plants, of insects and birds and animals, few can see the dreams of others, fewer still can interpret what they see. As with most things, some paye are more gifted than others. A paye's luminescence manifests when he delves into his own or another's hallucinations. A paye's soul should illuminate, rendering visible all that's in darkness. Of a paye whose explanations remain obscure, the others say *his soul is not seen, it does not burn; it cannot shine.* Namsoul's soul shines.

When the feathers dip in waves and lift the paye, let him float along their silken crest as easily as a leaf upon a sea of waves, he knows it is time. Once more he bites into the blueball.

To begin the trance, the horizon opens like a door.

The feathers, no more than swollen neutrinos, are capable of yawning into worlds. On the surface they are all the same, given he doesn't focus on any particular one. A mere glance allows the energy of the feather to reach out and swallow him whole. This is what happens to the others when they chew the blueball—they cannot resist the fluid array of seductive colours; inevitably one feather captivates and carries them away. A paye knows where each feather leads, its world suddenly cavernous as a whale's mouth, impossible to escape and endless and like no other. And there are millions of feathers. All this Namsoul learned before he could walk.

But they are only feathers, floating distractions. They have nothing to do with what he wants or where he is going. He closes his eyes and focuses on the electric gaps, the empty heliospace, the radioactive river they float upon. That is what interests him. He concentrates on the between.

The river is the black side of blue, long runners turning cerulean and Prussian and just as quickly back to black. Ordinary travellers (those who aren't paye) nibbling the blueball are swept up by the wavering—it takes some skill to stay with the fast-moving river to keep from falling into the magnetic woad of black, for they are beautiful and cloying.

Once he starts to fly, it happens very fast. He's out, way out, beyond the cave, beyond the hidden valley, well above it all. Here he stops. He is skilled. He knows what to do. He knows better than to travel fast. It's dangerous and reckless. He drives the blueball like a horse. Yanks it short. Forces it to hold back. The energy trembles under him. It quivers in his hands. He glances back down.

Below him the others sleep. Only Nabia and the dog are awake, placidly walking through the open field toward the river as though they haven't a care in either world. In the field, cattle and horses graze. She stops to stroke her horse. She's brought a root he loves. They glance up, the horse and dog and Nabia, to see him far above them. They watch him hovering, caught by the long arm of the moon.

The paye flies higher. At this level he can see the damage Youngerbrother has wrought. His cities, other tracks.

At the Milky Way the paye wait on the dock like travellers queuing at a ferry terminal. They bob this way and that to glimpse Namsoul as he flies through the heavens toward them. It's always like this.

The one waiting, the first one he sees, is his old mentor, Kamu. Kamu steps from the crowd and reaches out to help Namsoul, steadying him as he first steps free, knowing he'll be disoriented from the journey. The nebula sinks slightly under him. It's very different here from earth. The difference unbalances even the most practised paye. Kamu leads him to his cave. Namsoul hurries inside, for it is very cold. Although the paye of the Milky Way live in similar ways, the cave homes are as dissimilar as the air and light and rocks and silence.

While Kamu builds a fire to warm the gloomy cave, he shows Namsoul all he knows. Yes, it's true, Youngerbrother has seen them, but he doesn't seem able to control when he sees or what he glimpses. They chew the blueball and between them the fire grows. In it they see the fifth world and Youngerbrother. It happens very quickly, the visions soar in front of them larger than the cave. Wings of heat draw them in, allowing them to wander through the fire's Milky Way to observe Youngerbrother.

Outside one transparent office tower, workers spin through pin-wheel doors to smoke alongside dying pansies and a chilly fountain. No one speaks, worn out by a cliché of complaints, computer sex and corporate intrigue. Near a placid sea, Namsoul and his mentor watch an old man fish and a couple stoop to save dogshit in a special bag, while in another placid country a young man beats his wife, her head rolling as gently as an orange buoy above the waves of blows.

Gibson dreams, his face pressed against the groundsheet, a stamped and trammelled leaf, red with the hard work of sleep. The tent smells of wet woollen socks and damp canvas and heavy plastic. Awake, Ana listens to the river, then a far-off hunting hawk and the wind shivering through the trees. Icarus strolls along the river shoals away from the waterfalls on his way back to his tent. Hidden in the rocks, Hill and Maggie make love. Icarus watched Maggie leave her tent and run to the cache of rocks. He walks with shoulders raised to block their noise.

Namsoul and Kamu make no sense of it. They chew the blueball and wait. Great legions drift by, things past or yet to come. They stop the circus parade, hanging their heads to think. It's quiet again. Only the sound of their chewing.

Soon they observe Icarus in the act of seeing their world, and the paye look at what he sees. But Icarus sees nothing of interest. He's watching Nabia sitting alone talking to the river. The gift of seeing is lost on him. He sees without seeing, a video camera at an ATM indiscriminately recording.

Laird is also awake. He's followed Hill and Maggie and, watching them, beats his penis into a rag. Namsoul observes, "There in

the ugly one's head we may glimpse what Youngerbrother wants . . .
only it's worse than we feared."

"No," says Kamu, "it's as I expected."

––––––––––

In the beginning Aluna and Elderbrother lived serenely on earth.
That was before the great flood, before she created Youngerbrother. From the first, Youngerbrother was insatiable. He lied and
gorged, a jealous whelp, snuffling and circling, anxious to usurp
Elderbrother. Exasperated, Elderbrother implored Aluna to help.
Aluna agreed, designating the half on the far side of the sea as
Youngerbrother's and reserving this half for Elderbrother. She
washed the earth with a great flood but, while sheltering Elderbrother in a snowy paradise, she warned him, Youngerbrother
will return. Prepare for it. And she endowed Elderbrother and his
descendants with the gift of sight and the perspicacity to travel all
nine worlds. Youngerbrother knows nothing of this. In his blind-
ness, Youngerbrother imagines there is no other world, no other
reality. He's trapped in unknowing. He knows only what rises and
falls between his legs!

According to legend, the universe is waiting for Elderbrother's
descendants to reclaim the prodigal. No one knows how this can
happen, if Youngerbrother will ever be ready.

After the flood waters receded, Elderbrother's descendants jour-
neyed back from the snowy mountain paradise and came to live in
a jungle, beneath a canopy of branches and heavy vines that stretched
for thousands of miles and nothing grew along the jungle floor for
shade. The lower deck seldom saw the sun and the world was a sea
of trunks and clambering stalks where each mile unravelled exactly like the last, yet Elderbrother's people found their way without the help of stars or sun or topography and walked to wherever
they wanted as if drawn by a magnet.

Rivers, because they reflect Aluna's vagina, are sacred. A river
flowed through the jungle to the sea as beautifully as the Milky Way

drifts through the night. Green on all sides, a blinding green to eyes travelling from the monotonous brown jungle floor, it brimmed with splendidly crowned birds flaunting rainbowed tails, and fleets of monkeys wearing endlessly amusing masks, and greenery and herbs to cure disease or guide them to the immense beyond or help the hunters prepare the spirit of prey for their arrow. Life prospered along the shore and the only task left to Elderbrother's progeny was to praise Aluna in everything.

But when the paye travelled to the Milky Way, they saw the future, and as Aluna had warned, Youngerbrother was preparing to return. In his orgy, Youngerbrother had forsaken Aluna for other shabby gods, a healer trussed upon a cross by shamans without second sight, hucksters who couldn't read dreams but followed a greedy queen's centaurs, brandishing strange weapons and wearing skins of silver. The paye foresaw it all. The time, its blood. Cortez. Conquistadores.

Inevitably, the day came. The paye returned from the Milky Way and told those huddling by the fire that Youngerbrother was coming in boats the size of small mountains, as beautiful and many as clouds of butterflies. At times such as these, paye have the power to plant all they've learned in the minds of the others. Straightaway, everyone set to work preparing for Youngerbrother's arrival, knowing the malocas (villages of mammoth beehives: thatched huts, windowless and with a north-facing entrance, protected by a jaguar mask) would be burned and the hunters and elders, the children and women and paye enslaved or slain.

While the hunters and elders and women wove wicker barricades to defend the malocas against the invasion, the wisest paye selected a small group of protégés (Nabia's ancestral clan) to journey through the floating reality, along the high sierra, in search of the snowy mountain paradise, the world they'd descended from at the dawn of time (as the fifth world knows time) after the great flood receded.

As the protégés prepared for the difficult mountain passage, they completed their tasks knowing Youngerbrother would destroy their nation. While they packed the baskets and filled the travelling sacks, and those destined to stay behind whittled arrows, chiselled flinty heads and dipped them in venomous oil, they shared the blueball, knowing most of the faces across from them would perish and the world they loved would disappear. When it was time and the preparations were complete, friends and families said goodbye, aware there was no chance but this to send an expedition back to the source, in the hope of beginning anew. All would not be lost, the sacred would be safeguarded in the floating reality, the reality Youngerbrother walks through and doesn't see.

And it came to pass. Youngerbrother returned and took their half, claiming it as his. Queen Isabella's centaurs blew apart bodies with an innocuous powder fired from wands no bigger than a twig. Behind the absurd centaurs came lumbering herds of armadillos trained to spit heavy balls, which burst into blossoms and rained flames upon the malocas, until there was nothing left.

According to paye from the other worlds, Youngerbrother isn't finished. Even today he continues raiding the few remaining malocas sequestered deep in the jungle in search of survivors. These survivors are understandably wary, they keep to themselves, avoiding all contact with strangers, determined to preserve their identity. Finished plundering stones and wood and herbs, Youngerbrother conspires to steal their blood, pure as old seeds, for the vaults of pharmaceutical and biogenetic multinationals. Youngerbrother recognizes that this latest treasure is more valuable than gold. "Come, come, if you don't want your child to die of malaria, let us take a vial of blood. What's the big deal? What do you take us for?" Here again he travels as clumsily as his starships do the Milky Way.

Although their journey began before his butterfly boats arrived, the paye witnessed the fate of the malocas from observatories in other worlds. Nabia and her tribe are the descendants of the band of protégés entrusted to make their way through the floating reality back to the snowy paradise. Along the way they've observed Youngerbrother many times. Often his disease arrives before him. He's perfected it and no longer needs to bring it on a lead; it runs on

ahead, his trained messenger and scout. Where he goes, death follows like a crazed and tortured grizzly tied to a sadist's chain. Flocks
dwindle, herds perish, forests are flattened. Such is the way of
Youngerbrother. His seed has spread throughout the fifth world, a
rampant weed, thriving unchecked. Each fallen leaf roots afresh
and if a vermian thread of rhizome is cut, it will double, in the way
of worms. He is a husk issuing seeds to range like dust, like locusts—
rats, snakes, cancers of every sort.

Until now they have been safe. Youngerbrother has never sus-
pected the existence of other realities. He's remained in one world
and one reality, with little idea of the corollary realities drifting
alongside his, or of the other eight worlds and the myriad realities
circling these worlds. As he cuts the land like a surgeon to make
way for his farms, mines and factories, the magic escapes like blood
and some of it infiltrates even Youngerbrother. What else explains
his sudden ability to see? The paye and elders are afraid. Youngerbrother cannot be trusted. It's not his fault, he has no conscience.
This they also know.

———

In a flash, Laird awakes. Everything is clear. The black-eyed bitch
knows where the gold is. This time he'll offer her a pocketknife or
some glittery goober, maybe steal a tube of Maggie's lipstick, what
chick doesn't love orange axle grease? Icarus is a lightning rod; if
he takes him, it's bound to work. Befriend them, give them a few
trinkets, let them feel like they're part of the crowd and wheedle
her or one of the young punks into showing him the entrance to
the gold mine. What could be easier? (Such an old familiar loop.)

"Looking at the one they call Shitface is like approaching a dark
hole in deep space." Kamu chews the blueball. "Denseness, in his
case, is power."

Namsoul stokes the fire. "We're flying the between, the dark
space, the vast emptiness between the nine worlds. There is no star
chart, no sky master, no regular route."

"Youngerbrother uses another set of laws altogether."

"That's what I thought."

They fall silent. Namsoul scratches the back of his neck, and then Kamu scratches the back of his. One paye is silver in the firelight, the other paye dark, both bodies are lean as cats, their eyes the colour of oil. The paye enter a dilemma like a cock sliding into a vagina. By making love to a problem the answer arrives like a lover tenderly coaxed. For this they pass the blueball.

"They don't have a heart," Namsoul announces, as though it's the first time the idea has occurred to him, but of course he's voiced it many times, almost as many as he's heard others express it. Always it's said like this: they cannot fathom it.

"It's the problem, his basic problem."

"His heart broke, the contents emptied and the pieces went every which way."

"Look at how he treats the world he lives in. What other beast fouls his own lair?"

They chew the blueball. The cave stills, even the fire slows.

Kamu continues, "There's not much we can do, outside of trying to piece it back together, to transmogrify his heart, and him."

"Jaguars must come!"

"Yes, jaguars must come."

"And devour him. Then maybe he'll be conscious?"

Chewing the blueball, paye become the jaguar to devour disease and cure the patient.

"One way or another, Youngerbrother must see that what he does in one world has an impact on the other worlds. So long as he was only capsizing one reality, it was manageable—now he's on the verge of entering the real worlds. Devoid of a conscience, he is dangerous. He needs to be connected. Somehow. He works outside of everything else. He sucks life out of the world he lives in, he needs to know it affects everything. Things can't go on."

"Exactly. We have to bring him around."

The cave fills with sounds. Insects and birds, raucous and sweet, acrididae striking their matchstick legs against their spiny metal

shins, monkeys screeching, notifying others they've found food or
something curious to watch, noise of all sorts, creatures rustling
through the dark, dried twigs snapping underhoof, branches dusting some dark moving form. Abruptly it stops. In a great rush the
noise vanishes in all directions, and from behind out of the silence a
soft pad of paws, barely gracing the pulpy floor, edges nearer, silently
stealing the ground out from under them, pausing to breathe in a
purr, sending through the dried-out stone, stronger than our stone,
a flash of eyes green as glass. Cat's eyes, sharp and bright, fill the
funny-looking cave.

   Finally the cat, an ancient paye, Kamu's mentor, pounces and
devours Kamu and Namsoul. Beginning at the base of their skulls
and working up the back of their heads. At last they are jaguars. It
can begin.

Down by the river, Icarus listens to the dark, some shady underbelly stirring, yet when he looks, there is nothing there. Still he
knows. He feels something watching him.

   The jaguars reach the tents, so carelessly pitched along the muddy
scree, where Youngerbrother sleeps and sees and things are worse
because of it. As the paye have feared, seeing the other worlds
doesn't help Youngerbrother, simply gives him more to want.

   By the river, quiet in the night, Icarus surveys the sky, also silent
and black, Cassiopeia sliding slowly into view as if tugged by an
ankle across the midnight.

   The jaguars observe Icarus gazing at the sky, wanting to conquer it, to own it. Everything is one thing or another to use.

   Kneeling by the river, Nabia watches Icarus. She knows he sees
the paye as jaguars entering Laird's tent. She studies Icarus observing
the paye, as his literal mind imagines they are cougars. He cannot distinguish between a jaguar and a cougar, or a paye disguised as a
jaguar. She shrugs—he may see, yet knows little. His mind tells him
that what he is seeing is not what he sees but what it decides he must

be seeing. She wonders how long it will last, this sliver of space between his seeing and finally knowing. This remnant is the time left.
Her heart splits apart and falls like a perfectly halved melon, green in
the light, into her palms. She glances down, admiring the symmetry,
the seeds and perfect colour of the fruit, not in the least surprised
to discover herself broken-hearted. Youngerbrother can never give
Elderbrother back the world he loved. That world has vanished.
Ultimately, though, the two brothers must connect and face the des-
olation together. This convergence begins in the realm of dreams.
She returns to watching the jaguars. All hope rests with them.

The jaguars wait, one at either end of the sleeping mat, their
eyes the colour of limes. Laird gazes at the ceiling, unaware the tent
has changed. It is lifting off the ground. The flaps shiver gently in
the downdraft, the nylon floor bags and billows like a skin of water
gently blowing to waves. The paye lock the tent in the moon's
strong arm.

The jaguars' first task is to drag Laird to the plain of dreams.
There are no wars in Elderbrother's world—disputes are settled on
the plain of dreams. They are devoid of Laird's predilection for
hand-to-hand conflict, and even the hunt is handled in this way. The
animal is battled on the dream plain, leaving the actual killing more
symbolic than bloody, and (in Youngerbrother's phraseology) a done
deal.

Dreams to Youngerbrother are suspicious illusions, trivial diver-
sions, occasionally haunting but ultimately no more than wrinkles
to be swept aside and straightened with the morning sheets, only
taken seriously by the weak or deranged. Ironically, even Youngerbrother sorts through his life on the plain of dreams, unaware his
dream double carries him there when he has lost his mind to sleep.
Youngerbrother's consciousness never attends the plain of dreams,
he sends his dream double instead. These second-hand accounts
are hazy, incomprehensible and generally misconstrued memos
dropped about the office floor.

Kamu signals Namsoul to target the hearts. Youngerbrother has
many hearts. Where they've only one, he's born with as many hearts

as rivers have stones. Desire, lust, greed, revenge: these are his hearts. Bullets, smaller than fine grains of gunpowder floating through his body. In this light they appear beautiful; even dust in the moon's arm is beautiful.

Nabia feels control slipping. The realities are fluid now. Nothing is fixed or splendid or as it was, but changed and changing yet.

She watches the jaguars manoeuvring Laird's tent. Namsoul hopes to restore his heart, heighten its need to gravitate to light. In her dream she asked Namsoul to begin with Icarus. It might have been more successful, but events progressed too quickly, and suddenly Laird saw as well as Icarus, further than the paye had supposed he was capable of seeing. Things are very different now.

Icarus begs Nabia to look away from the river and the paye and world she is watching and cast her eyes and heart to him. He wants her to see his blood burning his veins, soaking him with heat. Icarus's love shines from him in a sheet of oroide, thin as foil melting over wedding rice, blinding him marvellously. If he weren't soaked like a sippet in a marriage cup of mead, he would see and act accordingly. Passion spoils him. Worse, he mistakes her anxiety for desire. Icarus should know better. He knows something about the art of divination but, inexcusably, he's forgotten everything. He confuses what he sees with what he wants to see. He sees without seeing. Laird has picked it up, the gift of seeing, snatched it like a wallet abandoned on a bench. Laird has snap enough for that, to see what he sees.

Once the tent is off the ground and safely floating in the moon's lean arm, the jaguars rest for a moment, content to allow the labour of lifting Laird to fall away briefly from their shoulders.

Nabia watches the tent floating like a leaf high above the ground. If he turned to look, Icarus would see it and begin to fathom the danger they are in. Instead he watches her, never once wondering what fascinates her, never turning to look.

The jaguars approach Laird. Laird is spending his gift of sight in searching the tribe for weak links, devising ways to persuade one of the young bucks to lead him to the hoard of gold. That there is a store of gold, he hasn't a doubt. The way is clear. Their lack of defences startles him. He pauses, suddenly afraid, unable to decide whether or not it is a trick to trap him. Laird understands tricks and traps and very little else.

The jaguars move then. One jaguar attacks from behind while another pounces from the front. Too late, he glances up. Perhaps it doesn't matter. The jaguars command long seconds in the air. They know what they are doing, they've performed this trick before. Time enough for him to consider them and his fear to swell.

He doesn't scream because his throat has drawn tighter than a dowager's purse; they're a tricky bunch. Confused, he wastes time puzzling over how a pair of black cougars managed to sneak into the tent. When he decides they aren't cougars, they strike.

Each cat devours separate parts. One feasts upon his brain, another upon his hearts. Equally tasteless, equally empty. They finish the meal with his penis and balls. Each jaguar crushes a ball between his teeth until it shatters like a soft walnut, spilling a taste of rancid fat over their tongues and the stippled ceiling of their mouths. Swallowing the gritty bits, they stare into each other's hearts. It is their turn to be afraid.

Laird glides down their throats, lumpy as congealed oatmeal. He cannot see, for his eyes are mushed and broken and his mind is on the fritz, although he's aware he's being eaten and the pain remains, pain reminiscent of a jungle cell with its sonata of electrodes playing upon his scrotum.

Once various loose parts hit the paye's stomachs and collect in a mishmash of what he used to be, Laird understands he hasn't died, but he doesn't understand what the paye are doing. He doesn't know that it's possible to make love or die in one reality while fishing lazily in another (everyone knows a hill is a hill and fish are fish, and everyone but Youngerbrother also knows there are other worlds where hills appear to be homes and fish walk about like men). All the same, Laird knows with a hunter's instinct that they will fail. They've only devoured members of their own placid tribe, docile even in defeat, but Laird doesn't fall apart in the same compliant way. One, he doesn't learn. Two, he is very tough. He has a built-in immunity to hocus-pocus. Laird isn't enlightened. He doesn't remember Aluna or the beginning, he isn't even aware that he is Youngerbrother. All he knows is what he sees, he doesn't know what it means. In spite of that, instinctively, he knows he will survive.

Laird's flavour permeates them. It isn't sweet. This is not a palatable business, nothing like devouring a young virgin to teach her how to love, or priming an old man for his dance with death. Laird's foul taste lingers in their mouth's trench, sour as gas. When he comes out the other end, his hearts resemble a jumbled string of lights, not one working, the majority barely screwed in. The jaguars instruct the cordate lumps on what it means to be a heart, the honour of such a position, a tedious task. Youngerbrother owns more hearts than ambitions or automobiles. It happened when he was conceived that his heart slipped and broke into a million billion quanta. While Youngerbrother waits for someone else to solder the fragments together, Aluna waits for him to collect himself sufficiently for the job to begin. The universe waits. Om!

Namsoul gathers the hearts and mashes them together; it is a sorry job. Laird's hearts remain separate and distinct, coagulated gravel attached by gluey, invisible cement. The paye are struck by this. Usually their work is beautiful. Even viruses and bacteria are magnificent; after all, they toy with life. Chewing the blueball, they ponder ugliness, how it comes about, reproduces, what possible use it has. This is dull work; they chew a little harder.

Words escape. Laird is shooting the shit. He knows what they want to hear. What he's really saying is fuck you. When they let go he will rise up unaltered. The stench of him is the same. He will be no more than what he is. All he has ever been.

Chewing the blueball, they tell him what he needs to evolve into, they explain this and other things, things he might understand; they leave out the complicated parts.

In a cave at the end of the maloca there is a crazy one, harmless enough, a paye gone awry, who couldn't resist the flight of feathers and now succumbs to endless terrifying journeys into them. He wanders screaming through the most wondrous day or night, communicating solely through that scream. Roaming the fields and forests or the river's edge, shoulders raised, head jutting like a heavy stone poised to drop, seeing nothing, avoiding even the children and dogs playing, he screams when no one expects it, when everyone's forgotten his agony. Utterly incongruous on such an evening, he screams, blasts from the inferno, reminding everyone that Youngerbrother has not disappeared; he is merely waiting. Tonight the crazy one lurches through the field. Although his screeching cannot touch the tent hovering in the moon's long white arm, he screams as if hoping to hold it there; he sees the jaguar's fear.

It's this business of seeing that the paye are concerned about. It's possible from where he is, the cushion he's now drifting through, to see all nine worlds. Not that Youngerbrother ever has, but as with many things and most especially here, it's possible and potentially catastrophic. No telling what havoc he might ignite, what blueprints he might unroll or what he might unwittingly (for it would certainly be unwittingly!) stumble upon—what mystery he might contrive to open. If from this innocuous cradle he should suddenly glance up and the nine worlds be revealed to him, the inescapable reality is that he has access to them all, and with the singular complexity of an atomic particle.

The jaguars carry each sorry heart to the plain of dreams to battle there. The plain of dreams is sacred, even a spiritually challenged rodent or roach divines as much, and a heart devoid of conscience has never found its way here. The event thunders through all nine worlds. Cleaves through and through them. Paye from all nine worlds arrive to witness the phenomenon. The stands are full and noisy.

The plain of dreams sits in the palm of the moon. It's a vast arctic plateau, warm and pliable as feathers and deep enough to drown. Laird's heart, the first one, when it arrives, sinks. Naturally, it hasn't the slightest notion how to float. Namsoul wades in, guddling the heart's aura, gently moving the air around it, as if reviving a trout. It sinks again. Namsoul shrugs. Of course, breathing is new to it.

Around each heart he places wings no larger than a pair of monkey's claws. These hairy hearts rise and fall like battered moths struggling to quit a candle's cup. Paye from the nine worlds sigh and silently remind each other not to expect too much. Things are difficult enough. Eventually all the hearts are bobbing, ugly dumplings on an oily bouillabaisse, blind to the crowded stands and betting booths, unaware they are the spectacle of all nine worlds. Let the battle begin!

The jaguars charge. The hearts, in fear, fly (badly), hovering above the jaguars. It's disconcerting to find jaguars eyeing their underparts. The hearts grow defensive and warlike. Territory is really what they know, they are oblivious to most considerations but who's on first. Although given their present predicament "first" has acquired an unfriendly edge.

The feathers turn the colour of blood. Namsoul expected this; he and Kamu have readied nets to fall over the hearts like webs. The hearts fly erratically, small birds, trapped, battering their wings against the webbing until some part catches, a wing, a claw, a neck. Battling to break free, they entrap themselves further.

The plain of dreams is scarlet, plush as papal robes, that strange audacious colour of danger and intrigue. The paye practise patience. They are not swayed; it has to be like this. Nothing else will satisfy the stupid little pumps, dumb as jaw-locked canines, where even in death the bite remains clamped and resolute. Laird is tedious. If he retreats, it's simply to advance along another avenue. The paye fight off yawning, chewing another blueball. If only it made sense.

The paye from all nine worlds confer. It's conceded that no matter what they do, Laird is impervious. His denseness is his best defence. The paye shake their heads, remembering other panhandlers and conquistadores. Youngerbrother is unlike even the simplest reptile. A reptile feels the heat of the sun in a stone and turns. Mountains, in their own time, move. Only Youngerbrother is immutable.

Yet Youngerbrother has begun to see that these few harbingers herald the coming masses. For the safety of all nine worlds Youngerbrother must make his way back to Aluna. It's what she expects.

In that instant, the paye from all nine worlds tell the jaguars what to do: the blueball, Aluna's tongue, has made everything clear. We must take our cue from Aluna and—as she set brother against brother—Youngerbrother against Youngerbrother, and leave Icarus to tackle Laird. Yes, toss Laird back on his bedroll to sleep it off like a bad drug trip and concentrate on Icarus. Icarus is experimenting with love, he may be retrievable. Certainly it will be horrendous work transforming Icarus into a paye, even a routine voyage through the other worlds with him in tow will be a daunting task, to say nothing of his journey through the miasma of his own consciousness to return to Aluna. What choice is there? With the inevitable rush of others, one of Youngerbrother's clan needs to be there as they disembark. Why not Icarus? After all, his seeing before the rest was Aluna's doing.

First, the jaguars will persuade Nabia to seduce Icarus. But it's amazing Youngerbrother falls in love, that he manages such a mystery—half asleep! The paye shake their heads. Tumbling off to sleep, Youngerbrother's dream double visits the plain of dreams and in a span of time returns to the skull to awaken the dolt, who remembers the waking world yet forgets the house of dreams entirely! This magic is what the paye need to open, the secret passage of the conscious mind where turning down one or another alley closes off the entryway as deftly as the shutter between windpipe and gullet.

As soon as Icarus falls asleep, they'll send Nabia to the plain of dreams. Matters of the heart are never accidental. When love collapses, the hearts agreed long before—love cannot exist but it begins and ends in this quiet white space.

———

Sweet morning frees the usual suspects: a bird's song, the river's and a dozen other off-key melodies, a childish wind teasing some arthritic branch, a far-off flicker badgering a dying tree. Icarus passed the night waiting on the river's jeering lip for Nabia's return. He glimpsed her last after midnight, walking through the woods, threading between the silvered trees, as though a fleet of iron chests were fastened to her shoulders and trailing miles behind. And he waited, night clinging to him heavy as her iron chests, though he ached to take on hers as well.

The rest are finally awake. One somnambulant has started a fire. Icarus glances over without interest, hoping only that when his eyes return to the river he will find her there. Instead he finds Laird, preoccupied, outfitting a cumbersome pack with dehydrated food, lipstick and fleece blankets, furtively hurrying as though to avoid detection. Icarus thinks no more about it. The others are consumed with rhapsodies of gold, but it no longer interests him. Nabia should be along soon. What else is there to care about?

Icarus has never been in love before. The unaccustomed nerves are charged to excess. His body rings with pain. He could stop it but the novelty holds him. No longer different and held apart, he soaks in the sensory jolt of love. Subjacent to Nabia is a feeling of finally having reached a plateau the world has been partying on for years. He's humbled, rejoicing at no longer being different but chagrined that it's taken so long. The feeling of relief is lost in the thought there is some flaw within—like the first time a woman touched him there and he ejaculated in her hand. The same uncomfortable mix of ecstasy and shame and pride.

Hours ago, when Nabia refused the paye, they hit her with their eyes. Their request is as unthinkable as her refusal. Here, at the tail end of a very long dawning, she stares at the forest floor and weeps. This is the first time she's disobeyed the paye. It hangs on her, this obstinacy, they see it casing her shoulders in a thick, ugly cloak of weeds, the sort that climb over trees and bones and debris and finally take them down.

"I can't," she begs them, "fuck Youngerbrother. Nothing is more repugnant."

The paye shield their thoughts from her, not out of kindness but to make her wary and worry more. This final debate is a formality, the paye strike her with their spears of light. Although they are silent, she hears a thousand others weeping in their blows.

Nabia's husband, Zipa, is the chief. Handsome as an elk is handsome, Zipa is a leader the elders and paye respect, a judge given to
understanding, incapable of deceit or shallowness. The paye have
sequestered him in an apartment at the furthest end of the wall of
caves. The thing's decided and Nabia has lost.

Zipa married her when she was fourteen. Even as a child, Nabia
was beautiful, with skin the colour of a high luminous moon, eyes
black, the sort that blaze and take command, yet quiet; at her slightest glance peace is settled at her feet. She is, after all, Aluna's copy.
Zipa is also weeping, dry male tears. Nabia feels each drop running
like molten tin from his eyes. She believes she will always love him.
With each jagged tear, Zipa asks her to obey the paye.

Already the paye are at work, changing her inside, switching
things around. The paye are removing Zipa from her special places,
and in his stead they're inlaying images of Icarus. The hint and whisper, the very smell of him. The paye leave nothing alone. It is hope-
less to resist. She doesn't bother hiding any small remembrance—
the only way to fight is to be quiet and give in.

Meanwhile the paye continue to instruct Nabia. Inside the clouds
they lay out various scenarios. This morning, however, the paye have
lost their sense of humour. They aren't snickering as they often
do when dealing out the learning clouds. Today the game is very
serious.

"There can be no wrong moves!"

They repeat it a hundred times. It's dangerous to get testy with
the paye. She works to control herself. It's not, however, a day for
self-control; she has difficulty remaining civil. Under usual circum-
stances the paye would find this unpardonable. Today, though, there
are already too many lessons pending.

Another thing: Nabia will become more like Youngerbrother.
The paye in their wisdom haven't divulged this to her, leaving her
unable to explain the discrepancies she discovers in herself. Small
wonder she blames herself, for she sees it, the disintegration, and
is appalled. The paye aren't certain it will be reversible, and they ne-
glect to tell her this as well. She has enough, they've kindly weighed,

to worry about, and besides it's not expedient to distract her from the task at hand. The paye are practical. Aluna and the blueball have taught them pragmatism.

Ordinarily she would avert her eyes out of respect, but she finds herself staring them boldly in the eye. The paye recognize this; her wilfulness is gaining precedence. While they hunch there, deciding things, she watches Zipa in his new apartment; she watched him at the entrance watching her. She's trying hard to not let go.

"First you must eat this." Namsoul hands her a root and a fistful of leaves. The leaves are prickly and bitter, tasting of sickness and poison. The dusty root is even worse.

"All of it," Nikko, the young novice, prods her. "Every last bit."

She dislikes this paye. Once she overheard Laird and Icarus arguing, referring to being pissed off. At the time she hadn't understood what it meant and tried to imagine peeing and stopping off. Chewing the bitter leaves and root, Nabia begins to understand.

The paye smile. Their heads bobble. Things are progressing, considering.

Zipa waits by the fire, burning Nabia's pillow and all the joy it held. Its feathers play along the flames and quickly turn to ash. Youngerbrother has begun to see. All bets are off. It's finally begun.

———————

Gibson says, "It's not like I give a shit about the gold. I don't."

"Yeah," scoffs Maggie, "we're all of us here for the sunshine of brotherly love. None of us here for freckin loot."

The sky is a funny red, air reeking of rotting deadfall and the stink of mountains thick as pine needles reamed up the snout. Gibson continues dipping a pan in the water, his back to the others swatting the surface with their pans like grizzlies fishing the shallow bank.

"Don't bother haulin that out," Gibson shouts at Newt, already preparing to weigh a handful of dust. "Right from the get-go that piece'a shit never worked right."

Dawn's all but finished. The birds are still working on it, chewing down to the milkbone of day. Sweetgrass smoulders in the campfire, dousing the air with dulcet smoke. When Ana calls them for breakfast, well-aged crow eggs skating sunny-side-up over a gallimaufry of Richardson ground squirrel and dandelion spears, it's quickly finished, only minuscule bones left to pick. Gibson takes a greasy plate over to Icarus, but he waves him away.

"If you're not gonna eat, least you can do is chop firewood or scare up some game. It's been the best part of three days you been draggin your ass like some old geezer on ice. Snap out of it. High country ain't the place to slack off. None of us got time or energy to piggyback some geriatric hypochondriac."

Icarus isn't listening. The words might as well be river noise as his brother yammering. He knows Gib's stationed behind him doing what he does when he gets mad, his head angled like it just took a blow and his right side aiming to volley back.

"Eat your goddamn breakfast and settle down to work."

Gibson walks back toward the firepit, stopping beside Ana to ask if she thinks he's getting worse.

"He's not any better. For one thing, he's not sleeping and for another, this last day or so, he's done nothing but moon around down by the river." Ana laughs. "He's acting more like a love-drunk teenager than a man suffering gold fever."

"Leave him to me," Laird whispers.

Icarus has lost Nabia. For a moment he thought he saw her next to the river, stooping to drink. Turned out to be nothing more than mist breaking apart, the sun punching through night's fading spread and falling face down on the water. Pretty as a mess of red-tailed birds.

"I got an idea." Laird sidles up beside him.

"Piss off! I'm not goin anywheres near that field. I'm stayin right here down by the river! You wanna go desert-stormin over there, suit yourself. Leave me out of it."

Icarus wanders the bank, searching one way and the other for her. Unaccustomed to pain, he is irritated by everything. He kicks the river debris puckered along the water's ribs, shakes his head as though working free some cumbersome rack roped to his crown. There's nothing there; at least, nothing shakes free.

Gibson watches him warily and it occurs to him that if Icarus is in danger, so are they all. But what, if anything, has gone awry? Icarus doesn't notice Laird stopping behind him. "I can help," Laird says. "I know what to do."

––––––––––

The air, gummy against a shoulder or cheek, feels inclined to stick, walking through it is arduous, leaving Nabia's steps easily traced, for glancing back it seems that her path hangs in space as though the air is batter and her body a spoon. Yet birds above her fly as freely as ever, and their song arrives unspoiled.

The dog hunkers beside her, tracking swallows, but he's too old now to give them any trouble. His head falls abruptly to rest upon her foot. Without thinking, she brushes her palm along the back of his head and he groans and closes his eyes. Behind her the batter folds in a sinuous crease stretching from where she's been to where she sits. Namsoul has fixed this. She cannot hide or escape. She needn't inquire why. Namsoul has the birds tell her again and again.

Youngerbrother won't leave us in peace. Soon he will ravage the yellow stones buried in the rocks, as though they are virgins and he is their god.

The birds, it seems, are also afraid.

Wasn't the land along the river once tropical? Now a green tongue licking brown, transient lips . . . forgetting for a time to breathe again, balancing in the purgatory of empty and forgotten, and squandered to shit. There, by the smell of river rot and fresh mountain water stumbling down the centre or lying back against the banks, flat, dragging its heels, happy to spool and suck the sweet mucky ribs before being dragged away, reluctantly letting go the slime and rocks, schlepping on like a weary farmer following his herd home, Nabia picks up and leads the horse to another fallen stump to sit and wait and wish she couldn't see. It's beyond her. It's important she realize this.

Icarus finds Nabia by the river, the dog asleep on the shady side, tired of trying to catch fish, the scene straight from an idyllic duster. When she sees him, Nabia rides the horse to the middle of the river. Its hooves break the water like glass. Watching her, Icarus kneels to pet the dog. It growls, gets up, shakes itself and settles down again, well out of reach. The horse is nervous, bobbing its head up and down and pawing the water with one leg.

He stands then, straightens his back and watches. She doesn't look at him. At first she doesn't hear him wading into the water. The horse shudders, and the dog barks, raises its hackles and growls. The horse sidles sideways and spins on its back legs, and still she doesn't look. The horse doesn't understand why she fails to give the signal to run. Bounding along the shore, the dog barks. The birds have left. The air smells of bitter smoke.

When he grabs the horse's withers, the animal rears up and she whispers to calm it. Dropping back down, the horse shakes, its legs trembling their length under the effort to hold the spot. The dog is in the water, swimming alongside them.

Icarus lifts himself up on the horse in one swift move, stationing himself behind her as easy as sitting a bike. The horse bows deeply, all four legs splayed and trembling, waiting. One small signal and it will send the stranger flying. When he kicks the horse, it doesn't respond but sinks lower, its fury suddenly black. Finally she nudges it.

Namsoul has Nabia take Icarus to the green where he first glimpsed her. The pallet, bordered by its browning cuff of bank, is idle and serene, a lea of flattened felt, waiting for the players to take their cue. Although he is too beguiled to notice, the park dances with jaguar eyes.

She might be the moon pooling on still water, the way she reflects day and night, so many things at once: in her eyes he glimpses a snowy winter's pass, a golden hive burning in the sun, a wide-winged bird scudding down upon a hollowed hum of running water.

"I never used to believe in love, I didn't understand about going outside of what I know, that out here is the real world, and it's the other one that's false. I never understood."

Nabia settles into the affair. The horse is in the woods, also watching. Not the dog, it's turned its back and waits. The woods are quiet, only the sound of Icarus grinding, his body slapping hers. Locked in his tunnel, Icarus is inconscient.

Icarus in love is no performance artist. He works hard at fucking. Like a bus driver on a disco floor, he grinds gears and backs up and lurches into overdrive. The paye orchestrate the comedy by interfering with Icarus's orgasm, they bulldoze him to the brink, dangle him along the hairy edge, drag him back, softened slightly, and punch him up for another go.

Nabia turns to reading his mind, cartoon strips combined with strip joints and centrefolds and a man dragging a small child into a public toilet, shoving him over the seat and bum-fucking him. She perseveres through the forest of cheesy videos to the reservoir of hearts, to begin the task of soldering these splintered pumps together.

She pauses, dismayed. Icarus's hearts aren't alive or working. His heart space is a dust bowl, his hearts are tumbled husks stolen over time by wind and sand and blown into a gulch of dirty pieces, crackled and emptied, with no idea of what they might have been or what they were intended for. She collects the hearts and lifts them to the plain of dreams.

It's new to Nabia, and old, this feeling she thought was for Zipa but here and now rises for another. This love, a volcanic mix of the two worlds, is more painful than she imagined possible. It helps her realize that Youngerbrother's half isn't easy. Love is difficult and brutal on this side of the world. There isn't a free ride, there's nothing soft or mealy-mouthed about Icarus's love, it takes the body whole and chews down hard upon it.

The horizon opens like a door. Aluna comes as a single ray of light, enters through their crowns and travels through their bodies to settle in their sex.

When he looks at her, and he cannot take his eyes from her, she is dipped in gold, and not merely a dusting but solid gold, of that he has no doubt. Plunging himself into her, he cries out, Oh, god, but cannot say more, love claims him completely.

The place where two realities converge is sacred. The paye suspend small golden ornaments there, gifts from Aluna, the scant pieces left from their life in the jungle before it was destroyed. The park, because it is where Icarus first glimpsed them, is now venerated. Trees run along the margins and river and a whisk of scrub brush scrapes the shore, little else. The rest is a cabochon of green. The paye discuss erecting a pyramid and attaching the gold to it but decide against it and settle on the aspen and cranberry willow mopping the riverbank.

In the sun, the trinkets play with the spokes of light along the water and for a second Icarus imagines the river must have overflowed its banks. Slowly he realizes it isn't a game of sunny billiards but baubles like Christmas balls scattered randomly.

The golden jaguars are more finely crafted than the pipe left in Gibson's tent. Some of these cats crouch or bound along the willow, while others hunt or lunge or seem to fly, if cats could fly; a score, satiated, drain from a branch in sleep. In the sun the charms appear transparent, as though it's possible to gaze through to the other side, as if the metal is glass. But it is gold and very real.

Nabia turns to face Icarus and through the dazzle of reflected bijous she is golden. The paye now are sure that Icarus believes if he possesses the gold he will possess Nabia as well. Satisfied, the paye grin. It's natural, isn't it, to take pleasure in a job well done?

———————

When the heart is broken it sometimes dries and disappears, and the area around it becomes a desert too. Nothing grows in it then; it sits arid and broken and dead. Life, even when the sky opens and rains down a flood, cannot return the place to green. The ground has soured, its lake another dead sea, home to nothing, sans microbes

or small frightened things, nothing save salt or some such bitterness. So Zipa lives on, a desert, impossible to kill or rescue.

Zipa kneels by the water's edge, washing golden jaguars no larger
than a child's hand. It is unusual to bathe a jaguar, for they're reposi-
tories and their patina is priceless.

"I don't want Youngerbrother to know us by holding what we
love," he tells Nabia, although she's no longer listening, and he
reaches out across the water, his hands like leaves waiting to be
blown from their branch by winter's approaching wave. Above him
in the low hanging popcorn clouds, the paye lounge, watching,
chewing the blueball. They are busy changing the feathers, spores
and quanta that make up Nabia's blood.

The water targeted with soft falling rain shatters Zipa's image,
making it more beautiful than ever. She loved this man, imagined
she always would, yet the love is leaving, like colourless mist from
the warm river.

There will be no going back (as if there ever could be, as if such a
trick were possible, as if the nine worlds and the galaxies between
could roll back into the invisible speck that is Aluna's mind). Zipa
can see it when he remembers her, but he doesn't like to remember.
Only when he catches a glimpse of her he sees the change, what the
paye are making of her, how like water turning to tea, one moment
clear, the next diffused and dark and impossible to look through.

He wonders how much sadder he can become. He cannot imagine an end. Youngerbrother will win. Zipa's only satisfaction resides
with the jaguar. They will leave their bite.

———

It's a while before Laird realizes, from Gibson's smile, that he's been
following him. Laird curses because he failed to notice earlier, and
walks back down the path to meet Gibson. "Hey," he says.

"Hey."

They're halfway along a rough stretch of rubble on the far end of
the cliffs. The slope is rough but raked and relatively easy to scale.

Of course, it doesn't last long—halfway up the slope it peters out
into sheer rock—but it's a natural place to start if a guy was thinking
about finding a way up to the caves. Laird smiles that fishy smile.
"Don't have nothin better to do than see what I'm up to?"

"Guess not."

Laird stops smiling. Squints. Smiles again. "I'm on my way for a
little walk. Nothin important."

"I can see that."

"Like I said, I'm in the mood for a walk."

"Nice day for it."

It's been pissing for the last hour. Both men are soaked and
chilled. Laird wipes the rain off his face, his smile tighter than usual,
and snarls, "It clears my head."

Gibson nods.

"You know how it is. Some days you need to get away from assholes."

Gibson nods. "Plenty of time for that once we're off this mountain."

Where before Gibson had some ideas, he wasn't sure. Now he's
sure.

Laird stuffs his hands in the pockets of his poncho. He looks back
down the way they came, thinking about things, kicking himself for
letting Gibson get wind of anything. "Look, I'm not up to anything
if that's what you're thinkin. Only wanted to have a look along this
side of the hill."

"Fine by me."

"If I come across anything, I'll let you know."

"I'll come along." He smiles. "Save you the trouble."

"It's not what you think."

"Yeah, I forgot you know what everybody thinks."

It's quiet. The wind lies at their feet like a dog airing its belly.
"Can't beat a view like this," he says, turning to face the broken sky
and remnants of a valley, green cut off by branches and rain.

"Never realized you were such a nature boy. First time in all this
you said."

He smiles. "I don't want to get into anything with you, Gib. It's only I got a real sense how to play this through."

"You don't say."

He lowers his tone. "Things'll go easier if I handle them."

"You don't say."

Laird leans on the rock as if it's a bar table he's pounded and will pound again, pissed at the barkeep's slowness in bringing the next round. "Hey, it's not that I'm playin my cards close to my chest."

Gibson lifts the water bottle to his lips and takes a long drink. When he puts it back down, he stares at his feet. "You got somethin you feelin a little bitter about, Laird, maybe you better tell me. Only don't start in shittin me. You know how I hate it when you shit me."

"There you go," he says, riled but stopping himself in time. "The thing is you don't know what you're messin with." Laird's face reddens. A jawbone, elk probably, caught in slag, falls apart like railcars suddenly disengaged by the toe of his boot. "There's things at stake here—things you don't know the first thing about!"

Gibson leans back, rests his shoulder against the side of a rock. The wind reels in a bit of the slack, nothing serious, hardly worth noticing, ruffling a stray hair, teasing it across a field of vision. Making the rain harder to like. "You're soundin a whole lot like the CIA."

"Don't go pushin meltdown. This here's a situation you hain't got a clue how to handle."

Gibson stays looking at him. He wipes rain off his face, like rubbing condensation off a fogged windshield; it streaks it some. "Needs your size of kid gloves, does she, Laird?"

"This hain't a time for egos but straight good sense. You got any of that you'll leave me do a job." Gibson smirks and Laird continues, "Icarus is playin us—he's over there right now cuttin his own deal. He's fixin on buggerin us good."

"Icarus is down for the count."

"You think that, you're dumber than I thought."

Laird turns, shouldering his cigarette from the rain to light it.

The sulphurous nip of tobacco smoke mingles with the fetid smell of wet clothes and hair.

"Hey!" Newt shouts in the distance, his arm waving like a sail come loose. "Hey, you guys!"

"Now what?" As he pivots, Gibson spies Hill and Ana and the others stampeding to join them. Something big has happened. Hill's out front, elbows tucked, knees going like pistons for a touchdown.

"This here is pyrite." Hill parks alongside Gibson. "But there's enough other traces to let me think we're close. Real close. You need to come take a look."

"It's not far." Clasping one side, Newt caves into a tripod, panting. "We've been working the east base of the cliffs."

They don't have to worry, there's still a good five hours of light. Inside, all hell's breaking. Soon as they find the first hint of dust, the lid'll blow sky high, however high that turns out to be. Laird's tapping into that, whistling, letting off a little steam. Besides, the rain is easing up, the sun's trying to poke through.

"There's something there, Gib! I'm sure of it!" Ana stamps her feet as if shaking free clumps of snow, and points, while the others wait in a small ugly clot, watching her trot aimlessly this way and that along the raked slope. Before she realizes what's happening, Ana bends over and vomits. Gibson leaves Laird and Hill to comfort her. "I thought you were finished with all this," he mumbles. Ana shakes, vomiting once more. She doesn't know if it's the flu or what, she simply continues vomiting, pausing occasionally to cough.

Unnerving to realize the body's miles of tributaries and runways, crude purveyors of fluids and combustibles, sense what the brain will not. Often the seat of reason is the last to know. Life must hit it squarely, rudely, before it will give over, admit things haven't gone as predicted. With so much the fault of logic, perhaps it's logical to heap this upon its back as well.

When she lifts her head, she cries, "Gawd, what's that, down there along the river? I can't make it out. It's giving me such a headache. Even in this light it hurts my eyes to look."

At first the trinkets wander in the wind like leaves and no one can see them. But when the sun hits the cats, caught like tiny birds on the current, their eyes are dazzled. The brilliance is unbearable.

A collective cry: "Holy shit!"

Although she sees the pretty baubles, Ana also sees Icarus, Icarus and a woman, and she wavers, stymied by a desire to retreat. Maggie sees the competition but focuses on the golden cats. The black-eyed bitch she'll deal with in due course. Instinctively, the group moves, sweeping Ana along, until they are running. No one thinks about how fast they are moving, simply that it isn't fast enough.

Nabia and Icarus watch his brothers racing down the sloppy gravel causeway, through the fringe of trees and diagonally across the green, aiming for the riverbank, cursing and stumbling in their heavy mountain boots. The bibelots catch the wind and shake, and for a second the runners stop as if suddenly frozen, and start again.

At separate times, quiet inner intervals, each member of the troupe has wondered why their perception kinks as if kept on a tinny band spronging out of shape, suddenly pitching them headlong into other worlds. It confounds them, this new ability to slip in time and witness events long past (what else can this other be but past?), yet view this history coterminously with the reality they like to imagine as present. *Goddamn!* If they were practised, they might be able to preview the future; the paye certainly do (easily done inasmuch as the future is simultaneous to past and present), but of course they are not competent at all. They've simply stumbled on some other world they assume must be already past. Forget questioning how a video may leave a string of gifts, take the money and run.

They see the gentle riverbank, its hemline of brush and wispy thread trees. There's Nabia and Icarus at the cozy end of screwing (seems they missed the rain down here), a horse grazing nearby, that dog again, a big guy skulking down the riverside, leaving behind bushes adorned in gold. And it looks real! Even this far away, Laird and Gibson know the colour, they don't need to be convinced, they only want to fix their hands around it. All the same, Hill and Newt are having difficulty. It's slowing them down. Hill likes his world calibrated as a carpenter's tape measure. Newt's a show-me kinda Petri plate. Now the universe has obliged, Newt panics like a child caught in a lightning storm. The situation is beyond *beyond*. What is he supposed to make of it?

There isn't any wind, the humming is merely the white noise of no return. The point of it, its jetty, nips like wind. Fools, waiting at the crossroads of cross purposes for a spinning signpost to slow and reveal the way.

Such times as these Hill takes charge, the designated driver, the sot sober enough to remember how to pull over and breathe into a Breathalyzer, he tells them in a commanding voice, "Gold!"

Finally it's Laird's turn, finally he steps into the centre, the empty pocket the rest have circled but chosen to avoid, and runs straight down the middle toward the litter. It isn't necessary for him to add more. There's a lottery, a windfall embedded in the word! One marvellous word! People think *love* and *sex* and *death* are words to stop the fucking traffic—flood the brain, the blood—but it's gold, gold, that hits fools harder than any other hammer.

Before the others reach them, Icarus slips from her arms to free a tiny golden cat from an overhanging branch. The act is automatic, and momentarily his concentration slides from Nabia to the intriguing metal. In his grasp the bauble feels like glass and he can't resist reaching for another. He doesn't notice Nabia dissolving as simply as wind or mizzle in the sun. When Icarus realizes she's not there, he searches the ravelling river cuffs but Nabia has disappeared. All his life he's dodged women, treated them like wind or rain or crows. Now here's a woman ducking in and out the way he's always wanted and he'd rather slice open his chest and tear away his lungs than spend another second separated from her. He's aching to find Nabia and he's aching to find the gold. The paye finessed this, they've made Nabia and the gold one in Icarus's mind. He also expects to find her when he finds the source.

Laird grabs miniature cats three and four at a time, a field hand picking fruit more efficiently than those who've worked a lifetime in an orchard. Gibson takes a share, Hill also scores high for innate ability. Still everyone finds felines to love and hold and time to reach for more. No one considers stopping to rest until all the ornaments are stripped from the trees and willow bushes, and every cat is claimed. Amply placated, they no longer wonder how *objets d'art* slip from one reality to another, like bunnies down a burrow, or whether it might not be the other way round, and *they* are the playthings who have slid through the pesky wormhole.

"Like I said, first we check out upstream. See it wasn't carried downstream." Laird squints into the sun. "Comprendez, amigo?"

"If you had half a fuckin brain," Icarus tells him, knowing he's pushing it, knowing like as not he'll get more than a verbal slur in return, "you'd see the obvious place is the base of those cliffs! There's no mine longside this river, that's for crappin sure!"

"What? You think those ol farts climbed cliffs high as those and set up the Lost Lemon Mine inside a cave? You think that, you are certifiable!" Laird spits to prove his point.

"I didn't say up by the caves, shithead, I said the base."

The air is magnetic Velcro. Molecules, dandelion fluff and bugs stick to it, nothing moves. Riding on top of it is an unaccountable hum, although there are no high wires or power stations for miles.

"I dunno . . . could be the mine's upstream. Makes sense. As much as anything makes sense." Hill's size gives him confidence to challenge anyone, but even Hill treats Laird with respect. Laird's tricky as a friggin hand grenade. "One thing for sure," Hill volunteers, hoping to defuse the situation, "I don't care if they're Moonies or Zen monks or Potawatamees, they got a shitload of gold and I mean to make em show me where they dug it out. Look at these gold cats!"

"There's a mine all right," Laird snarls. The blue temple vein bulges slightly, the eyes narrow.

"Goddamn," Hill drawls, "we need to sit across from them and ask them where in hell they're hidin her."

"You see them, then, when it suits you, Hill?" Icarus is curious. He can't control when they come and go. He doesn't believe Hill can.

"No. I guessed you could."

"Not so I can count on it. Fact is they fade in and out worse than a cheap car radio."

Gibson rubs a cat in the cup of his hand. "It's got so I see them most of the time, but the reception's scrambled, only every so often it pops up bright and clear."

"I'd like it to stop," Ana says. "It's like having a mud-splattered windshield and you can't make out what you're driving into."

"What we need is a go-between." Maggie smiles at Icarus. "From the looks of it back there, you're getting super-friendly with the natives, well, one bitch anyways. Maybe we should appoint you our ambassador? Who knows what you'll come away with?"

"Fuck off."

"Obvious first thing we need to do," Gibson decides, "is talk to them. Right off the bat, ask them where the mine is."

"No way they'll talk. Leastwise not about that. I'm tellin you."

"Maybe if it's you," taunts Maggie, "they might. Aren't you the stud muffin makes all us girls pee our panties?"

Icarus stays focused on Gibson. "Gettin them to talk is another story altogether. Most of the time I don't have a clue what they're goin on about."

Laird runs his tongue around the inside of his cheek, moving tobacco. "We'll get to them in good time. First we suss out upstream, like I said."

Maggie saunters by, a spunky kid wandering into a burning forest, leaning into Laird's ear, knowing he calls women slits and claims he'd as soon pay for it as have to put up with it, knowing he'd curl up on hot irons to fuck her. "Hey, Lardy?" her voice a cheap piece of fluff tickling the back of his ruby neck, "why don't you freck off up the river, you're so sure? Leave the rest of us track Sticker. Seems he's got the inside lane."

Before Laird has time to reply, before he can backhand her, the light changes, slipping behind the haze the way rain draping a leaf will fall without dropping. Even the bushes hunkered on the shore are dull again, disappointed and sorry as leaves dumped curbside. Cloaked under that, Namsoul fades in, faintly at first, for a quiet drink along the river bank. When he lifts his head, water spools from large ivory spikes the colour of brass, skin dissolves to blackened fur and the eyes turn lime then lemon then lime as if serrated aspen leaves turning back to front, spring to fall, with every glancing breeze.

Laird's body instantly sinks to a fighting stance. No one else moves, even those enthralled, fear takes their hearts to pump and bang about the heads.

All my years, Hill wants to tell Maggie, all my years mountaineerin, huntin, I never seen a cat this close! And never a black one! Never heard of a black this far north! He needs her to appreciate how rare the event is but he can't speak, and from her expression it's evident she intuits some singularity.

Laird will savour killing this runty specimen. He's never tasted cat, but tough or not, he'll eat every piece and tan the hide. It'll make a damn fine show on the side of the shed.

The ol man claimed a mountain cat stinks worse than bear but this cat stinks of resin, of musky fungus. In the second it takes Laird to aim his 30.06 Remington, the cat disappears, vanishing behind the remarkable light, leaving a small but perfect indentation in the sandy bank, uncommon in its detail.

Studying the print, they squabble about the divarications between cougar and panther and bobcat prints, and who in hell is better qualified to say, and settling that, they settle down to arguing about whether or not it was a cat at all.

"No way it was a cat!" Laird pronounces.

"I know a cat when I see one." Here, Hill has no doubt.

"Listen, there's shit goin down here you hain't got a clue about. That was no cat."

"Well, then, Laird, you mind tellin me just what it was?"

"Them."

"Them! Them? They turn into cats, do they?"

"They do."

"I took you for a lot of things, Laird, but I never took you for a fool."

"Fool or not," Icarus cuts in, "Laird's right about this. It wasn't no ordinary cat."

"I never said it was some ordinary cat."

"They do things, all sorts of things that don't make sense, but are a fact . . . as much as anything's a fact."

"Goddamn." Hill looks to Gibson. "You got both brothers off their nut."

Upstream, nine miles south of the headwaters, they discover another stretch of feline artifacts, and three streams converging, similar to the confluence depicted in the old prospector's map.

"This ain't coincidence!" Gibson looks at the streams and then the map and then the streams. "This is fuckin unbelievable is what it is!"

"Biggest day of my life!" Newt whoops, sending Maggie into spasms. "Ohmygod!" Maggie grabs Dallas and they gad about dancing in a circle, shrieking, "We've found it! We've found it!" Dallas soon stops and joins the rest, bent like bedlamps over the shoreline, panning for gold. Quiet as high voltage light bulbs.

Ana stares at the lump in her pan. Mustard with a funny tint of green. Laird grabs the pan out of her hand. "WhadItellya! WhadIsay!" Gibson and Hill take one look and resume panning, moving so hard and steady the water turns beside them as though they are wheels. Laird scours the shore, no longer a man but a metal detector, freed to roam on its own. Icarus wades into the centre of the convergence and, holding his divining rod, stands still as a bronze crane. Newt can't decide where to begin. He runs from stream to stream picking up gravel and rocks, staring at each handful as though waiting to hear the stones speak.

"What has to happen," Laird informs them, "is I need to take charge!" He looks around to see who, if anyone, objects. No one's focused, or if they have, they make no outward show. Laird chuckles to himself. This is great, it's open season then. Right over their fuckin heads. "Alls I'm sayin," Laird jabs the bank with a twig, "is here's where we need to set a sluice!"

Newt snorts, a nerdy long-suffering dissent. "A sluice is illegal without a permit. I thought we agreed to avoid drawing attention to ourselves?"

Laird fires Newt a look and returns to his map. "Could have the whole thing operational by sundown."

Maggie stops doctoring her blisters. "Jeezus, Neuter, why'd you tag along if you didn't think we'd be puttin up a freckin sluice without a freckin bloody permit? Don't be so freckin bloody constipated." Maggie has troubles enough. Her primo top-of-the-line freckin boots have rubbed her ankles and heels raw. She administers a combination of blasphemy and moleskin.

"Just don't go blaming me." Newt studies the sky, clear and blue as a California swimming pool. "All it'd take is a fire ranger patrolling or the RCMP running an infra-red drug search—don't come whining I didn't warn you. Something big as that'll show up from air. Might as well wire a beacon and a flare to it."

Silence, as it often does, follows Newt. Laird fixes his attention to the ground: first he imagines a boot encountering the side of a fat head; after that he pictures a fist pulverizing an expensive set of porcelain crowns. Newt, feeling something in the air, hunches to cover the back of his neck. When Laird swacks the ground with his twig, tired puffs drift up and down, irritable as a hound forced to move and doggedly winding back to sleep. The air reeks of heat and cedar and pine droppings grilling to rust in the sun. Heat hangs on their shoulders, pushing the fork of their necks, drumming down upon their heads until its weight sinks into their bones and melts there like lead. Joint and marrow lost wax.

"The important thing to keep in mind," Newt drones on in a professorial tone, "is we can't risk detection. Comprendez?" (Mimicking Laird, badly.)

The others ignore Newt. It's easier now the heat boils each sound into one liquefied squall of flies, mosquitoes, crows, their insatiable nestlings, and Newt.

"Another thing, who appointed you starfleet commander?"

"Shit," Icarus groans, stepping in front of Laird. "Don't go mashin mushhead. Save it for when we get back to earth. Here in space, we have to behave. You know the rules on *Voyager 2*."

Hill's arms rise like a forklift as he backs up to tour the site. "If Laird wants a sluice here, he can have a sluice. Where's the big deal? It's not like there's a shortage of wood or labour."

Newt twists on the log, lips a sour but tidy insignia, disdain disguising defeat. When he closes his eyes he imagines himself a Spanish monarch astride a gargantuan steed parading through the rabble. "Do whatever you like. I couldn't care less."

Laird starts collecting his gear. "Shouldn't take a slew of pussy-power to build a sluice."

Gibson hauls himself up, hands jammed in his back pockets. "Laird's right, the girls here and Neuter can jerry-rig one in half a shake. The rest of us need to be out doin somethin useful. Checkin out each stream."

"No way I'm helping if that's what you're asking."

Laird grins and spits sidelong. "That's a relief, Snooter Neuter. We want the friggin thing to work."

"Gib's right," Icarus says. "It's got to be up one or the other of these streams. Funny though, my stick here hasn't moved, not one iota. She's stone cold. Where's the sense—with the rivers converging same as on the map . . . logic says it's here—but the stick's sayin we're nowheres near. Bitch is, there's nowhere else it can be. Not really. Unless . . .?" When he jerks his head up like an animal drinking and suddenly startled, he whispers, "They're sending us on a wild goose chase! It's back at the cliffs—inside one of those caves!"

Laird swears, "You and those goddamn caves! There's nothin happenin up there outside'a couple three old bags weavin rugs."

"No," Icarus says, leaving the river and heading back downstream. "No. I'm right. About this I'm dead on." And he begins running. The rest watch, incredulous, but something in the way he runs, his absolute certainty, forces them one by one also to start running. And the harder they run the more they feel the correctness of it. Soon the entire group, everyone but Laird, is running flat out over terrain too rough for much outside of hiking. Never mind, Icarus won't slow down, he refuses to turn around or listen to reason. Laird hesitates, pissed off, shouting after them, "There's nothin in those caves! Not at that height!" The others are a good distance ahead and can't hear him. Laird spits and shouts louder, "Good riddance! I'm happy to see ya go!" In the midst of his harangue, Laird glimpses the edge of what Icarus sees. Laird sees it whole then, a cave with an unexpected shimmer where it should be dark, and before he has time to measure possibilities, he begins to run, behind the rest and not likely to overtake them easily, only certain that he will.

Once they see them coming, the paye order everyone to leave the common and return to the caves, and when the last crippled old woman has laboured up the ropes, the paye order the ropes and ladders raised. Children and dogs collect along the connecting corridor and mothers sit the toddlers to dangle their legs over the sides and giggle at the clumsy men and women searching for deadfall and branches in hopes of constructing ladders; yesterday the old women and children cleared the easy-to-reach branches, leaving the inaccessible ones to tantalize the visitors.

Icarus and Gibson and Hill hack down skinny spruce, swearing and cursing that they could use one of the chainsaws lost in the drop instead of making do with three yuppified camping saws and a piece of shit-Gucci-fucking mountain axe. More goddamn high-end high-tech crap than goddamn high-rent dentists take to goddamn Everest! A continual flow, repeating.

Dallas asks, "I still don't see why we don't start down at the other end—down on that raked gravel slope? Be a whole lot easier. Messing around here is fucked."

Hill stops briefly to explain, "We'd waste a day or more haulin timber over there. There's nothin at that end but saplings and up where we need it, sweet fuck all."

Front and centre, Newt coaches Maggie and Dallas on the art of stripping bark, drawing their ire when he explains it's like skinning rabbits—a lot he knows about that—and, following his orders badly, they drag the trees over to his work station from wherever Hill and Gibson dump them. There they attempt to work a hatchet well enough to peel bark or finish some minor detail, harmless and unnecessary. Maggie, of course, doesn't see the need to strip the bark and vents loudly about futility and work for freckin work's sake. Their arms and legs are scratched, there is mention of this also. Newt, a frustrated architect, takes it badly when Hill, a full-fledged finishing carpenter, tells him to piss off and leave the construction entirely to him. "We want the goddamn thing to hold!"

Laird shouts across at Hill, "Don't think tying it that way'll hold!"

"Come on over here," Hill tells him, "and I'll show you how well!"

Meanwhile, Ana, kooky as ever, runs in Chicken Little circles, ostensibly searching for sturdier limbs or to save the trees, screeching for everyone to think what they're doing!

From the Milky Way the paye watch. The stands are filled, the nine worlds have descended—despite the crowd it's silent. Namsoul and Kamu huddle in the centre chewing the blueball. Adrift in the straits of Youngerbrother the paye are profoundly apprehensive.

Although Youngerbrother plays at reason, Youngerbrother is a dog barking at a distant noise, knowing nothing of what it heralds: an air-raid or a nuclear holocaust or a passing ice cream truck. Younger brother cannot fathom what trouble is actually afoot. Fatuously, he believes he can master every mystery. Here he holds marvellous faith.

"Youngerbrother longs to return to Aluna," Kamu says, "it's why he's always hungry, gorging is his way of filling this emptiness, the gap."

"Even he knows this much—he has caves commemorating it."

Namsoul hands Kamu a gourd of white powder, he stirs the stick and they pack their gums with paste and gaze upon Aluna. Aluna kindly wraps herself and the paye in a strange thick dust, for if they gaze on her directly, as close as this, they'll detonate. Even so, they see.

How can it be—*Aluna loves him*!

"Eventually," Kamu explains, biting the blueball, "Youngerbrother will ascend, he must. The sun and moon coexist and so must we, brothers, one on either side of Aluna."

Namsoul shakes his head. "It's possible that even if we drag him kicking and screaming to live with Aluna, he'll roll like a dreamer and fall back to earth."

"Chew a little harder." Kamu smiles. "We have our work cut out."

Namsoul posts Nabia in the front of the cave. In the heavy afternoon she slumps like a mermaid tied to a mast, her eyes dried wood, her hair torn and blowing. The dog by her side watches the paye. He's seen this before, a sacrifice. She won't be tossed down a mountain or tied to a rock, her heart won't be torn from her chest and eaten raw, she'll simply disappear with this foreigner who reeks of clogged bowels and tobacco and fly spray. For the dog there is no question which is worse.

Nabia waits. Once Youngerbrother is distracted, mollified like a wanker with a virtual reality cartoon, the paye will begin to recast Icarus. It's no simple makeover, no easy conversion, transforming Icarus from Youngerbrother into a paye. But even Youngerbrother must be capable of such transmogrification. His mother, after all, is Aluna.

———

Suddenly the cliffs are incontrovertibly gold. In the bloated sun, Icarus cannot move, overcome at finding her. Her eyes are all the world.

Hill pushes away from the ladders he and Gib are constructing and strides over to Icarus. He fixes his eyes on Maggie and Newt still working on another ladder (a sorry mess of weak links unlikely to support termites). "Icarus," he says, still not looking at him, "you want I should thump you a good one?" With Hill it's hard to tell when he's joking. Icarus joggles his head, halfway coming to, realizing he's been standing motionless for God knows how long. "No," he says, "I'm fine. What round is it?" Hill smiles, clipping him on the shoulder, sending him forward. Icarus braces himself to keep from falling, grinning, aware if he doesn't shape up Hill will kick his ass clear up the ladder. "A little zapped, I guess."

Gibson grumbles, "Leave him behind with Neuter and the chicks. He won't be much use, not the way he is."

"Fuck that!" Laird snorts. "It's time he got with the program. The nother thing—once we're up top, we separate. Sticker and Gib, you take the left wall, me and Hill'll take the right. Neuter, you keep watch down here with the women. Soon as you spot the first sign of shit you yell on up. One thing for sure, you can holler." Laird sets a ladder against the cliff. "Once we zone in on the motherlode, everyone's gonna be wired—only there's no buggerin off on your own. Things can't break down bad as that. We work as a unit. Pack up and go home right fuckin now you got other ideas. Every military incursion requires discipline."

"Forget ditching me." Maggie elbows in. "No way I'm missing the party."

Ana staggers up to Laird. From the looks of her, she could be sleepwalking. "We have to stop doing this!" The rest freeze. No one can believe what they're hearing. Hill motions to Gibson to get her out of harm's way while Ana continues raving. "It's wrong. We need to leave them alone. It's where they live. We're going into their homes. . . ."

Gibson tows her over by Hill, explaining quietly, "We need to get up there before sundown. Nobody's got time for much outside of that. You understand, Ana, no more monkey business?"

"Gib, it's all wrong." She looks across at Icarus. "Why don't you tell them? You know it better than me."

Ana leans back to study the caves and she glimpses Nabia. Nabia looks sick, and it crosses her mind the entire tribe may be ill. When she catches Nabia's eye, she decides, no, she isn't sick but something is terribly wrong.

"Hang on," she tells Gibson. "I've changed my mind, I'm coming too."

Gibson's busy, and offhandedly responds, "If you think you're up to it, hon."

Hill examines the ladders one last time. Rechecking the braces and the safety blocks, he doesn't want anyone getting hurt because of bad carpentry. Newt follows him, scrutinizing and auditing; the few Newt put together had to be discarded, which may explain Newt's assiduousness.

"Hello? Is anybody listening?" Newt looks around and resumes his lecture on ladder safety and the need for Maggie to stay below and hold them.

"Will you freckin shut up and climb."

The caves are beautiful at sundown. The tribe gathers outside the dwellings as if preparing to greet guests. Oddly, though, they can no longer be seen. Not fully at least. Icarus and Laird and Ana perceive the caves as apartments, but fail to see the inhabitants. They detect rugs and pots and utensils, the accoutrements of life, while the residents are as void as if the settlement were uninhabited, a display in a museum rather than a living, breathing village. They catch sounds, flecks of conversation, disconnected and foreign, and an aroma of fish. There is in fact food, not a feast, but they've interrupted them at meal time. Again it could be a display, one that pipes in fragrance and amplified sound effects, hoping to enhance the overall effect.

Laird swoops off the ladder, over the protective ledge, scoping out the settlement as he docks, debating with himself which cave to ransack first. Icarus disembarks in search of Nabia. The rest arrive slightly stunned and slow. Overall, there's a stultifying quietness and while Hill and Gibson mumble about where to start, Laird aims for the centre cave.

When he enters the apartment, Laird doesn't register baskets, never mind the queue of creels along the entryway or earthenware jugs or the handwoven rugs rolled out in front of him and draping the walls. Laird spies the braces, those huge beams supporting the walls, and the rocks behind the rugs.

"Only, it's tricky to know, close as we are, how close we are." Icarus follows his divining rod into the cave, convinced Nabia has taken control of the stick and that it will lead him to the gold and subsequently to her. The stick steers him to the east wall, snaking in his hands with such force he has to fight to keep from losing it. Motherfuck. "Looks like we're zeroing in on Golonda," Icarus whispers to keep a lid on the roiling inside.

Gibson takes time adjusting to the darkened space. Before anything else, he sees the kind of stone, and he begins to hum. Hill, coming through the doorway, blocks the light, forcing Laird to switch on a flashlight, and when the wedge hits a wall, there is a collective flash of tears.

Hill tells them, "Never pays to get ahead of ourself. Not yet anyways."

Their bodies, flailing with such force against the rocks, resemble swimmers crossing heavy waves. The walls, for as high and as far as they can reach, scuffle down around them until they must climb over the debris to work.

Finally, Hill steps back. The interior could have suffered a bomb blast. Gibson stops as well. "What you thinkin? Cut bait and move on?" Hill tosses a stone down on the pile. "Can't hurt to look further on. This hole's runnin dry. Don't need to work all night to find out that much."

"Could be," Icarus says, "we're right over top of it—or we need to circle out. I'm thinkin circle out."

"Fuck off!" Laird rips down more rock. "It's here! Closest I've ever come!"

"Close doesn't cut it in our line of work."

Hill gnaws the inside of his cheek. "Alls we're pullin down here is jack shit."

Icarus turns and leaves. Like cicadas moving on, the mob vacates the cave, dividing now into two groups, one to travel east and the other west, to investigate every cave. No one is happy or willing to stop or aware they haven't eaten all day or that the sun has set and it

is instantly black, blindfold black, and they must work by the light
of fires set inside the caves. They are driven by some other kind of
fuel. Hours pass. They burrow into night as they burrow through
the caves. Fires burn down and are built up again until the air inside
the caves and out along the avenue is filled with smoke and dust, and
still they do not give up.

The brattice has been wrenched from the sides of the apartments like teeth from their sockets, and strewn, leaving the walls
pocked with hammer-holes and long, deep gashes and the floors
spoiled with mounds of mullock and timber thrown chaotically.
Inhabitants cower in the corners of what used to be their homes,
heads bowed; only the occasional child watches. The paye have
turned their backs on the inevitable. Old women, long past weeping, weep.

"We been through every fuckin one and nothin!"

"It's here," Laird says. "Somewheres. Probably starin us in the
face."

"It's nowheres near here. We need to go back and check along
the bottom rung of the cliffs."

Laird starts working another wall. "Gib, you start in bellyachin
and you and me'll need to have a go-around."

"Tellin you facts is bellyachin?"

"There's only the one cave left." Icarus is almost too tired to
stand. He leans against the entrance to the cave, watching the sun
come up, numb to everything but how sore and hungry he is.

"What cave?" Laird asks him. As far as Laird can see there is no
other cave. They've gone through every friggin one. He's been clear
about that.

"Oh," he sighs, "that one down on the east end, hidden behind
that ridge of rocks."

Laird leaves the cave to stand on the corridor, studying the ridge
of rocks reddened by the morning sun. "What cave? There's no cave
there!"

"Yeah, there is. It's where they make em into medicine men or
whatever it is they call them."

Laird runs now. He can't see the cave, it's hidden so well, but he'll find it if he has to tear the ridge apart. Fast as Laird runs, Icarus arrives at the ridge before him.

The paye's cave is concealed behind a rubric of rocks that jut and wind to provide a natural maze, an ingenious barricade. It's dark, therefore, protected as it is; even when morning douses the ridge, the cave behind its palisade is never touched. The entrance sits high under an awning of slate and descends from there a good long way down. Once inside, the cave is profound, winding back from one emptiness to another. All of it is dark. There is no light, no small spear reaches any part but is filtered by the ridge and blind of overhanging rocks, and the blackness is frightening.

"Hell!" The divining rod vibrates so vigorously that Icarus nearly loses his grip. Taking on a life of its own, the rod plunges, pulling him down to the ground. It wants to dig in. If he weren't gripping the stick so cruelly, he'd convulse. Ashen, eyes scrolling, he appears on the verge of an epileptic seizure.

"It's here all right," Laird groans, sinking to his knees, as though struck down by a passing sniper's bullet. "We got her now."

"Has to be."

"Has to be."

When they descend into the paye's cave, gold spills like tinselly wax down the grotto. It shines in the fierce white cones of their flashlights. High along the roof, bats beat the dark into a great stir, and sounds like leaves caught in a whirring fan descend around them. No other noise but the commotion churning far above. Silence wads their ears in deafening rolls. Their lamps, weak in comparison, hang heavy in their hands as if about to drop, while a four-letter word runs torpedo wild, round and round, never registering, never firing, simply running on and on. One moves and the rest burst to life, each grabbing the shingle, digging free its crusted wax to push into their faces, sniffing, tasting and gazing down into it as if the metal is actually fluid and teeming with beasts.

Laird presses his cheek against a wall and stands silently communing with the stone in it.

Icarus waves his flashlight over the cavity, and they all see what he sees, a great Vatican of gold. The view is fully and utterly rich. The basilica's Byzantine dome is a cosmos of mosaics blinking with the violent pitch of a thousand gemstone eyes.

No one is breathing. They've reached the motherlode. There is no time for shouting. Their joy is too immense. Slyly, they each slide the chunk they clutch into their pocket and reach for another and another until their fingers are raw and their pockets burst at the seams and empty. Only the cave goes on, opening onto other greater caverns leading further into the mountain, honeycombing, opening and opening on other larger, deeper cavities, crusted with the stuff. Only then do their eyes narrow and focus on one another, silence falling as the noise of cascading rocks and the stir they've created gently fades.

———————

Gibson and Hill stop raking the interior of the cave; they rest against the rough wall, hoping to recharge. The cave is stifling, each breath brings the other man's outflow. If they had energy left to speak, they'd rail against Laird, off on another wall, pulling down fuck knows how much!

They dream of tossing fortune like petals to the wind and showering city streets with powdered luck. Their minds have divided to accommodate these freewheeling dreams, no longer connected but independent and prolific. These dreams prove a better fuel than food or sleep.

"Then I'm gonna get me a couple three Bengal tigers and let em roam around the place. And a herd of zebra."

"A submarine. Always wanted my own submarine. . . ."

The gold no longer stacks in the middle of the cave or out in front but each day's work ends in a covert trip down the snaking ropes and ladders lining the cliffs and through the darkening woods to be hidden there. Long gone any thought of fortune shared. Buried under greed and avarice, such altruism suffocated early. They're

united only in frustration, universally stymied by how small a dent
. . . how trifling the amount they can extract in any given day.

"Hang on, you guys! This isn't fair!" Newt and Maggie bitterly
attempt to keep up to the unnatural pace. It's beyond them. Everyone understands there will be no catching up, no better way. This *is*
the way. Get on and be quick. No time left to carp, to explain or
prove a point or hold any lesser, weaker miner up. The race is on,
the leaders well out in front.

Icarus keeps to the cave, riving down its walls to spread along
the floor like goods fallen from a speeding truck. He is cold and
senseless and angry, with no idea why. His energy is profound. If he
begins to slow, Nabia arrives, at least the memory of her skin glancing his. When he touches the rock, he imagines that he is touching
her. But Nabia is cold. She can't stop shivering. It's the paye's fault.
They are hard at work rewiring her imagination, installing more
memory, upgrading, preparing her for the next and final stage. The
child inside her is no bigger than a gob of spit.

Icarus senses the paye near him now. He grasps that it was the
paye who set him like a robot to work upon this wall, hammering
and tearing down; he also understands that while he is distracted,
the paye climb inside his brain and lift him out and carry him away.
It's why they've come today—they want to take him flying. This
trip won't be the usual casual jaunt around the cave. This will be the
first time Icarus leaves the planet. It will also be the first time Elderbrother has carried Youngerbrother to the Milky Way. Another kind
of family excursion through the countryside. Buckle up.

The paye stir the gourds of white paste until the motion eddies
and in the eddies Aluna drifts. They pack their gums and prepare.
When they take him flying, the paye keep Icarus in the middle.
Namsoul takes one arm and Kamu the other; it's important he feel
safe. The blueball helps him to relax. Icarus can see himself back
working on the wall, he knows that he has come apart and this part
has come away with the paye. He is slightly exhilarated. He knows
that the part left working down below is seeing, remembering a
plush sedan and a mouth fixed and bruised while a drill digs through

shaky reefs of decay. He knows, too, that the part left behind is trying to make sense of what is happening in the only way it can, by
tossing up images, past remembrances like skeet pigeons in a vain
attempt to answer this current phenomenon . . . but he knows that
other part will never comprehend that he has come away and is
flying with the paye, one on either side. He's flying somewhere
beyond the imagination and he isn't high or sick or crazy but sane
and straight and sound, maybe for the first and only time.

From the Milky Way they see the galaxies latticing the universe
like vines twining a trellis. There is order and peace. Avoid the
holes, swiftly bump around them, black or white. Either way they're
tricky little flues.

When paye fly, some stand, arms apart and wide, canting, and
others hunker, their arms knotted down around their knees, a few
lie back to float like sea lions bobbing and flibbering, but together
they travel in a fluid raft. They are flying to the far end of the universe. It isn't easy even for a ray of light, and they are only paye.

"Christ, Sticker, you damn near hit me on the fuckin head." Gibson shoves him, not gently, and holds up a fair-sized chunk of rock
to show him. "Watch where you're pitchin this shit."

"This here's the problem. Exactly like I been sayin," Hill informs
Gibson, "we need tools! We're doin ten times the work and gettin
nowhere. To say nothin about safety."

Newt keeps on chipping. "It's only a matter of time before someone gets hurt. I've been saying it till I'm blue in . . ."

"What we need," drawls Gibson, "and far as I can see, it's the only
way, no other way'll work—we need to draw lots to see who goes
back to base camp for gear."

"Lots! That'll never work!" Laird swings back his arm and keeps
hammering away at the wall he considers his.

"I don't know," Newt says. "Nothing else has."

Icarus slips, sending a small avalanche down the wall. The shin-
gles punching the ground recoil, causing shards to fly like sparks,
bombarding Laird. Laird rolls like he's pitching a ball and delivers
his response square between Icarus's cheekbone and jaw. "Whoa,

where was that comin from? I was mindin my own business!" Icarus wavers on one leg, collects himself and returns the blow to Laird, same velocity, opposite side. They could be playing catch, the rhythm that they keep.

"This won't get us anywhere!" As Gibson intervenes, they turn on him and he catches it from both sides. "We need to keep clearheaded," he yells. "It's the primary thing." Each brother, convinced he could make short work of the other, glares at Gib. "God knows we got enough needs figuring out."

"Gib's right," Hill tells them. "We need to settle who stays and who ships back to base camp for tools and supplies."

Laird tells Hill, "One thing sure, it won't be boy wonder."

Day sinks to evening but they continue arguing. Countless times they brawl and settle only to brawl again, until by dawn's dreary light they are exhausted, some badly bruised, ignoring a mélange of sprained and swollen limbs.

Once the idea of drawing lots is generally accepted, the business of sortition begins. Ultimately certain names are dropped, deemed perfidious, but dropping one name quickly results in another being jettisoned until the hat is empty. This repeats.

"I'm sick to death of all this fighting," Ana shouts. "I don't want my name in the hat. Don't even put mine in."

"And me—don't put me in either." Maggie sighs "God, I can't barely stand let alone traipse hell'n gone back to base camp only to turn around and crawl back here lugging tools and crap. Besides, round trip, it'll waste a good two weeks. Nobody's going to be helping Newtie pull in my share."

Tedious rounds of sniping persist until, during a meal of fried deer mice (they found a hundred or more nests in the cave) and desiccated chili, the group agrees to draw lots from those names bloodied least or those who've altogether refused to participate.

Ana throws up her hands and stomps away. "I said—don't put my name in the hat! Is that clear enough or what?"

Newt hounds her. "There are only a few names that everyone agrees on."

"Well, not me is all I can say. But why don't we all go back? You guys keep saying you can't do much until you get the proper gear anyway."

"We can't waste a good two weeks of prime weather. Besides, someone's got to stay behind. No way we can leave the place undefended. There'll be just as much trouble deciding on who should stay as who should go."

"Why not all go back, take what we can, and register our claim, we can fly back with the supplies after? Now that makes sense."

Gibson cuts in to set her straight. "We're not leavin here with a handful of what we could. Besides, by the time we all traipse back and see to business and arrange return transportation, anything could happen. No tellin. God knows someone's bound to get wind, and by the time we get back here we're liable to find any number of asshole heli-hikers settin up camp, stakin a claim, cryin nine-tenths and all that bullshit. No, it's the one thing every one of us see eye to eye on—we don't say shit till we're good and ready. Once we hit town and register all hell'll break loose. Even you gotta know that. The whole entire thing's sky high and outta control then. No, we keep a lid, a tight goddamn lid on it."

"Like I said, not me."

"There's no one else. What? You want this fightin to carry on until one or the other of us gets killed? Laird or Icarus or me, one or all three of us are bound to end up in serious straits."

Ana isn't stupid, she sees the truth in this and reluctantly agrees to allow her name to stand. And Ana and Maggie win, or lose, depending on the point of view, and, although Ana remains convinced the draw was fixed, that there were only two names, she concedes that, for the health of everyone, the issue must be quickly settled, and she agrees to go along. Not so docile, Maggie balks. "Where's the point in sending us? We're the only ones that don't want to go."

"There's the point."

"Christ, the little we'll bring back is hardly worth the effort. Send someone capable of carrying a ton. Dallas, what about her?"

"Dallas's name went in but it didn't get drawn."

"How many names went in—exactly?"

"We told you—there were three."

"Three? And all of us women! That's not fair. No way that's fair."

"Life hain't fair," Hill tells her. "Leastwise she tried to be, this go-round."

Worn out, Maggie curls up on the rock-strewn floor. "I don't see why anybody has to go. Why can't you make do with the tools we've got? Boys and their freckin toys."

Hill and Gibson and Icarus and Laird and Newt and Dallas stare at her. It's impossible to fathom her lack of understanding.

"Food," Dallas says, "and other supplies like flashlight batteries. Even you gotta see that much."

"No way we're goin all the way back to base camp for batteries! Besides we still got some left. Make freckin do. And food, hey, there's always fish."

Push *play* and Newt takes off. "Maggie, if you seriously want to get seriously rich then you have to do your part. Number one, what we're up against here is time. Time! If we hope to get anything out before the season ends, we need tools and supplies. Those tools and supplies, sweet Maggie pie, are back at base camp."

"God," she groans. "What were you guys thinking? Why didn't you bring them in the first place? Like none of us have nothing better to do than hike hell'n gone back to get them for you. What were you thinking leaving them behind?"

Icarus refreshes her memory. "They didn't believe me is why. They thought I was up my ass is why."

"What's the big deal anyway? Send whoever wants to go? Hey, I'm outta shampoo. You know what, if I didn't have to come back here packing your freckin crap, I'd love nothing better than to get back to freckin freeways and shoppin malls."

Again Hill and Laird and Gibson and Icarus stare at her, silently.

"That's the problem," Dallas clues her in. "Nobody trusts that whoever does go will come back—at least not before they've kicked ass to the nearest land titles office and filed a claim. Minus your name and mine—you can *freckin* take that to the bank, Magpie."

Maggie sits up, leaning on her elbow to study the men staring down at her. "You are a slimy bunch of pricks. It's plain Newt's the only one halfway straight enough to be trusted to go there and come back."

"Me?" Newt squeals. "Well, yes, yes, obviously. I'm the one best qualified."

"Newt's a lawyer," Ana tells Maggie. "No way it gets to be him."

"If not Newtie—who can be trusted?"

"You two!" Dallas draws a picture. "Plain and simple, Magpie, nobody worries about either one of you. Ana's too fuckin straight to ever cheat friends and family and you're too bone lazy to take a step further than you have to."

Newt takes it upon himself to explain. "Our work would be cut in half if we had a better drill, some explosives . . ."

"Explosives!"

He waves his hand and shrugs. "Not to worry, it's no big deal. I packed them like they were hundred-year-old eggs."

"You're not serious."

"Explosives!" Ana stops, stunned. "Nobody told me you guys brought explosives!"

Gibson raises his arms like a bandit surrendering, "Don't get yourself in knot, they're packed better than Grandma's fuckin crystal."

"Explosives," Maggie repeats.

"You can't seriously think I'll have any part of this. You know me better than that. What? Are you guys planning on blowing up the countryside to get this gold?"

"What are you thinkin, Ana? How do ya picture us gettin it out? This isn't some Greenpeace fuckin picnic. We're out here raping and pillaging, we're prospectors, we're not on the fuckin *Rainbow Warrior*, we're not goddam Sea Shepherds, we're prospectin here. Prospectin requires a certain amount of damage to the scenery. It's the way it's gotta be."

"I can't believe what I'm hearing."

"Mother of fuckin Christ, what in hell's name did you think we were out here doin?"

"I'm outta this. I wash my hands. The whole thing makes me sick. Sick."

"Don't talk stupid, Ana, you know as well as me there's no packin up your loose marbles and scootin back home—not now. Not after we found it. This isn't a fuckin TV game show. You wanted to play, now you're gonna have to fuckin play. This is the real deal. Laird and the rest of them aren't gonna just let you trot on down the road. So just forget that fantasy."

Maggie bobs up and down, hitting herself with her fist, some crazed flagellant. "Like you honest to God thought I'd haul explosives like a freckin donkey? I can't believe you'd ask me? Me?"

"Listen," Icarus says, coming toward Maggie and Ana, his arms open, palms out. "Will you help me?" They stare at him like corralled ponies. "I need you to help. You're the only ones I can count on." He approaches them like a cowboy with a rope in one hand and a sorry lump of sugar in the other. They know the trick. They could escape, but instead they stay quietly staring at him, listening to his soft sucky sounds. "I'd never put either of you in harm's way, you know that. If I thought there was the slightest danger, I'd never go along with sending you. Only we need the explosives. We do. We gotta have them. And much as I'd like to go myself, I can't. You two are the only ones that everyone trusts enough to do this. Don't you realize what that means? How important you are to us?"

"Right," Ana snorts, "so important you'll let us haul explosives up ten thousand feet, down ten thousand feet, across a chasm and God knows where else—sky high no doubt!"

"Ana, have I ever asked you to do anything?"

"God."

Maggie approaches him, nudging his shoulder, "Why don't you come along? That way you can carry the crates of freckin Grandma's crystal and we can keep you bound and tied—make sure you don't go buggering off to the nearest land titles office."

"You know all the ins and outs of why and how come I can't go." He motions silently in Laird's general direction.

"No way I'm bringing back explosives! Wipe it from your minds. Besides," Maggie waves the list in the air, "most of this shit we can do without. Why in hell do we need four different kinds of batteries? Another thing, this entire lottery's been rigged. How about we do five outta five?"

"I'd feel a whole lot better if I was going back with you."

"Not in a million years, Neuter." Gibson shuts him down.

"It's difficult for me to believe," Newt harangues Maggie and Ana, "that the two of you will know what to bring, despite my lists and instructions, in spite of my non-stop lectures. You will forget something, guaranteed."

"The thing I hate most is the chasm," Ana discloses, barely able to speak.

"That? After what we've been through? It's nothing."

"It'll be what gets me. See if it isn't."

"Ha!" Laird snorts, digging out a tricky bit of rock. "A little crack in the rocks no wider than a whore's cunt."

At base camp, Ana and Maggie demolish tins of canned apricots. The empty tins roll around the campground like hollow bees. There is no fire; it died long ago. The air smells of coffee (real, not powdered roots!), bitter from standing too long over a rocky stove.

2

There is no push to hurry back. Instead they wander down to swim in the cold lake, both marvelling over the luxury of shampoo and cream rinse. Neither mentions the crates waiting or the inevitable trip out in the morning. For this brief afternoon they act as though tomorrow will never arrive.

The novice, Nikko, accompanies Maggie and Ana. At first he isn't interested in either of them. The unattractive, clumsy way the sun marks their skin has to be a sign Aluna doesn't favour them, branding them with great white barber-pole stripes along their upper arms and breasts and buttocks, haphazard slipshod swipes, nothing as delicate as Nabia's tattoos or his. To say nothing of the stink. Their food floats through their pores in waves which payé travelling from the Milky Way say resembles the stench drifting from their fast food joints. Not that Nikko can imagine a restaurant or fast food (isn't most food fast? fruit or nuts? roots?) but the smell wafting from the pretty bodies provides some clue.

Skunk lilies, he refers to them each time his gaze drifts to the women swimming in the pond. Something in their shape fascinates him, draws him all the same. Even though he swears he won't look, he looks again. Strange, their beauty. Skunk lilies, he swears, loud enough to be heard if they were listening.

Initially it's Maggie he finds fascinating, but this shifts as he watches Ana, the way she rouses her hair from her neck to cool her back, resting her head to one side. She isn't attractive—she isn't. It's her oddness he finds fascinating. She's a foreign insect, one he's never seen but heard terrifying tales about, some paralyzing many-headed bug, capable of opening unexpected parts to devour a dewy blossom from behind. Danger has its appeal. Didn't Namsoul and Kamu warn him? They knew, as he knew, how susceptible he might be.

He forces his eyes away, knowing that while his eyes are not looking, his mind continues to watch the body leaning back to dip that hair in and out of the sparkling water. There's her laugh, close to something snapping, a twig or spear. Although he's never visited Youngerbrother's maloca, he's overheard Laird refer to bars and getting drunk and brawling, and her laugh reminds him of what he imagines the floor of such a place to be, long after the brawl, emptied, littered and broken apart like the forest after two jaguars have met and fought, before the birds return. There is a loneliness in her laugh that reaches him and makes him ache. He is lonely too.

If only he could will himself to be seen. Unfortunately, he hasn't the power to pull back the screen blocking their sight. The paye fixed that. And Ana, when it comes to seeing, is benign. Like most of Youngerbrother, Ana filters what she sees. Rather than cherishing the gift, she tries to lose it—as if she could.

Youngerbrother has the ability to gild his world. No matter how often his scribes tell him his chances of winning the sweepstakes are one in a million, Youngerbrother intrinsically believes that applies to everyone but him. He swaddles himself in a belief that he is better than he is, protected, chosen, beyond the rules, beyond mortality. Nothing applies to him, only to others. That is the true condition of Youngerbrother. Only mediums, schizophrenics and depressives suspect otherwise, and those Youngerbrother drugs and chastises. Ana is a depressive. Because she's been told for so long that she's wrong, she doubts herself, doubts what she knows, what she sees, placing her trust in society like a circumcised girl defending the right of old men and women to use a rusty razor.

Although she won't glance his way, not even casually, Ana senses him hunched on the rocks watching without watching and she's apprehensive. Ana wants to believe that if she doesn't sense Nikko, he won't exist.

On the return trip, Maggie chooses to take a shortcut, along a rough sheep trail winding through a tricky pass. Ana finds herself in serious trouble. She slips and falls and clings for her life to the side of the treacherous slope. Nikko takes the form of a root, catching hold of her ankle and holding her fast while Maggie reaches down to haul her back to safety. Once the worst is over, they can't account for her good luck but speak of angels and fairies and a few dead relatives and finally a friend they used to have, who OD'ed.

"Good thing," Maggie says, "I was packin the freckin dynamite."

———————

"One or the other of us must've been awfully good in some other life. There's more gold in this warren of caves than in the whole of Mother Russia!" Dallas digs both knuckles into Hill's shoulders, punching the tightly knotted muscles into leavened dough.

Hill grunts his reply. That and more, it insinuates.

"More!" Her laugh seems incapable of stopping. "We need a team of mules or oxen."

"You and your goddamn mules. Mules won't make it past the first rock slide. Thought you'da snapped to that by now."

"What about a helicopter? Why not buy one!"

"Neuter'll never get his hands on a chopper without a proper licence. According to Gib, Laird has connections through his soldier of fortune days and he might wrangle one. But Laird's as likely to bugger off with a guy's stash as hand it back."

Dallas works the muscles harder. "It's smart to stick with Newt. Wouldn't surprise me if the other three are hatching something. They're brothers after all."

"What are you sayin?"

"Wouldn't surprise me."

"You're crazy. Gib'n me played ball together."

"Blood's thicker is all."

The gold, because it can be picked like peaches espaliered along the damp walls, fills their sacks with stones that split the Gore-Tex. They are forced to devise a tremendous slide to get it off the cliff. Hill and Gibson build barrows to haul it to tunnels dug deep in the forest floor, but these feeble tubes overflow with more gold than can be spent in two, possibly three generations. There's gold to feed a dynasty. Still, there is no thought but *more*.

"Gruel's ready, if you're hungry?"

The porridge resembles a pot of epoxy. Laird shakes a spoonful over a bowl, he shakes again, finally he takes his hand and runs it down the spoon, the epoxy now sticking to his hand. Again he shakes, the porridge comes away to plop down on the ground beside his hiking boot, white plaster mixed with straw as though he's preparing to whitewash an adobe.

Newt knows better than to laugh. Instead he looks away, distracted by the rest of the work crew leaving the cave. Gibson and Icarus walk into the light, brown as prairie dust.

"Christ, Neuter," Laird complains, "I thought I sent you out here to whip up something to eat. I'm not lookin to mortar up the cave. Not yet anyways. Not without you in it."

Accident or not, Icarus bumps into Laird and sends his breakfast flying and Icarus and Laird circle each other, clockwise, counter, clock again. Between them, jellied moulds of bluish mucus, spat upon a browning platform, transmogrify to stones. Icarus, zapped from overwork, weaves, flopping this way and that, a towel in the wind with no snap left.

"Stand still so I can nail ya one."

Laird seizes Icarus's neck and twists it until the body, like a plastic stem, follows him.

"Leave go, asshole."

Laird kicks Icarus's legs out from under him.

Above, the sky is completely blue, rubbed with the whisper of the moon's faint thumbprint, fading quickly from view. The wind reeks of sweaty pine, and beneath the heat there is a sting of autumn, an unnerving chill even in the sun.

Laird hunches over him, a starving hound ravaging its kill. "Next stop oblivion, little brother. See how ya like it there."

"Hang on a fuckin . . ." Sidelined, Icarus feels drugged, shot through with some nuevo sister of cocaine.

Cheap tin spoons scrape the barrelled bowls of tin as the others hurry to finish and be gone.

It feels like he's lifting a cement truck, but finally Icarus manages to right his arm and reach around. It's taking so long, his muscles are mush. When he finds the shin, he uses it to push off and grab Laird by the balls. Laird lifts instinctively, beautifully, off the ground, spewing a compilation of profanity. Icarus brings in his other hand and hangs on good and tight. Laird, trying to wriggle free, twists, seizing Icarus by the hair, kicking into prisoner of war mode. The two begin another duet. Hard as he pulls, just so hard does Icarus squeeze. The boys begin to roll, another fandangled inflatable gone awry. Laird slides his hands down around Icarus's head, driving his fingers into Icarus's eyes. Icarus wobbles, and the world, his world, revolves.

Laird won't bother with fists or boots, nothing easy now, but grinds his hands around Icarus's head, content as a miller milling grain. Icarus supposes he's okay, that he'll be steady on his feet any sec. His eyes close again on all that he might do. If he had the strength, he'd yell for help, ask the bouncer to steady him a bit. Quick as that, he's nodding down to sleep.

The paye's influence is the cosmology of intangibles. Inevitably, intangibles leak like Chinese takeout, and sometimes reach the desperadoes squatting far below, holding the bag.

A gust shudders through the leaves beginning to turn, spins along the grassy valley, kicking up swirls of dust and seed pods and dressing the sharkfaced rocks with every souvenir it snags along the way. When the zephyr envelops Icarus, he comes to life, a pugilist determined not to give way. His revival catches Laird off guard, allowing Icarus time to slam the diaphragm. Laird leans into him like an old man tossing his chemotherapy and Icarus batters him with a rapid set of blows, mainly to the side of his head, one reaching into the open mouth and taking out a tooth. Icarus leaves him then and returns to the cave. Nabia is waiting in the rocks.

There's a place not far from the valley green, a shady treed spot along the river's edge she wanders through when things are in turmoil, as they are now, a place apart, where she visits lost moments, words. This is where she invites Icarus to meet her so they can be alone.

The child grows. Even on a cloudy day, she feels its warmth shining from within. Nabia is big enough to float away, fat as the clouds that bang up against the cliffs and stumble to catch on the sharp-tongued peaks for a time, that pitch and sway, end broken or jostle free to tumble somewhere else to fall apart. The child fills her belly, swims as if kicking free of a very small pool. She lays her palms flat and lets it boot her hands from their resting position—it's a game they often play. The child reminds her of a puppy she owned as a child (of course in her old world you never *owned* an animal), the way it worried and nipped at her heels, trying to bring her down, preparing itself for adulthood and hunting deer.

The child gives up, to rest, suck his thumb and survey the surrounding soupy nucleus. He's weary, already bored. It's the grind, the sheer effort involved, the vast futility of it—after all, it's a very small pond, growing continually smaller. No matter how he tries to push or stretch it out, or how he coaxes or prods or knots himself about, he never manages to shrink but grows forever bigger. He doesn't want the responsibility or the aggravation. It's come to him—the answer.

Aside from Christ and Rosemary's baby, there have been other trans-dimensional births. It's not entirely without precedent. Achilles, Cygnus and Arcas. Juno turned Arcas's mother into a bear, and Arcas years later unknowingly shot and killed her. Jove then turned Arcas and the bear into a constellation. Not entirely smooth sailing. Not surprisingly, Icarus wonders how his progeny will fare. Will it float between the two worlds as smoothly as children of mixed cultures? Will it, with the dexterity of a tiny golden cat, be equally at home on either side? Or will it, despite its mother's gifts, be unable to survive in its father's world, lacking an essential meanness?

"Icarus," Nabia whispers, "your brother intends to kill you."

"Don't worry," Icarus tells her, "he's way too busy to care about me."

Gibson and Hill and Laird burrow like grubs into the cavern's side, finding that as far as they can tunnel into the interior, the mountain is gold.

Gold spills from sacks, from reckless skeps that from a flying distance resemble a careless farmer's stooks, row on row, strewn and forgotten along the valley floor. Harvest in some wacko world. Pretence of private ownership has vanished, supplanted neither by brotherhood nor by a generous change of heart, but swept asunder by the colossal extent of the find. Just the work of hiding it exhausts them.

———

Ana stops to listen to the wind catching along the deep craggy throat. Her senses have absconded, she faces the worst of it with immobile muscles and a weakening bladder.

"Come on, don't let it bother you. We haven't got all day."

Maggie waits on the opposite side, one foot planted on the bridge Gib and Hill made months ago. She bucketed the bulk of supplies (the assiduously packed and wrapped—like freckin robin's eggs—dynamite, and drills and related gear) across by herself, in a series of difficult transfers made increasingly awkward. She's been back and forth a half a dozen times. Much as she likes to work, she's as mad as that.

"We're almost there. Besides, it's not that bad," she calls back to Ana. "Really." Lying through her teeth.

"Bridge! What bridge? A few twigs, three rotten logs, an old rope, one Gib and Hill thought well enough of to leave, is not a bridge! Not in my mind, perhaps in Burma, perhaps prisoners of war might be induced to believe such a shoddy noose is a bridge—not me!"

"Come on!" Maggie shakes her head, quickly losing patience. "Get over it! It's not like it's your first time, you made it across twice already." She bites her lip, to restrain herself from adding, fuck knows not once today, when I coulda used some help! But quietly relates, "Remember, both times you were fine. A piece of cake both times."

Nikko hovers, hidden in a swarm of blackflies. If she listened, she might realize the wind is nothing more than his voice, repeating again and again to come along. Eager to do what he can, Nikko joins the battery of blackflies buffeting her face and arms.

"Chop, chop. Get a move on."

Ana inches nearer the makeshift bridge, whining with each small unwilling step. "Such a flimsy piece of shit I've never seen! Amazing it's still here! It's a miracle it hasn't blown down!" When she reaches the bridge she stops, holding her breath, afraid to set even that free. Tears find a path down her cheeks like blind fingers feeling their way along a stony wall.

"If you aren't careful, I'll come back across and push you. I wouldn't really. Honestly, I was only tryin to get you to lighten up."

Ana doesn't feel Nikko take her hand. What she feels is strangely relaxed. Certainly her shoulders loosen and the back of her neck and lower back release a long train of tension. He allows her to stand a while to savour the tender air cooled by the river. The air is sweetened by flowers falling to seed. The chasm below must be beautiful, she decides. It must have wild chamomile or meadow-sweet along the river's brow. When she thinks of it, she imagines herself walking over cushions of blossoms. In the same instant she sees herself lying on the fat pillows, covered with greenery and flowered streamers and drifting along a sluggish stream, rather than the torrent below.

In this dreamy state, she allows Nikko to lead her nearer the bridge. She can see him now. He is handsome, with eyes that pierce straight through her. When she looks into them, they frighten her; she won't do that again. Still she follows him. She hasn't any way of stopping herself. She's let go of everything but his hand.

At the threshold she pauses, struck by how closely he resembles Icarus. This likeness is no accident, paye shift shapes, reassembling features in one or another order, whatever is required on any given day. Today's task proved remarkably easy. The young novice bears a certain resemblance to Icarus, and it required very little to accentuate it.

It doesn't escape her notice that he holds her hand, or that he pulls her close to him; this can only be a mirage. Icarus cares nothing for her but the mildest friendship. If she were to die now, she tells herself, she would die exultant.

His voice is warm, very like Icarus's yet wholly different. She discounts the differences, the strange accent, its clipped consonants and foreign cadence. Instead she concentrates on the similarity, hearing only that.

Before he leads her onto the bridge, she pauses to study the small spade of sky as though expecting something to break through the pearly veil and carry her away. The wind, what little there is, remains a constant gentle stirring, the birds, a fistful of sparrows, gossip nearby, and nothing else intrudes on the deafening hum of nothing.

Leaves caught by the wind pull away from the aspens—in the next breath their covers will be down around their knees. Closing her eyes, she waits for his lips to visit. When he nudges her gently to begin, she responds. For once she is completely relaxed. "Thank you," she whispers, and follows.

Ana imagines that she's walking through a fog of nothing. No matter how she searches, she can't see anything but fog. She has no way of knowing, but she supposes that she may be dead. She hasn't a body, not one she can make out. If she could see, she wouldn't mind nearly as much. Being unable to see is worse by far than fear or pain, or what she remembers of pain, and it's not in the slightest like being blind. For she can see what there is to see, and what there is is fog!

Weren't friends supposed to greet her? Angels or at the very least dead relatives, dressed in shimmering white light? It's not remotely like she's been led to believe. Where was there any mention of fog and nothingness? Very well, there was talk of nothingness, but who supposed it would be visible? Who imagined it would be real? Globs of nothing, tracts of it, who guessed it held the universe together? Neither gravity nor electric energy—nothing whatsoever! Whoever thought it might be worth seeing?

Nikko studies her. Her thoughts are clearer. Where before they hid behind, he can't really say what it was, a murkiness, that has been swept aside, and she appears open as never before. She hasn't the slightest notion where she is.

Nowhere, oh, endless eternity called heaven, paradise—what names Youngerbrother attaches to reality! Even those dreamers expecting golden pavement arrive in fog, but for a hapless few it's vast fields of clouds. Of course Youngerbrother will see what he wants, resolutely missing what is there. Clouds then are castles. With such clarity as that, the foghorns must be harps. Small wonder Youngerbrother succeeds, when reality so rarely interferes with his dreams.

Death, he decides, for Youngerbrother is an opening. This he considers hopeful, as hopeful as anything he's gleaned from Youngerbrother. Obviously, Aluna has tried to help them.

When he speaks, he expects she might be able to hear him. It would make sense, wouldn't it, to allow the two realities to meet here, where it's safe? What harm could come from it here? Imagine the good.

Nikko tells her, "We only come to this holding camp when we've lost an animal, a family pet or a favourite horse. Sometimes they get stuck between the animal and the human realm." When she doesn't respond, he asks, "I suppose you know I can't interfere? That you've arranged your death long before you were born?"

Ana hears the inner dialogue of her life, her view extends only as far as she has gone, the ground she covered, only as far as that, no further.

Where else but hell?

Namsoul and Kamu take her then. Ana doesn't see them as paye but wild cats. The plain of dreams also frightens her. The stark white icebergs are more like a bad abstract painting than a place. Namsoul allows her to wander freely, to make herself feel at home. And strangely, Ana does. She feels as if she's been here before, many times. Namsoul shows her then, floating far below her, the chasm and the makeshift bridge, and the woman standing perfectly still, halfway across.

She watches the woman prepare to take another step, and lose her footing and fall and in falling, Ana, and the woman falling, both see it is her fear she has tripped upon.

The tumbling human pinwheel turns on a negligible breeze, starfishing limbs descending, carried earthward as if she were not inching her way toward a fuzzy schism.

Ana no longer sees the paye disguised as cats. She only sees the woman that she used to be, falling. And when she hits the ground it will be like in a dream, waking with a start, but not waking there, not ever there again. Not here. Some other place.

———————

It's that time of night when the world turns black and blue. Trees, swollen in shadow, cry in the wind and small scrabbling noises claw through the undergrowth and fallen leaves. Trees will wake to find what leaves they owned down upon the ground, eloping with the wind. A night of change, of turning, where summer reels to autumn, a night that separates dusk from dawn as though by a year or longer, when in one small blackened time a season flourishes and departs. No mistaking, the turn's been taken and summer's flown.

Difficult as it is to leave Ana, Maggie must go for help. It's improbable, in light of the fall, its height, the jagged overhang of rocks, but Ana may have survived. Maggie struggles against a wave of nausea. Ana could be in great pain, hovering between life and death in that shadowy netherworld. Maggie dangles over the edge to try and catch a glimpse, as if the view might be a pretty fish leaping in midair to be hooked or captured in a net. The body, through the tangled bush and rock and moonlight, is nowhere to be seen. Immobile certainly. A limb, perhaps, is all she thinks she recognizes, but it's difficult to read from this height, and the limb is oddly splayed, foreign to a human form now twisted and possibly removed.

"Get your freckin ass up outta there! This is grizzly country! No way I can make it back to camp without you!"

Maggie is alone, in dense mountain terrain, miles from anything or anyone. She has a week before she reaches the others, a week alone, managing entirely on her own. Grief and hysteria and fear ignite like leaking propane to envelop her.

————

"How do you mean, fell?"

Gibson's face burns down to a mask of sadness and anger and it's impossible for Maggie to look at him without slipping back into grief as well, but it's the other, the eyes behind the mask she cannot bear. Ana, she's come to realize in those eyes, was her only friend.

"I think there were a couple cats down there with her."

Maggie pushes her hand and lips against her teeth. She doesn't want to cry. Not until it's finished. If only she could trade grief for hate.

His knees, always weak, feel it first. His mind, like a starter shot to shit, can't connect with the notion of her being dead. Ana was supposed to live to be ninety and wheel him around. Who'll attach his morphine drip when the time comes? She can't be dead. Not just when they hit the motherlode. Where's the sense in being stupid rich if she's not there to help him blow it? Besides, she handled the books, the taxes, insurance. Without her how's he supposed to find his passport, the spare set of keys? Ana can't disappear, drop off the planet like some fucking bad tenant.

Gibson remains stationary, unable to move, although move he must, even he realizes that rudimentary fact. This insight carries with it a fresh wave of anger, uglier than the last.

"No way she survived a fall like that!" He says it to himself, flatly, as though reading a headline, hoping that through repetition it may register. "Even if she did, she wouldn't've lasted the night, let alone made it six more days."

Finally the anger arrives, like the cavalry edging near the crest of her unhappiness. "Either way," Maggie cries, "it doesn't frecking matter! One way or the other, dead or alive, we have to get her out! No way we can leave her for cougars or bears or worse. She's one of us!"

The rest collect along the corridor leading back down to the paye's cave. "Either way," Laird yells back to Maggie, "she can stay where she is. If she's still breathing—which I doubt—she won't live through the vexation of hauling her out. And if she's already dead—which she probably is—where's the point?" Said to rattle Gibson. Finger him as smoothly as a two-bit accordion.

But Gibson is in shock and the remark doesn't come close. Instead he considers it, matter-of-factly. If she's dead, if she's dead, bobbles like an inane pop song, he can almost make out McCartney's whiny nasal.

"Laird's right. There isn't much we can do," Dallas sighs, "but say a few words and scatter something over her on our way out. It's on our way anyway. Anything else boils down to a waste of time and energy."

"No." Maggie is very definite. "The little bit I managed hardly counts. If she's really gone, we have to cover her so no animal gets to her."

"Probably already have. Won't be but teeth and toenails left by time you get there." Laird's lingered long enough and turns back to the cave's entrance. "Hard," Laird says, "to think of some cat gnawing that pair of tits."

"You fucks! You dumb fucks, you can't leave her down there—it's disgusting! I won't let you!"

Laird's ego is beaded with hot buttons, a big one being authority, another one any kind of threat, even a certain tone. Maggie, whether she is aware of it or not, has hit more than one or two. When he's really pissed, his voice plunges, travelling low to the ground like a flame following an oil-soaked fuse.

"You figurin to join your little friend?"

"Look," she says, too mad to be scared. "One way or the other you'll be in the same boat. Either way you'll have to account for her and me! Either you come and help—or you'll be explaining to my folks and hers what exactly happened back here. And you better believe they'll get the law involved. You know my old man. One way or the other, you'll have shit to deal with! Rich or not! Don't think you won't!"

Laird gives her a good long second look. He had no idea she was so feisty. Regular little shit-kicker.

Maggie unzips her pack and removes a stick of dynamite. She wasn't sure why she bothered bringing a few sticks, only that she figured they might come in handy if she encountered a grizzly or a cat. She holds the stick in one hand, her cigarette lighter in the other. She has everyone's complete attention now.

"Maggie," Newt says, "how's freakin out and blowin us to hell gonna help Ana? We're all of us undone by the news but I don't see how this is any kind of a solution."

"Where's Hill?" she asks, finally aware he's nowhere around and he'd be a help at a time like this.

"Out combin the cliffs lookin for you," Dallas replies.

Frustrated, she shouts at Newt, calls him a few names and tells him he'd better come and help her with her friend. "Be a man for once in your sorry life!" she holds the stick of dynamite up to her lighter, and stares drunkenly at the fuse.

"Maggie," Newt pleads. "We need to calm down. God knows we're all distraught."

"Distraught!"

"Maggie." Gibson walks steadily toward her. "Come here, girl, I know how you're feeling. . . ."

Maggie tunes him out. She flicks her lighter and fixes her attention on the flame.

"The cold truth is she's dead. . . . Our girl's dead. . . ."

Gibson's voice cracks and he stops and looks at her as if to say he's with her and she might as well go ahead and blow the whole goddamn lot of them sky fucking high. And the days of mountain climbing, alone, the nights too worn out, too afraid to sleep, catch up and she begins to shake.

"Ana's dead." Gibson slides his arm around her and she falls against him, exhausted. "I need to face it same as you. We both have to understand that trying to haul body parts outta that ravine won't help her now—we have to resign ourselves is what. Hard as it is."

"I can't believe she's dead."

"Hard as it is . . ." repeated to himself.

"I read somewhere," Maggie tells him, "the spirit stays a while in some kinda holding tank and the outpouring from those left behind helps the spirit on its way . . . do you think we might be able to help her somehow?"

"It's too bad about the drills," Dallas carps, stumbling back into the cave, "but thank Christ you remembered the dynamite. It'll go a long way to helping our work load."

———————

"The important thing," Laird says, "is to be shut of here before snow flies."

Whittling by the fire, he finishes a couple three neat little dowels for the crates he's built to transport his stash. Laird's decided to go in with Newt, for the first mile anyway. After that, time will tell, but he might as well let Newt arrange a fly-by. They've all come to recognize the wisdom of sticking together, at least until Newt gets a couple of helicopter loads back to earth. Better to deal with Newt flying the chopper than explaining to some good ol boy soldier of fortune what in hell is in all the crates they're airlifting out.

"Be nothin to fly in here," he says.

"The problem isn't getting aircraft in or out," Gibson explains. "The problem is getting out in the first place to arrange the chopper. That needs co-operation, something we're short on."

"It was stupid sendin that pair back for supplies, when it shoulda been all of us goin out." Dallas smiles at Newt, determined to ingratiate herself. "We'da been back by now!"

It's early yet, they're waiting for the pot of starling soup to boil so they can feed and get to work. Supplies are low; Maggie left most of the replenishments back at the chasm. She's still out cold. Hill gave her the last of his opiated hash, combined with three of Newt's Seconal. Gibson and Hill are constructing another crate, similar in idea to a Haida box, God knows how many that makes, and Icarus is mooning over the fire. Another thing Laird can't figure is when Icarus finds time to build that flood of crates, but there they are, finished and waiting for him to load. What the hell.

"It's high time we got organized!" When Gibson stands to make his point, he arches his back and twists his neck, sore and stiff— he's been pushing himself, it's clear. "We need to get our asses out of here. Sooner rather than later."

"Gib's right," agrees Hill. "I saw geese flying a V yesterday. Early as this means winter's on her way. Any day we could wake up to a foot or more of snow."

"It's not gonna snow." Icarus turns from the fire as if from a book he's reluctant to put down. "Not for another month. Probably be longer."

"That a fact?" Laird sends a pine flake flying. It dances on a tongue of fire, curling like a leaf, blackening to ash. "You got a hot line to the weather channel?"

"I can tell is all. No more'n a heavy frost."

Gibson tosses his pine needle tea onto the fire. "On your say-so we can count on a motherfuckin blizzard any time."

Laird leaves the firepit to circle his latest bank of gold. In the early morning sun it shines like hubcaps heaped at an auto-wreckers. He spins on his heels, finger pointing, arm bobbing like an insolent crow on a high wire. "A load big as mine needs a s-61 Sikorsky. We don't want to be comin in'n out any more than necessary." His eyes weld to slits. "More trips mean fuck-ups. Clean'n quick's the key."

Maggie stumbles to her feet, groggy, feeling the effects of the drugs, the time she's lost. Medusa hair, suture-swollen lips and a face webbed with painterly scarlet strokes suggest a serious run-in with an aggressive cat rather than a down sleeping bag. She approaches Icarus. "I dreamt we left without you. The day we started back, you weren't anywhere around and instead of staying until we found you, we left!" She swings around to charge the rest. "We left without Icarus!"

"No way we'd get lucky as that."

"Promise me, Icarus, whatever happens, you won't go buggering off without letting us know where we can find you? Promise, okay?"

3

Her hand fits like a shell in his. Coiled in a tiny nautilus which he brings to his ear, it carries the rush of waves, of wind. Icarus stares at her face for a long time, as though she were a reflection. Mightn't he be gazing at the moon's face, on a dark lake, that any wandering cloud could pirate away?

They are supine on the valley green, not far from the tribe, as he was that first day. Crones smoking fish drape limp fillets on the drying racks, children and old men mending nets slump over their work as if only napping, and others, splayed along the banks, fishing, rest as quiet as the fishes loafing in the nets. Nabia nestles next to him, her eyes following a ridge of clouds, while Icarus strokes her hair. "Tell me again about our child." This has become a favourite pastime.

Nabia giggles and places his palm on her belly. "Wait, you'll see, he'll swim by like an otter looking for fun, see if he doesn't kick at your palm. He's unbelievably strong."

"What shall we call our little bull?"

"I don't know . . . we may have to wait until we see him."

"I'd've thought he'd've told you."

"Oh, this son of yours is very picky. I suppose you were as a child?"

"Me?" Icarus shakes his head. "I didn't have a clue. Before you, I was lost. Basically my whole life."

"Let's start with the names you like?"

"Anything but Icarus."

"In our language you're called Namaku."

"That's nearly as bad—what does it mean?"

"Jaguar Lord."

"Whoa, I'm a regular underachiever, me. Alley cat's more like it."

"You may not know you are a Namaku—but you shall be. Namaku is your destiny."

On the horizon, the paye emerge riding the blueball. The blueball shades the sun and from a distance the paye appear as flames around a god's head. No more than a mewling cub in its mother's mouth, Icarus is carried by Namsoul and set down upon a couch of clouds, and he understands they intend to teach him something. His mind's a blank, but that, Nabia reminds him, is a good thing; it's what the paye want, a clean slate. The paye put the wind in front of him, the wind that ruffles nerves, that lifts the edge of mountains and turns them upside down, inverted tusks to lean against and ponder. Inside these cones are layers of scrolls stored flat one on one, the history of the fifth world. These records are written in Aluna's blood, but when Icarus studies them he doesn't see blood but gold. Fibres, veins of gold hold the mountain together.

Icarus feels like an iguana, cold, his head and throat the blue of Navajo beads, clawing to climb free of a glass tank, slipping and sliding back down, unable to break through to the side he can clearly see. Stand on your tail, his instincts shout; yet stretch and jump as he may, he cannot break free.

Laird observes the goings-on from the vantage point of the caves. From where he stands, it's hard to tell what's happening on the green. With so many things intersecting, it's confusing, and bottom line, he doesn't care. He doesn't focus on his brother and a beautiful woman making love, or paye working over some skinny dude, but on the gold. Laird sees Icarus diving into a goddess made of solid gold, and the love pouring from Nabia isn't invisible: it's like molten ore spooling over the valley floor and riverside, turning air and sky and conifers to autumn gold. Laird feels cheated, and asks himself why Icarus is perpetually favoured, why Icarus should have this last best share?

Nabia suffers a sharp spasm. "The child," she tells Icarus, "is kicking like a colt."

Along the corridor of caves, Laird's rage intensifies, sending flocks of swallows fleeing the rocky bluffs in a fluid noisy graph, reminding one another, in their patois, that it's time to journey south.

Nabia tells Icarus that when the time comes he must help, and she tells him exactly what he must do. Icarus has been midwife to horses and heifers, and comforts her by saying he knows his way around a little bit, and Nabia grabs Icarus by both shoulders and suddenly neither one can see for laughing and tears.

Ricocheting off the mountain walls, Laird's curses reverberate, the fresh cancelling the old, skewing the words until there's only noise, a scratchy snarl feeding back between the blue ceiling and brown floor, grunge kicking back in a tinny garage. In a blind sweat, Laird plunges down a ladder, parachuting off before the middle rung. Elbows fixed like he's crawling on his belly, he careens along the ragged path cutting from the cliffside through the woods. Sealed in the vacuum of this tsunami is a lifetime of jealousy.

Sensing danger, Icarus rouses his attention from Nabia and their future to survey the scene. In the distance, he spies Laird slicing across the field. Laird's soul is as bony cold as Pluto's unknown moon. For as far as Icarus can see, looking at Laird, loneliness rolls like bare, stubborn hills. It's all there is to his brother! In place of venom, this opens something else, something wholly unexpected: the emotion that doubled for years as malevolence is actually a boy's love for an older brother, perverted. Where only a moment ago he viewed Laird as dangerous, Icarus decides now Laird's imminent arrival is an auspicious new beginning for the brothers, and what better, more advantageous time to reconcile than with the pending birth of his son? Two new beginnings. Icarus waves to him, inviting Laird to join them, yelling out his brilliant news.

Laird interprets every kindness as stratagem or an overture to battle. That Icarus is feigning forgiveness and pretending to come to terms with their years of estrangement boils down to dupery. Icarus inviting him to share in his great and lasting joy is another subterfuge. The scam enrages Laird. He isn't deceived or deterred. His hatred descends completely to black. It's full-scale war.

Laird has a good steady arm. As a little boy he played at being a knife-thrower in the circus. It's a skill he continues to hone. When he's within range, he hurls his hunting knife. The whistle in the air is as familiar to Laird as his own voice. Icarus also recognizes the sound and veers to cover Nabia and the child with his body. The flat of Icarus's left shoulder stops the blade, and almost immediately his back is hidden behind a cloth of cerise.

Laird takes her by the hair and swings her off the ground. Nabia slumps like a goose dipped and plucked and hanging from a hook in Chinatown. Smack to the face. Her nose, a pomegranate split in two, suddenly pours juice. Smack to the ear, the belly. As the child begins his descent, she quivers beautifully, a high pitched fork, tuning or silver, and drops as if plummeting from a bridge.

He meets her on the ground. In one quick jerk, Laird hunches over her, as though he's shat his pants, fighting to yank what appears to be a stuffed woollen stocking through the awkward opening of his dirt-stiff Wranglers. He fumbles fitting in, and pushing his way through birth's prefatory effluence, he roils like a fish flung upon a glassy deck, and then it's over. Dazed, he staggers up, dumbly looking this way and that, a drunk searching for a door, his penis sagging from his open fly like a rip-off Mapplethorpe.

Icarus is in trouble, weaving up a great white bend toward a radiance beyond. Kamu reels him back. Namsoul reels him back. Together, they tinker with the wreckage as though life and death are parts of a very tricky motor to be tweaked and greased in anticipation of a high-speed and genuinely deadly race. Icarus crashes into consciousness as though he's struck a wall. First the gushing through his head, then Nabia's crying reaches him.

"Our child," he realizes. "Our child."

The birth is harrowing, the way it bowls like a gale through a narrow liquid pass. The child is free and Icarus sees what Nabia cannot. Yes, the child is beautiful and wearing Nabia's face but born too soon, and blue, the cord a noose wound round its neck.

Icarus lunges at Laird, knocking him to the ground. Icarus's store of anger is absolutely black and will not be assuaged. Even in

death, he vows, his arms, his fists will flail on. Hate, especially hate
revived, is a supernatural fuel, unnatural spleen with no other need
but murder, to exterminate each morsel, each vagrant atom, to
leave nothing to contaminate the universe, but destroy it all.

He considers the advantages of a knife, its finer points, its pure
hands-on pleasure, the ease of a blade. He reaches his good arm
round and grabs the haft, yanks the dirk from his back, and charges
Laird, who is curled up on the ground, knees against his chest,
struggling to rise. Laird's hate is tempered with pleasure, the taste
of victory still sweetly wasting him. The child is dead, the woman
beaten to a pulp—these facts dilute the poison of an otherwise
deadly sting. His legs and balance signal a man duelling too soon
after, dazed and spent. The curved carapace is no impediment, this
war is not fair. There are no rules, no mean civility. Icarus lifts the
weapon swiftly and brings it down. The man sinks beneath the blow,
the knife breaks through skin, crushing some underpinning bone.
Raised again, the blade delivers vengeance with the steady cadence
of a woodcutter until the skin is gone and bones and backing pulver
ized to meal nearer grain than spine or ribs. Blood soaks the ground
and the other three.

Laird is sorely afraid. Death is no more eventful than leaving the
fifth world, but for some, particularly those convinced the fifth
world is all there is, facing it is a horrendously big deal, stupefying,
demoralizing, the catalyst that pushes them over the final drop.

Icarus crouches next to the body. Even though he wanted this,
even though he's responsible, Laird's death is not what he anticipated. It's the shoddiness, the unabashed baseness, he is ill prepared
for, and watching it unfold, he understands that Laird is unprepared
for it as well. Perhaps, Icarus decides, we all hope for more from
ourselves and our gods! Possibly we intuit there should be more?
Conceivably this might be construed as hope? Or room for hope?
Hope, if it is hope, masquerades as strange fish, flying from his
mouth and eyes and ears, pouring out his asshole, penis and belly-
button, hope deformed and twisted, devoid of light or breath, fish
all the same, bottom feeders, mud-encrusted prehistoric piranhas.

Hope hybridized, melded to despair, forms the metal of the man.

In spite of cracked, broken bones, Icarus runs the short distance to the river, carrying her and the child, grieving for both. His son is dead and Nabia is grievously hurt. To help pull himself along, in order to ignore the pain, he recites the tortures he had in mind before Laird's body gave way like shot fabric and would take no more.

At the river's edge he sets the child down and wades into the water with Nabia, to wash the worst away. Through the sleepy trance of pain she perceives birds wheeling in the air, a sublime kite drawing infinity's flattened eight round and round a cloudless sky.

Along the shore there is a tree that stoops like a derelict carrying too many shopping bags. It overhangs the river, as though a great unseen burden swings from its trunk. When it was young, too young to bear such weight, it stopped some beast and wears its reward now in the broken back, bending as if to spew, fated never to straighten but for the rest of its life face the interminable river.

Icarus lays Nabia beneath this tree and tries stuffing her vagina with bits of moss to stop the flow of blood. Then he works on the nose, daubing it with rags of moss. The bank sinks beneath them, damp with mosses of many different shades of lime and amber thick as newly thatched hay. The infant waits, on the plush beside her, to be rubbed with beeswax and honey, herbs and sweetgrass, and ferried to the sacred burial ground in fabric as fine as smoke. When the uterine hemorrhaging worsens, he sops it with his shirt and makes a pad of grassy mosses mingled with a layer of birch leaves. And he begins to weep.

There must be as many varieties of fear as love. Are they inter-linked and mated, these different kinds, twined like DNA, each necessary for the other, cleaving one against the next in order to survive? Are there any forms of love that are free of fear, and fear, is it ever very far from love?

Icarus cradles her in the warmth of his chest and bids her sleep, in a endless solfeggio, free of grief and pain. The world outside is blocked by the fast approaching night. The riverside is reduced to a cinema of shadows. Dusk soaks the river and high trees in a reel of indigo and brown and of course, black—if he doesn't look closely, nothing surrounds him save black.

His scream into the murk sends thousands of sleeping bats raining down upon them, but nothing else returns in the falling salvo, certainly nothing like an answer or assistance, nothing but a resounding echo, and the great resounding unending black.

A heart broken badly is irretrievably altered. Sometimes a life cannot be recovered like something simply dropped, no easy matter of rewinding a spool of thread. In his small small world nothing remains unaltered but his love for Nabia. And she is gold. "Love," he whispers, caressing her hair with his lips, "is the ninety-eight percent. The black space holding the rest together."

Icarus's intestines groan like timbers on a fighting ship. The night air shakes down around his shoulders in chilly gusts, wending through the wool and fleece and skin without a sound until the bones turn to frost. Falling upon the ground and blades of scrawny grass, it builds a hairy coat. Before his eyes, air turns itself to cloth. When he opens his mouth to yawn from cold, his breath stains the air with a mauve dye that falls finally back over him.

It is quiet now, the birds have bedded. There may be coyotes later when the moon returns—oh, it's the wind that's died, that's made the difference. Without its noise, the air falls quietly to the ground, rich with fragrance, rotting vegetation, aspen, spruce, poplar and pine moistened with the work of hardening off, the last luxuriant smell of closing down for winter sealing every living fibre in its own peculiar paraffin. When the leaves drift through night's glimmer, they might be petals passing, they are the colour of the sun, the air could be bringing spring, but they are leaves, lost, and the wind is down. It will rise again, winter will arrive, but tonight, in this moment, it's possible to forget. Forgetting is the drug of autumn, its poignant tug, forget, forget, that's all the air, the quiet air, will hum. Pay no heed, let go, forget.

The shadows are moving . . . it must be the paye coming to help. "Hello?" he calls and waits and calls again, "Hello?" It's too dark to decipher much, but regardless, he waves his light back and forth along the stretch of river, leaning into the gaping black like a ferryman hanging over the prow to search for sight of shore. The long cone probes the chasm with weak luck, a poor beacon losing itself on a dark and crumpled sea.

Icarus shouts, "Over here! We're over here!" hoping the paye will come. Failing that, perhaps Gibson or Hill will see his light and come to his rescue. The flatness of the mead, softened by night, reveals nothing, and he suspects he may have been mistaken. Perhaps he caught a glimpse of an animal passing, perhaps it was no more than the play of light. What light without the moon? He searches again.

"Who's there? I know someone's there. She's in trouble . . . in terrible trouble. I can see her slipping."

As the words leap out, they form their own larger world, a world he can wander through as easily as a forest, and he understands—Nabia is dying.

Her breathing is faint and Icarus feels her leaving, each breath stealing more of her away. Perversely, Icarus calms down. He bends to hear her say, "I won't be far away, I'll stay inside of you until Aluna calls us." Nabia's last words to him are, "Don't be sad, my love, I'm simply leaving my body to live for a while with you in yours."

In that moment her body becomes weightless and rigid as windfall and his own heart opens in a tremendous updraft. Surrounded by light, there is no sorrow, nothing like grief, simply oneness and illumination.

Icarus must wait, like the ground before a quake, for the shaking to begin—his time has finally come.

In the beginning there was darkness, only sea and darkness.

"Looks more like a babe asleep in the woods than our Stick."

"No," Gibson tells Hill, "it's how he looks when he's sick."

Hill leans over Icarus like an intern questioning the surgeon's diagnosis. "You tellin me he's sick then?"

"Only that's what he looks like when he is."

"Has every reason to be sick." Hill stretches his back and looks away. He doesn't have time for this. If Icarus is sick, fine and good, haul him back to the cave and leave Maggie take care of him. She's next to useless now, best thing she can do is nurse Icarus. Nothing she'd like better. The spring in his heart that was hers has finally run dry. "We should be gettin back," Hill tells Gibson.

Gibson nods, but doesn't move. Instead he looks around as if expecting something. The morning is cooler than either man would like. He and Hill are both listening. With their heads tilted, ears elongated, they resemble coon hounds tracking a scent. There's a noise in the mountains. Yes, there it is again, a bugle, and the two men exchange glances. Neither says a word; they stay quiet, listening. The bugling continues, answered by another bugle from a mountain ridge further away. Gibson takes a deep breath and looks down at his brother asleep on the ground next to the river. Hill lets out a sigh and says, "There's elk bugling. You know well as me what that means."

Gibson nods gravely and leans down over Icarus and gives him a good hard shake.

Hill says, "Means we're in for it. Elks bugle this early in the season means we're lookin at a early winter. No two ways about it."

"Icarus," Gibson calls. "Wake up. What you think you're up to here anyways?"

Icarus rolls his head and opens one eye. Hill tells him, "Guess we don't need to ask what happened. Guess we don't need to act surprised. All the same, in case you didn't know, Laird's dead." What he doesn't say is that Gib took it pretty bad. That he stalled for a good long time alongside Laird, like he was stuck in heavy mud.

Icarus opens the other eye. He stays lying there, staring up at Hill and his brother. What he has to say is written all over him. Laird had it coming. Laird got what he deserved. All the same, Gibson is struggling. Much as he'd like to beat the living crap out of Icarus, he knows he hasn't the strength to lift his arm, let alone reach across and strike him. Gibson looks at the sky, and back over at Laird, and quickly away.

Hill shrugs. "I suppose it was a case of self-defence. Suppose it was bound to happen. Only a matter of time."

"You'll have to bury him." Gibson stands a shovel in the ground next to him. "We'll leave you to see to him. We've buggered around here enough for one morning."

––––––––––

Winter snow is in the wind; by nightfall the sky will be blizzard white. Here, at this altitude, the first snow seldom leaves, but hardens in the wind and builds. By morning there'll be no getting out. They'll be forced to settle for the season, kill what they can to keep them through the worst of it. They can't eat rock. By spring . . . but that's a long way off. First winter and whatever she decides to bring. On the fire roasts a feast of deer mice, a mother and her ten children. Tomorrow may bring a gopher or sparrow.

In the distance a band of coyotes cry, tantalized by the wind and its smell of man and fire. The sky is hidden behind the falling autumn fog, the sun hangs barely there, a misshapen eye swollen blindly shut.

No one needs to incite the surviving cabal, they are already crazy. Outside of this murine feast, no one's eaten in days, or slept, yet they continue working, unable to close their eyes without quickly staggering to stand, driven by the need to press on and bag more gold. They are insatiable, with no appetite for any meal outside of stones.

At the back of the cave, the paye huddle, old men smoking and gambling. They are no longer amused by Youngerbrother's hunting prowess. Youngerbrother, they've decided yet again, is a fool. Namsoul and Kamu ride on Icarus's shoulders. As Icarus hammers the rock, the paye take him travelling through the quantum field of stone, along Aluna's veins to the cosmos of her heart.

Gibson pauses, stumbling over a jacket stiff with hoarfrost that he recognizes as his, one he'd let Icarus borrow. The frost signals time has gotten away on them. Could be days, weeks, since they began packing up to leave . . . but each attempt to actually head out ended in a muddle, it was always one more handful, one more and one more, until time simply got away. "Could be we won't get shut of here before snow flies."

Newt says, "I told you, haven't I been saying. . . ?"

Gib shakes his head. "Probably time we get winterized."

Hill stops working. "Bound to be elk and sheep wanderin around grabbin what they can. Last minute shoppers stockin up before the big blow. We keep our sights straight we can rack up a few head. Worst comes to worst, we can take down a coyote or two."

Gibson nods his agreement and tosses the jacket to Icarus. "Wear the fuckin thing. Don't leave it layin around. Another thing—quit moonin around like an arse missin his hole. We got our work cut out, if we hope to survive this winter." He pauses, tight-lipped, and finishes, "One thing for goddamn sure, we can't afford to lose any more of us."

Silence descends, and remembering, they plummet several fathoms. Regret is both sacking and stone.

"Let's get this show on the road," Icarus says finally and walks out of the cave, slipping into Gibson's jacket.

"Where's the sense going when the weather's liable to turn? Why not wait?" Maggie paces the length of the cave. Along the walls her shadow lumbers, monstrous and broken, a grotesque puppet, as the fire carves her features into a jack-o'-lantern. "At least wait until it clears?"

"That," Newt elucidates, "may not happen before spring."

Collecting their gear, packing up, excited, falling into familiar patterns of preparation, Hill says to Gibson, "Whadya say we start off lookin for those bulls we heard a while back?"

"What about us? Someone has to stay behind with us."

Hill waves her away. "Sit tight, Magpie, we'll get Sticker back before this flurry kicks up."

Dallas stands watch, her face as grim as it's ever been. Once the four men are out of sight, Dallas begins shoving the rock back across the opening. "Much as I hate the dark, I hate the cold more."

"I can't frecking believe it!"

"Hill knows what he's doing."

"Famous last words." Maggie flops down next to the fire. "Up this far, a storm can come up quick as anything. Weather's different here." She pokes at the fire, "And where will we be if they get caught?"

———————

Icarus, Hill and Gibson, with Newt some feet behind, slog through drift after drift, each man swearing loudly, each damning the storm and snow and winter to hell. Finally, when it doesn't stop, they concede and take time to find wood still dry enough to burn.

"Won't last."

"Not this soon into the season."

"A day or two, outside."

Sadly, they've been going in circles for hours now. If they weren't exhausted they might notice the familiar surroundings, altered slightly in a fresh covering of snow. If they were clear-headed, they'd know as much.

After a skeletal main frame is finished, they leave Newt to complete the shieling while they head out in separate directions to hunt. In this weather they won't find a lame mountain goat. They'll be lucky to come across a dead raven. Probably end up melting snow and boiling spruce needles and dead moss.

Cold and complaining, Newt works to insulate the frame of scrawny aspen, fixed with pine roots and pressed against the lee side of the mountain. He stuffs what moss and grass he can find in with evergreen fans and around these bricks he packs snow in an effort to mortar it. His fumbling fingers are dumb with cold and this frightens him; he hurries more.

"Just don't be all friggin day," he shouts to the mountainside. "Get your asses back fast as you can."

There is an indistinguishable point when danger presents itself. Those who tease the edges of it in order to survive know that, long before it arrives, it sends its emissaries—ask those poor souls awakened in the dead of night and running for the seashore at Herculaneum and Santorini. It settles in the unconscious, this tingling sense of dis-ease. Those tuned to it awake. Hunters, of course, are supposed to hone this sense to such a point that it acts alone, without direction. It's startling to fellow hunters when it fails in one of their own. It's unnerving to realize the skill is not inborn as they convince themselves it must be but remains wayward and wilful and not to be taken entirely for granted. *Attenzione!*

Icarus stops, looks around. Something feels very queer.

Naturally, the hunter in him surfaces. He forgets to breathe, his pulse slows and his blood pressure drops as though he's been immersed in freezing water but it's instinct alone that turns down the valves, shuts off the need for noise or breath.

There is in hunters a sense of when to attack. Timing, as in comedy, is the essence of it. Yet no matter how crucial, it cannot be totally taught and hinges on an understanding of the moment, an ability to open to it.

Here he holds back, rather than advancing—it isn't time. He studies the desertscape of drifts. There is no sun, it's hidden behind a frieze of icy clouds. Slowly he makes his way ahead. Ordinarily his footsteps might create a grinding crunch, but his movements are so deliberate that they cancel most of that. The wind has returned and brought with it a lot of noise, lifting the snow from the reefs to weave around his head. While screening his vision, it erases the sheet of steps that mark the way back out.

The print surprises Icarus. At first he can't believe it's real. He tells himself it must be the result of snow falling from a branch. But there is another, and further along, another, each perfectly pressed as if in wax. He crouches down to look. They're fresh. His heart begins to pound.

He feels the cat's proximity. Watching him from some nearby tree or rock. Icarus forces himself to move slowly although he impulsively wants to lurch about and look.

The cat watches, flattened to the high rocks behind him, the rocks he passed through only moments ago to check the prints. Everything is silent as the powdering snow.

The air around the man is draped with cords of disappearing fog, yet the cat is free of that as though it doesn't need to breathe. The eyes alone decipher the man's smell. Perhaps the reek is infra-red.

Before Icarus turns to take aim, the cat leaps through the curtained air with the same easy power it has racing over ground, appearing not to distinguish the slightest difference between earth and air. Landing on Icarus's shoulders, the cat anchors both front paws across his throat and face while the mouth takes the crown.

Examining the paw's cushion, Icarus considers for an instant the darkness of the leather, the long ridiculous fur, their unaccustomed softness, oblivious to the needle-fine claws erasing an epidermis. It's moments before he realizes the implications of a puma upon his back. Of course he knows it instantly, but oddly it takes a while, then resonates stupidly, like a clanging bell strapped to a bovine, before it bothers to register.

Eighty percent of the time Icarus is instinctive. Inevitably, whenever he needs it most, he is not. Rotten luck. Although it may have more to do with other forces at work.

When he grasps a fraction of his dilemma, he decides, contrary to hunter's lore and Cub Scout guidelines, that there is no point in pretending to be dead. The animal tastes his heart beating in his blood, and furthermore the animal doesn't care, one way or the other, alive or dead, the meal is the same. A sobering thought.

Another time he might have sworn, wasted energy shouting out for help. After all, the others can't be far away. Gibson won't have ventured far from the lean-to in this weather, knowing worse is on the way. Shouting for help would be a sensible thing . . . but his ego intervenes, precisely when he needs it least. Perhaps that's why saints and know-it-alls instruct the rabble to curb their habits, as habits have the irritating knack of surfacing when needed least. The cat triggers a reptile lodged in Icarus's lower skull, the base cell affiliated with swagger and conceit. This may be accidental on the cat's part, pure luck (whatever that may be), nothing more than chancing to strike an opportune button, an argument for word processors and chimpanzees.

Single-handed, him against the cat. He likes the ring of that. Pictures himself a hero. The image floods his brain, ruining every sensible cable and motor neuron.

In the cold the cat chewing through his skull feels oddly distant, the crunching sounds well removed, rather like a plaster cast breaking beneath a mallet in another room, painlessly reverberating as each slender crackle quickly joins another until the entire surface is a mess of hairline fissures tottering toward perfect disintegration.

Once it breaks through, every tinge of trouble disappears, although if he could see his face, he'd realize he resembles a monkey at a Chinese feast, skull opened, allowing the guest of honour to pick away, while the hosts laugh at his exquisite grimaces as the chopsticks strike various cerebral centres, eyebrows waving ribbons to the wind, lip curling in a fiendish grin. What can he be thinking?

Suddenly he's a boy again, running through a field of winter rye, chasing a small spotted dog further into the newly risen crop, the sky a clear blue vacuum inviting him up.

This doesn't last. Unexpectedly the pain arrives, obliterating all pleasant thoughts, bringing racks and stakes, a plethora of medieval toys to scrape each remaining moment.

Provocative thoughts roam freely through the brain. Perhaps it's merely a matter of activating particular centres. Perhaps, as some psychobioengineers suggest, God lives in the right frontal lobe. Possibly it's more, time or some similar curiosity, time running out and pirouetting like a professor hurrying his students, cramming the important points into their thick skulls before the final exam, information they'll need for admission to the other side. Who knows? In any case, notions such as he's never dreamt before sail through his brain, concepts fly about like term papers rattling in the wind.

The cat secures its haunches against the small of his back, pushing its back claws into his ribs, and settles to sample the crown and spine, weakening him, sapping what strength he has left, his power draining through his legs as he fights to keep from falling. To no avail: soon he topples and the cat climbs all over him.

By the time Hill arrives, followed immediately by Gibson, the cat has quarried the face and shoulder. What flesh remains hangs from birch-white bones like strips of bark, and the flesh, papery brown, curls delicately away.

Both fire, miss, and take aim again. Gibson can't decide which to kill, cat or brother (years ago they'd made a pact to take the other down same as they'd do for any horse or dog or wounded game but suddenly it's not possible). Hill shoots, but still it doesn't stop. He fires again. Again the cat acts as though it felt nothing more than a bead of hail bouncing off its hide. If cougars laugh, Icarus believes he hears this one. When it turns its head to face him, its eyes are jubilant.

Oh shit! moans Icarus. Hill fires again. His bullet lodges in the beast's forehead, square between its sharp lime-yellow eyes. The cat doesn't blink, simply returns to the work of wrecking fibula and bone.

Gibson rushes forward, slashing at the beast's back with his hunting knife until the blade slices the cat's ribs and lodges in the lungs. Before he can wrench the knife free to try again, the cat's mouth twists impossibly around, seizing his forearm. Its teeth sink in as if his bones are softened taffy. He screams with the unbelievable pain, and struggles to free himself. The cat holds both men. Hill has time for one shot before the cat turns and leaps for him. He aims and fires, the bullet enters through the cat's temple and ricochets from side to side, up and down, coming to rest along the back wall of the brain. The animal slows, its strength declines like floodwaters falling back. The eyes close, open briefly and shut again. Finally the beast cries out, a long terrible shudder as the bones and muscles shake and stop.

Hill leaves Icarus locked in the cat's embrace. There's no point even checking. Gibson's arm needs attention. Hill rips the end off his shirt and gets busy. The bleeding takes some work to stop. Hill tells him, "We gotta get outta here. Much blood as this, God knows what'll show up next."

Losing consciousness, Gibson mumbles, "We need to get Sticker. We can't leave the kid."

Looking this way and that, Hill heaves Gibson over his shoulder. "Icarus is dead." On his way past Icarus, he stops. He'd like to do more than give him this one last look, but he hasn't got time. "Hope you understand," he mumbles and moves away.

Icarus senses it coming, the pillowing bunks between the highest peaks, as if pinned. Gradually the pillows collide, sending heaps of swanny down breaking through the valley floor. Beautifully, its feathers drift over him. One by one they land upon his legs and lashes until the sky has filled with feathers, the mountains disappear behind the bedding, and he lies covered by the white.

After the dreamy pillows empty, the blizzard begins. Great howling winds arrive to harden even the gentlest fluff, tossing every sublime thing against the rocks, taking leaves, what's left, those yellowed bats hanging ready to drop, and mounds long fallen, tearing them until nothing fine remains. Even the downy whiteness breaks when gusts fling it whirling down in drifts that bury trees. Chasms and other passes slam shut, and Icarus is inexorably buried.

———

The fire beckons. In spite of the building storm, perhaps because of it, the wind, plucking the tarp of branches and boughs stretched across Newt's lean-to, enrages the flames, lending an illusion of comfort and well-being while generating a roaring, dangerous heat. A feeling of snugness pervades the shabby scene. Hill tends Gibson, washes his wounds and avulsions with melted snow and iodine and wraps them with whatever he can find, caribou moss and a little powdered goldenseal left at the bottom of his daypack. Gibson cannot sleep but groans with pain, his moans rise and sink, well up and fall away, following the rhythm of the raging wind. For the others the sounds are linked, as though he somehow rides the storm, his fate perversely coupled with the onslaught.

"He's as big a baby as I've ever seen," Newt points his chin in the direction of the patient. Newt's face shines with sweat, apple red and black from the fire's heat. Gibson lifts his head but before he manages the strength to ask how bad he is, sinks under a sudden downdraft of pain. "How's Icarus? Is he okay?" Hill tells him once again, "Icarus is dead." Newt warms his hands over the fire, and the scene, its stench of smoke and men mixed with winter's smacking grunts, might be a page fallen open, unchanged, from some prehistoric chronicle.

Namsoul and Kamu approach Icarus gently, breaking the fog softly. Youngerbrother has never been this close to seeing at the moment of death, and the time after, as they are all aware, is a very iffy predicament, an unpredictable queendom where anything can happen.

4

From where Icarus sits, nothing looks promising. Although he knows he's nowhere near, he feels as though he's going home, waiting at an unmarked bench for a bus, sans schedule, uncertain of the fare—who cares?—he's left his wallet, abandoned everything, including latchkey and bus pass, he can't remember where.

The bus, Icarus realizes unhappily, is wandering aimlessly through suburban streets he vaguely recognizes and wonders why he ever bothered to record when they meant so little. Returning to one, ambling down another, narrow, quiet, abandoned in the workday world, children away at school or daycare, not a kitten or dog left to shamble about, still the bus grumbles around the never-ending neighbourhood. In the distance he can see flat farmland, the city's end, while the bus continues its meander. There are no other passengers and he isn't altogether sure about the driver. Little else is clear but of this he has no doubt: he is on the wrong bus and travelling in an antithetical direction and although it feels that time is fevered down and motionless, he's actually travelling lightning fast to another destination. Things aren't going well, he perceives that much. Whether riding on a lawn mower or a jet plane or jitney in Jakarta, the vehicle is moving and there is turbulence. Suddenly he is thrown somersaulting down a chasm as narrow as an air duct.

The village is a sleepy spiral resting between three bald hills. Its streets circle a hub dispensing hardware, dry goods, farm machinery

and alcohol, hooked at either end to chapels, one of white slatboards
and the other of variegated stones, representing adamantly opposing Christian faiths.

The hotel stands bleak as Hitchcock's twin on the crest of the
first bald hill, the entrance to the village from civilization. Slouched
across the third and last hill, the one leading into the mountains,
rusts a desolate Pegasus service station with one working pump
but no gasoline and a convenience store attached that peddles
fly-specked bags of Cheezies and potato chips and very little else:
scented pine air fresheners in the shape of Christmas spruce trees
to hang from rear-view mirrors, Milky Way chocolate bars and
antifreeze that, judging by the dust they've collected, haven't moved
from the day the addition was installed.

The hotel and gas station and its convenience store snag real
estate brokers and other lost and misdirected fools, the usual mix
of weekend hunters, enviro freaks, rock climbers, birdwatchers,
criminals and prospectors, like flypaper protecting the sugarbowl
village below. There are no cordial you-are-here maps, no visitors'
centre dispensing handy leaflets with directions or fishing tips. The
locals are a taciturn bunch, with a surly, disagreeable curl to lip and
brow when greeting anything out of the ordinary. It's too much to
raise an arm to point the way; they feel it serves the wayfarers best
to discover the route for themselves. There are no cafés, no drive-
through restaurants; even the hotel provides nothing of the kind.
Any of fortune's fools with luck ill enough to lodge here overnight
will retire hungry, the innkeeper won't supply a sandwich, and
although the faucets turn, little pours but air and there's scant hope
the innkeeper will feel inclined to turn the water on. Not surprisingly, the rooms are desolate and empty and often cold. Little more
than a bed, bad, of course, possibly a window overlooking one or
the other balding hill, possibly a dresser, but the drawers will be
jammed and of little use. There is no bathroom but a row of buildings outside, around back, between the burn pile and the sty. Even
there, little care has been taken for the comfort of a visitor. All the
seats are in a row, holes crudely cut from a rough plank and placed

carelessly over an unsteady frame where, forfeiting privacy, guests sit cheek to jowl, one of many levies imposed, to contemplate the warning label on the tin of lye provided in lieu of paper and hand towels.

There is a melancholy humour to the rooms, the sheets are seldom laundered and the rooms are rarely cleaned. In each some reminder of the previous occupants remains to share with current guests, the way another set a palm upon a dresser that will not open, the dust colonized around the mark, how long ago? And who?

The halls go on too long. Again, expressly planned. A visitor that cannot find his way easily is unlikely to return, discouraged by the winding, aimless climb to room or fire escape or the meaningless passage for the simplest convenience, a towel, still damp, unclean, yet stored away, far along the hall.

Nor are there telephones or television, not even an old wireless, nothing to enliven or amuse, no release or diversion—apparently the room is meant to provide amusement enough. There is no morning newspaper placed outside the door, no small square of chocolate deposited on a freshly plumped pillow (certainly the small dark lozenge is not chocolate). No breakfast. No coffee, tea or Sanka.

The innkeeper is a drunk, his wife as well. The children, the endless marauding brats, starving thieves, lurk behind doors and wardrobes for the opportunity to help themselves to any trifle, novel or banal.

There are dogs, snarling drooling jackals, and arrogant cats that are lazy and negligent and positively indifferent to the packs of mice and rats that root and loudly entertain within the walls and decomposing floors. Oh, let's face it, there are lice and fleas in everything that should be warm or clean, and is neither, but home instead to a host of leaping nipping pests. What will pass for curtains holds some other living, flying demons and the bedframes and sills house spiders and the like. As if that weren't quite enough, the roof leaks, never politely but violently, and the windows seldom close, or if they do will come roaring down upon a finger or a thumb never to lift again. In a similar fashion, the doors, if they can be locked, will never be unbolted. Although it may seem counterproductive, the innkeeper long ago discovered that any fool unable to vacate a room is as good as gone, and often life, or rather, death, accommodates him beautifully.

Nothing grows around the hotel. Wind picks away at the bare ground and lifts what little it can hold to shove inside a guest's collar. Every corner, every nook hides some piece of ground to flaunt and fling about, happily or cruelly. The sheets, the frames are protected too. No surface is neglected or forgotten but all touched and remembered. There is no comfort, no inviting shred; all has turned the colour of old cheese, exuding the aroma old men, socks and mattresses muster, a reek that refuses to evacuate but lingers, the very stink that bites and finally brings down even a stalwart steely synthetic fibre, the stench that will finally conquer even stone.

Oh, it took years of unaccountable trouble to bring this hotel to such success.

Caught between the prickly Porcupine Hills, the village saves its best to share among its own. A smile is seldom wasted on a stranger but stored to spill among the regulars fondling the bins of nails and screws in the hardware store, or buying sacks of seed or talking hail insurance on a cream can in front of the general store. A placid village where every denizen reads every other with endless curiosity. No detail is forgotten but referred to in each scathing glance. No amount of dust settled upon an indiscretion cancels it, the village owns a collective memory that files each incident in perfect order and keeps intractable account.

A thoroughly rigorous system rules the streets and homes and chapels. There are no wrappers left to tumble dry along the road; each day jells in an aspic of order. There are no raised voices but monosyllables traded in low modulated tones, or reserved, not uttered at all but swapped in a whisper that reaches under every door. A village like a thousand others, not in the least unique. A collection of well-oiled hinges and expertly metered drapes that never close but passersby wonder what's transpiring behind the veil, and quickly set about discovering. A quiet place harbouring an investigative mind, twisted like the hills, until all that might be green and pleasant is gone with the never-ending wind, a village where every day is Sunday, dressed and polished and waiting in the front row to be chastised from the high and solid pulpit. There is no charity or mercy; selfish generosity marks what was spent and when it was returned, the date and interest well recorded.

Beneath it all, through every blade of bone-dry hay, blows the interminable loneliness that visits crowds poking through the bin of one another's lives, as though each life is nothing more than a scuttle of nails or screws to be fingered well and used. Pain cracks the faces painted shut, weathers every eve, gutters down the pipe of lines beside each frowning lip. Pain must be the howl of wind hoovering between the hills. Come winter or spring the sound remains the same, carrying God's own repartee.

Into this village Icarus descends, home at last, the prodigal returning, with a million memories kaleidoscoping his drowning mind. Life has a way of crossing paths. Not only stars and comets collide, but atoms and less important things will in time cross paths.

Picture the hills the bus bumbles through, not average, middling eastern hills, but high enough to be considered mountains in Vermont or Inverness, clean and bald and grand, whipped with grooves where wind and time have knocked about, exposing sandstone monuments and gravel. Behind the hills soars a range of mountains, bladesaw grey, over that a sky that never stops but parades a cartoon strip of corn continually popping and pouring down between the upper peaks.

The sky this morning is the shade of pink reserved for pike, slit throat to fin, a hint of scaly opalescence glintering in the horizon's pearly underbelly, soiling fast-moving clouds, roiling continually on the hopper. What other things are obvious, besides the air, only the moist smell of dawn, the fragrance of dew deserting those exuberant birds, scattering more notes than there are leaves to clamour with the wind. The air is full of work, the sweat of song and dew, departing. There are more songs than branches to perch upon—sadly there is no wood but streams of scrub or silverwillow snagged along the coulees, songs as varied as a forest, blending in the morning air as beautifully as falling leaves do in other places.

Occasionally a flock lifts and veers across the pinkened sky, forming there a melancholy stain like an enormous leaf blown against a stucco wall, then turns, widening and tightening into a tumble of other pictures and falls away behind the hills and disappears, as does the pink, quickly fading to the blue that hides behind the clouds. Still a shade of colour tints the lowest part of the ceiling where it soaks quickly in. The sun has come, a ball as bloody as a gallstone, removed and hastily set down upon the flattened tabletop of hills.

The traveller doesn't notice. Sunrise now, no matter how touching, is treated with the forbearance given any other obstacle. When the light comes, it will be easier to make his way. Making his way is the concern. There's little time for little else.

From his private capsule, he gazes down upon the far-off farms and ranches and nearby village. Nothing sleeps, each small chimney smokes and along the paths dogs wander, following men to a barn or shed or truck. In the fields, along the far slope of hills and the flat plain stretching after that as far as he can see, combines and threshing machines feed like tireless black locusts having supped the night, their headlights even in the dawning light waving about the fields of grain as though errant siphons, searching, hungry still. Each farmer works to save what he can. Harvest must be claimed before the winter, already settling along the mountain passes, collapses down upon their heads.

Nearby slopes are shared with herds of cattle, grazing until they drop, and horses, ravenously working the starved and dusty ground, concentrating on the impossible task, dazed as the women in the cottages putting up preserves.

Amid such labour he will slip into town barely noticed. Where a week earlier he would've caught the eye like a cat's claw snagging a smooth stocking, this time of year, this time of day, no one has time to care. *Bonne chance.*

Dawn is clear, the long-drawn-out sunrise wiped to streaks of red stain smeared every which way, as if with a sloppy rag. He sees nothing more than what a crow in a Bruegel painting might, and still the world below beckons like a pretty quilt, some softness fixed to break the fall. He doesn't chaperone the bodies ploughing through the dawn field, but rather his past, a jumble of images tossed like old sweaters overflowing a drawer.

The innkeeper's daughter shows him to his room without a second glance, remarking only that he bears some resemblance to a spit-poor farmer who works a field of rock miles out of town.

It's quiet now, and dark. Somewhere deep inside the wallboards, mice or other rodents work, excavating, re-creating, establishing yet another order. Disorder. Better suited to the state of things, more in keeping with the tremendous momentum of decline.

Icarus finishes pacing the long and winding hall, pausing by a leaded window on the landing, beautiful once, to gaze across the town wedged between the hills, past the other grassy drifts, at the dark white jaw of peaks. He is quite dead, quite back to his old self. What, he wonders, next? Ah, there, at last he feels a small quake, a sorry flutter of feeling.

Drawn by a jigsaw of memories, he leaves the hotel to meander through the town, which spills like coffee grounds down the backside of the hills and out through acres of salt flats. Desert snakes and wayward cicadas sporadically cross his path and larks still sing. Their songs have grown longer, Morse-code dots and dashes pitched from any bush with strength to hold itself and some others, featherweight or not, in this fried melon sun.

The spit-poor farmhouse and barn are boarded up, but despite that, it's apparent that someone lives in the small bunkhouse at the rear. A pungent smell of cooking grease bastes the air, and the ditch beside the step has been excavated and turned into a garden, well tended, with varieties of peas and beans and garlic.

The kitchen reeks of cooking and is very dark. The light from one small cluttered window reflects along a wall of hanging iron cookware. The sink is of sunken cast iron, aged a shade of green or

grey and even in the dark it appears to glisten damply as though
dappled with moss. The stove is iron also, darkened as if rubbed
first with coal, then with oil—in a shaded corner it shines and holds
a cauldron and a giant kettle. Both give the impression of being cold
and seldom used. In the middle there is a long wooden worktable
covered with bowls and steamers.

The ol man peers through the tattered screen door, his apron
stained with blotches the colour of black tea. The eyes, well hidden
behind pouches filled with small kernels the size and roundness of
papaya seeds or BB pellets, are coated in a thick blue vellum impossible to decipher. The face, although very old, is smoothly wrinkled as
if belonging to an ancient shar-pei rather than a man. The brows are
coarse and grey and grow upward toward the dome, as if to try and
help to cover it. The hair, what is left of it, is a brittle make of grey
drawn back in a ponytail that ends somewhere between the shoulder blades. One hand holds a cleaver, while the other grips a long-
necked goose, the two burdens dangling on either side with the
unbalanced weight of badly outfitted shopping bags, and between
his chin and shoulder he clutches a cell phone. He doesn't glance at
Icarus huddled on his back step, but gazes through the torn screen
to some distant place, concentrating on the conversation and what
is being said a thousand miles away. He doesn't bother to nod or
smile but nods continuously for the other end.

Anxious for the conversation to conclude and his business to
begin, Icarus rubs his face, hoping to contain his excitement, as if by
keeping his hands occupied he might restrain them from reaching
through the tattered screen to grab the cellular toy out from under
the ol man's chin.

When he glances at Icarus briefly, it's to shake his head, indicating he'll have to wait. His eyes quickly fall away and he lowers his
head to follow the conversation away from the stove and into the
darker part of the kitchen, where he sets the bird down on a chopping block and, talking into the phone, nodding frequently, begins
the business of gutting the bird and skewering a long stick through
the beak and what seems an extremely rubbery neck. The ol man

has done this job a million times. He could do it in his sleep. Once the goose is hooked, he finishes plucking it and dips it in a sauce the colour of betelnut juice and hangs the bird along a rack strung with other birds dripping a similar sauce.

Icarus shuffles on the back step, miffed and confused, debating with himself how to catch the ol man's eye. Ordinarily he would leave—he's never been a patient man—but this is no ordinary day. Instead of leaving, he studies his boots and the state of the ol man's wooden steps. It happens naturally, understandably, as the conversation drags on, that his concentration wanders, his thoughts drift to sandbars of their own, childhood and a string of themes that bob like bait atop a dead pool. He's so absorbed that he doesn't observe the ol man approaching, unsmiling, distracted still from the previous conversation, not quite finished with it, but pausing at the screen door to look again at a distant invisible shore.

The ol man leans for the door handle, his face calm as shadowed water, and it occurs to Icarus he may not recognize him. He resolves to introduce himself, to speak slowly and project each syllable as if switching a recording to a very slow speed.

"What? Don't you recognize me? It's me, Icarus." (If he wore a hat he'd run the brim between his fingers. For the first time in his life he regrets seldom wearing one—finally he comprehends their use.) "Only I thought you'd want to know, I hit it. Used the stick, witched for it like we always said. Just like you taught me." He pauses, smiling, his eyebrows rising to extend like awnings. "I'm a rich rich man!" He waits again, smiling, shuffling helplessly on the back steps. "Only I thought you'd want to know." The ol man moves, he fully intends to shut and bolt the door in Icarus's face. "I wanted to drop by and say . . . we were on the right track all those years, only we got it ass-backward. The gold, I wanted to tell you, the gold, it's her blood, here on earth, that's why we wanted it so bad. You know, because somehow we knew."

The paye hover in the background as Icarus prepares to leave. It's obvious that he no longer belongs, he waddles through this world like an alligator dragged out of water, awed by the buildings, by the hardness of people, their strange way of greeting, their machines, their noise. Even the blueball tastes grainy as the glaring day and night. Here gravity is hostile, it hobbles him. Like an acrobat suddenly forced to juggle columns of torches alongside pyramids of balls, he works to balance gravity and control his final flight.

The oldest wizened paye groans deeply, and sighs, and his breath blows back across the others like a long and winding beard. "We must return to Aluna, her other arm."

"Yes," Namsoul and Kamu repeat. "He's nearly ready."

"Yeah," he nods.

Time for one last glance back at what used to be his life. It is a broken-down skiff, tethered and thoroughly waterlogged and no longer of use. Goodbye.

Icarus slumps. If it were possible, his shoulders might altogether fall away; the pins clamping them together appear to have been pulled, the same with the spinal column, which drains into the knees, again not safe but buckling beneath the weight.

Bugger that, Icarus sighs, relieved it's time to board, and nods to the driver, telling him the rear right tire looks ready to blow. The bus driver continues reading an old newspaper as though he hasn't heard. He bears an uncanny resemblance to Namsoul in middle age, with a balding head and a sardonic scowl.

Icarus sees her, blocks before the designated stop. The summer's day has disappeared, replaced by a prairie winter. Snow drifts across the pavement in horsetail clouds, whipping round the bench. He clangs the bell, raises his arm and pulls again. He must get out. Nabia is barely visible for snow. The wind lifts banks like a sea rising to drown ships as great as city blocks. He leaves his seat to wait by the door. The bus dawdles on the icy patch, and finally slides to a full stop.

"Nabia," he screams, pushing through the snow to reach her side. "Nabia."

He runs in circles, but can't find her in the snow. When he passes under a lone tree, a great shelf of snow falls away, covering him completely. For a brief moment he disappears behind it, transformed in an instant to a veranda pillar, but gradually it drops away, flouring him with moulting clumps of stucco that leave him very wet and completely cold. And Nabia is gone.

If he can sense his way, follow it rather than his thoughts, he will travel like the hunters and paye through the storm and find Nabia. He needs to become a paye hunter setting out in search of game in a forest stretching unchanged for hundreds of miles, where the green-ery above creates an impenetrable canopy, without a hint of sky, and life springs high among the arms reaching for the sun and below all is brown and bare and identical, where the hunter walks for weeks in every direction with each unfolding mile exactly the same, yet when the hunt is finished returns straight home with no stars or sun to guide the way, no variant landmarks, following only some inner compass. Yes, this is the test, to find his way to her sealed in a hurri-cane of spinning snow, everything outside the centre hidden by an unending glacier, no life, no green, nothing moving that isn't white. A thousand shades, all white. Even the sky is white, falling to bits. He isn't afraid. Fear doesn't enter into it. There isn't much to see, nothing moves save each long tendril of the wind's mane delineated by snow.

But Nabia is here, she is the light breaking through, come to take him home. They fall into each other, branches of one trunk, their kiss the life within life. They ride the moon's long arm to the Milky Way and Aluna. Below them the earth becomes a pearl lost on a drape of matchless beads. He relaxes and looks around, marvelling at how wondrous it will be to wait on the pier of Aluna's bright sea for the next generation of conquistadores to arrive, as they inevitably will, and to intercept them, as paye on the Milky Way greet the ferry now.

————

The landscape is completely altered. None of what Gibson and Hill intended to use as markers stands, but every stamp upon the

skyline has vanished in a disconcerting white, peaks and valleys flattened beneath a Sahara of shifting floured dunes.

Hill and Newt drag Gibson through the drifts. The slog is treacherous and filthy but each man, even Gibson in his stupor, pushes
himself, hurrying to beat the odds. There is no talk of when the
storm will break. The storm will not give way. Cold exsiccates their
eyes and nasal passages. Less than fifty feet from the cave, Gehenna
opens, letting fly its festival of demons, determined to drown the
men in snow or wind.

The cave is blindfold dark and when they blink the black hood
never lifts. If they touch their eyeballs, they cannot glimpse the finger. The only light emanates from their own corneas, burnt with
ice-coated ramps and gold. Searching the cave's vaulting for glint
of it, their breathing rolls along the high rocky walls as though
hammering a thin sheet of very tall tin, and the bodies frozen near
the entry are sidestepped and forgotten.

Days and nights dissipate in an unending mirage of gold arriving
on scarves of snow, winding through the cave like a tide, bringing in
its wealth of kelp and seagrasses, or rocks the colour of good whisky.
Whisky at least they used to drink and have forgotten now. Thoughts
of food, of fire and warmth have given way to the golden world that
bears them, as if upon a golden swan in a mad king's cave, to a paradise where every desire's fulfilled, there are no limits, no depriva-
tions, only abundance and silken opulence. One moment the cave
will be a harem in Persia, the next tide brings a Chinese entourage,
complete with rugs and concubines and jade. A craving for a fountain with a nightingale is fulfilled before the craving has begun. The
paradisaical worlds are real and the cave nothing but a dowdy dream.

Death arrives gradually, dribbling a freezing elixir through their
bones like a dentist numbing roof and jaw, gradually feeling defects,
leaving the hum of an innocuous drill and stench of porcelain and
root burning down, quieting the cave, restoring it to mice and bats
and wind.

Perhaps someday strangers will find this cavern and wander past
the trail of bones to scrutinize its tricky amber walls. Stranger yet,

even if no one ever stumbles past, the story will leak out, for tales of gold travel invisibly from one world to another. Paye say, to emend schisms, myths must intermingle. What else is myth but a layering of tales, separated in telling from events, yet expanding nearer truth with each rendering, like escaping perfume filling a very great cavern, one molecule and another, until the air is finally altered.

The following books were crucial to the genesis of *Icarus*:

Hugh Dempsey, Tom Primrose, and Dan Riley, *The Lost Lemon Mine*. Edmonton: Lone Pine Publishing, 1991.

G. Reichel-Dolmatoff, *Beyond the Milky Way: hallucinatory imagery of the Tukano Indians*, Los Angeles: UCLA Latin American Center Publications, 1978.

G. Reichel-Dolmatoff, *San Augustin, a culture of Colombia*. London: Thames and Hudson, 1972.

G. Reichel-Dolmatoff, *Shamanism and the art of the eastern Tukanoan Indians: Colombian northwest Amazon*. New York: E.J. Brill, 1987.

G. Reichel-Dolmatoff, *The shaman and the jaguar: a study of narcotic drugs among the Indians of Colombia*, Philadelphia: Temple University Press, 1975.